The Charlemagne Accord

Andrew Clawson

© 2025 Andrew Clawson *All rights reserved.* No part of this book may be used, reproduced or transmitted in any form or by any means, electronic or mechanical, including photocopying, recording, or by any information storage or retrieval system, without the written permission of the publisher, except where permitted by law, or in the case of brief quotations embodied in critical articles and reviews.

This book is a work of fiction. The characters, incidents, and dialogue are drawn from the author's imagination and are not to be construed as real. Any resemblance to actual events or persons, living or dead, is entirely coincidental.

"The Byzantine church of Panagia Kapnikarea" and "The candelabrum at Panagia Kapnikarea" are photographs by George E. Koronaios (cc-by-sa-2.0)

Get Your FREE Copy of the Harry Fox story *THE NAPOLEON CIPHER.*

Sign up for my VIP reader mailing list, and I'll send you the novel for free.

Details can be found at the end of this book.

Chapter 1

Kyiv, Ukraine

A barrage of missiles blasted through the night sky. Harry hit the dirt.

A gravelly voice chuckled without humor. "They are not shooting at us."

An orange glow from the missile's tail fire lit the muddy roads and flowing river on the outskirts of a Ukrainian city under attack. Harry got off the ground, staying low as he brushed dirt from his sleeves. He turned to look at the man behind him, sitting in the stern of a small boat. "Can't be too careful."

"A careful man would not be here."

Hard to argue with that. Harry crouched as he looked around. The river flowed behind him. Armored vehicles were parked in a line against a low-slung rock wall. Helicopters rumbled in the distance, their navigation lights moving steadily across the darkness. Sporadic gunfire punctuated the noise from the nearby front lines.

"I won't be here long." Harry's breath fogged the chill air. "Now what?"

The bearded man behind Harry had smeared dark face paint on his nose and forehead. Only the whites of his eyes glowed in the moonlight. "Now I leave. I will see you soon, if you survive."

The burly man spun his small boat around, vanishing into the darkness across the river. Harry swallowed, his throat dry.

A small, open-top Jeep drove past not far away, its engine whining softly. There were two soldiers inside. Russians, both wearing white-and-black snow camouflage fatigues.

White and black. He lifted his arm, clad in white, black, and blue camouflage. He spun around, but the man who had led him here was gone. A man who had given him the wrong color camo. Another Jeep rumbled by and Harry watched it move. These soldiers also had white-and-black camo on. No blue.

He needed to get his hands on a pair of white-and-black fatigues. His Pakistani-American heritage made him stand out as it was. Without those same color fatigues, his life expectancy could be measured in minutes. The front lines of Russia's invasion of Ukraine were only a few miles away.

A tank roared its approach in the distance. Harry pressed his back against the stack of wooden crates providing cover. This morning, he'd woken up in a soft bed on a yacht in the Black Sea. A yacht owned by the exiled Russian oligarch Evgeny Smolov. If pressed, Harry would say Evgeny was a friend, though the sort of friend who might toss Harry to the sharks if Harry was no longer useful. One of Evgeny's personal helicopters had ferried Harry—along with a shipment of black-market arms—to a field outside Kyiv. The Ukrainian soldiers waiting for them unloaded boxes of anti-aircraft missiles, replaced them with several briefcases filled with cash, and then loaded the missiles and Harry into a waiting truck. One stop at a Ukrainian military outpost later, Harry found himself clad in the wrong color fatigues as he sat on the back of a motorcycle, clinging to the burly, bearded man whose idea of subtle infiltration behind Russian battle lines consisted of racing his bike at full speed across barren fields.

At least Harry was still alive. For the moment. This was only the first step of his mission. A personal mission that had begun when he'd found a message inside the lost crown of Charlemagne the Great. A message indicating there was another message waiting in a centuries-old church in Kyiv, Ukraine's largest city. A Kyiv now controlled by the Russian military.

Gunfire chattered nearby. Harry went still as loud Russian voices and harsh laughter filled the air. He didn't speak much of the language, but clearly someone had a strange idea about how to have fun. It soon faded, and he peered around the crates. An imposing monastery peered back.

In daylight the golden domes and pointed spires might fill believers' hearts with joy. The imposing walls and colonnaded bell towers would cause the faithful to pause and look to the heavens. Tonight, bullet holes and darkness turned this destination for the faithful into a grim reminder of all that was wrong in the world. One bell tower was reduced to little more than rubble, while many of the stained-glass windows were blown out. He looked at what had once been a beautiful sanctuary. Now the harsh mobile spotlights of the Russian army displayed the church's charred pews and scorched marble floors.

The Russians were using this holy place as their operations base and a staging point for attacks on the Ukrainians. Harry shook his head. *That's not my fight.*

He was here to locate an image of Charlemagne in this church which dated back to Charlemagne's time and was a cave monastery, meaning it had originally been built inside existing caves. Over time, as it had grown, the outbuildings took hold while the caves were forgotten. Caves he hoped contained the next step on the royal path he followed. All he had to do was get past a small army of Russians and then hope he was correct that the message in Charlemagne's crown pointed here.

"Stop wasting time," Harry told himself. Another Jeep went past, dirt flying as the tires churned in the muddy road. Harry's gaze went to a large tent across from him. Its front flap was pulled open and light spilled out from it, reflecting off the dented bumper of a rusty pickup truck parked just outside the tent. A man was inside the tent, sitting on the edge of a cot, brushing his teeth. Nobody else was visible in there. Harry's eyes narrowed. *Those could work.*

Harry stood and stepped briskly across the muddy road, acting as though he belonged. The darkness would shroud him and his wrongly colored uniform. He stumbled over a frozen clod of earth as he walked, his shoulders hunched and his head down, just one more soldier stuck out here in the cold. Harry paused at the tent entrance, then stepped inside.

"*Privyet.*"

Harry muttered the word and walked past the soldier, not giving a clear view of his face.

The soldier offered an unintelligible response, still brushing his teeth. Harry twisted to keep his back to the man, went back to the flap and let it fall loose. The soldier did not look up. Several empty cots lined the tent's interior.

A flashlight on the ground beside one cot grabbed his eye. A big flashlight, all metal, and when he picked it up, darned heavy. *This will do.* He turned toward the man still brushing his teeth. The soldier reached for a bottle of water as Harry walked closer to him and lifted the flashlight.

Bang. The soldier dropped to the canvas floor. Harry moved quickly to strip the man's fatigues and hat off before removing his own and stepping into the stolen gear, taking care to make sure his ceramic knuckledusters made it into a pocket of the uniform pants. Now he looked like a Russian soldier. Which left one problem: the actual Russian soldier lying at his feet would soon wake up.

Harry ran to the tent flap, lifted one corner and peered out at the truck parked outside. It had a metal cover over the truck bed. The sort that locked from the outside.

He dropped the flap, pulled the shoestrings from a pair of combat boots under one cot, and in short order the Russian soldier's hands and feet were bound. A pilfered sock made a decent gag. Harry pulled the still-unconscious man to his feet and manhandled him out of the tent, then dragged him into the shadows outside it. He looked around, listening carefully. Nothing. Harry hauled the man to the pickup truck and hefted him into the bed. He ran back into the tent and grabbed a couple of blankets, which he threw over the soldier before snapping the lock shut. It would keep the guy from freezing and it should keep the noise down. Harry glanced at his watch. At most he had fifteen minutes before that guy could become a problem.

Harry pulled his camo hat down low on his head as he stepped out of the darkness and walked toward one side of the monastery. The message from Charlemagne's crown ran through his head.

Locate my Father where Anthony of the caves led his disciples. My Father looks upon the true path.

Anthony had been a monk who lived in what today was Ukraine. He'd died a thousand years ago, having founded two cave monasteries, both of which still stood today. One was in Kyiv, the other here in Kharkiv. The message on Charlemagne's crown had been written by the king's personal abbot; *my Father* meant Charlemagne. Now all Harry had to do was find a king who had been dead for a thousand years inside a sprawling monastery filled with Russian soldiers.

One corner of his mouth lifted. *Nothing to it.* Frozen dirt cracked under his boots as he moved toward the monastery entrance, passing a line of tents and hastily erected metal sheds along the path. A soldier stood guard outside the monastery entrance. Harry looked to a massive hole in the monastery wall, a hole well away from activity around the front entrance. A hole with no guard posted outside.

A Russian soldier stepped out of the metal shed beside Harry. The man never looked at him, never stopped as he walked across Harry's path and kept going, his eyes fixed on the pistol in his hands. A pistol, Harry noted, in the process of being loaded. The shed door whined as it closed. A shed door with an unfamiliar Cyrillic word on it. Harry reached out and grabbed the door an instant before it clicked shut. He couldn't say why, only that his gut told him to stop it from closing. He peeked inside. "Would you look at this?" he whispered to himself as he slipped inside and shut the door behind him.

Shelves of weaponry stretched out before him. Row after row of automatic weapons, with boxes of ammunition stacked alongside, and other boxes with writing on them. He went directly to one with lettering on it spelling out a word he thought he knew. He lifted the lid and confirmed it, reached in and pulled out two grenades, which he stuffed in his pockets. An adjacent larger box contained rocket launchers; the ammunition was helpfully stored nearby. Harry had no use for a rocket launcher right now. If things went sideways, well, at least he knew where to find them.

The wind kicked up as he walked out of the armory and headed for the monastery's gaping wound. The guard stationed at the front door never noticed him keeping close to the shadows. No one challenged Harry as he slipped inside, moving past the rows of charred pews and overturned chairs to an interior doorway, which was intact. Harry hesitated and pressed his ear to the door before touching the handle, the carved wood cold on his skin. He listened for any sign of movement on the other side. Nothing.

A skin-tingling metallic screech sounded when he pushed the door open enough for him to slide through into a stone corridor. The door protested again when he closed it, though this time it was muffled by the noise of airplanes overhead. Flying low, from the sound of them. Harry turned and walked deeper into the monastery. Dim yellow lights along the ceiling guided him. A painting sat propped against the wall to one side, the nail from where it had fallen sticking out of the wall at eye level. He paused to verify it wasn't Charlemagne before moving on. The lights overhead flickered weakly as his shadow danced across the walls. The next painting was a saint he didn't recognize. Eastern Orthodox Christianity was not in his wheelhouse, not by a long shot.

No matter, for his target was simple. Charlemagne. Harry had seen enough images of the man to make recognizing him easy. The hard part was knowing where to look in this place. His research hadn't uncovered any paintings or sculptures or other images of Charlemagne inside, though that didn't mean there weren't any to find. The path laid out by Agilulph was meant to bring him here. Too bad Agilulph never counted on Russian forces occupying this holy place.

Light beckoned as the hallway dead-ended ahead. Bright light, the sort a military-grade spotlight would give off. Harry moved to stand in a shadowy alcove as the corridor ended. He leaned out to see another corridor running in either direction. A closed door waited on one side, while a chapel with high, curving ceilings and statues lining its walls was on the other. He headed for the chapel.

The doorway behind him banged open. Harry straightened his back and marched rather than walked, never turning to look as the harsh Russian words of several men filled the air. Harry stopped, turned sharply and stepped back as he saluted the three men passing him in the corridor. He waited until they disappeared down a different hallway before he took a breath. *That was luck.* And hoping to keep getting lucky was worse than having no plan at all. His watch revealed nearly five minutes had passed since he'd locked that soldier in the truck. Ten more and he'd be pushing what little luck he might have left.

Four statues were in this chapel, but none were of Charlemagne. Cross this one off the list, and he truly did have a mental list of all the larger rooms in the monastery. Rooms where worshippers would gather. Rooms built to impress with their statues, paintings and other iconography. Including, he hoped, a representation of Charlemagne.

The muted noises filtering in from outside seemed to intensify as Harry completed his circuit of the room and returned to where he'd saluted a minute ago. Moonlight turned red as it fell through an unbroken stained-glass window to paint the marble floor beside him. He walked to a large passageway to his right, behind the pulpit, and darted into the dim passage before breaking into a run. It was a long passage, as it connected the main church to a second one, and from there additional tunnels would connect the second church to smaller spaces. Such was the nature of cave monasteries. They began in natural caves, and outbuildings were gradually added so that it became a large complex instead of a single structure.

Harry's destination was a slightly smaller, square church. Nobody was inside; he saw only rows of empty pews and another vacant pulpit at the front. Oil paintings covered one wall, and a golden chandelier hung above the central nave. Stained-glass windows let weak light inside. The oil paintings were of religious men looking rather miserable. No

Charlemagne. Harry's next move was through a doorway under one window depicting a giant cross. The doorway took him to the adjacent structure. Harry opened the door—this one was thankfully silent—before moving quietly across the stone floor. His watch glowed softly in the darkness. A watch with a tracking device in it. The Ukrainian soldier who'd dropped Harry outside this Russian camp could track Harry's location so he knew when Harry was approaching their rendezvous point. That soldier should be waiting to get Harry back to safety soon.

At least the guy had said he would. Given the flat terrain here, he'd see Harry coming from a long way off, but if Russians were chasing Harry would the guy truly wait? Probably not. Harry's best chance lay with the soldier's greed and fear. Greed for more of Evgeny Smolov's weapons, and fear of Evgeny's retribution if he failed. He shook his head and pushed the worry aside. Find Charlemagne first. Another doorway stood in front of him. Harry pushed the door open.

A platoon of soldiers stood on the other side. A dozen men turned in unison as Harry stepped into the church. One man stood at the head of the troops, barking orders.

Uh-oh. He saluted.

The man at the front shouted at the assembled soldiers, and all the puzzled faces turned away from Harry to look back toward their leader, each man shouting a phrase Harry didn't understand. Harry fell into line, mumbling nonsense that was lost in their voices. The commanding officer turned on a heel and began marching toward a set of tall doors along the church wall. Two soldiers ran ahead to open them so their leader did not have to stop. A gust of air flew into the chapel and Harry's breath turned to steam as he kept pace until they were outside and the tall doors clanged shut. Or one door, at least. Harry turned to find one of the doormen had set his gun down and was cursing at a stuck door. A solid kick from the soldier got it closed.

Exhaust billowed from the row of tanks and armored vehicles waiting outside, each with headlights glowing and engines running. The two door-holders ran back to their places, passing Harry as the platoon headed for the vehicles. The bright vehicle lights made him squint against the darkness.

He stopped marching. The troops continued. Harry ran for the closest cover he could find. He dove behind a metal container, the frozen ground rattling his teeth as he crashed down and skidded into the darkness. He hit the container wall, leapt up and looked back as the troops marched on. None of them turned back. No flashlight beams landed on his face. He watched until the troops rounded a curve in the road and vanished.

Safe, for now, but he couldn't stay hidden behind a metal container. What was this thing, anyhow? The corrugated metal was streaked with dirt. He leaned around the front again to find a single door set into the front of it. The sign on the door showed a Cyrillic word. *Armory.* Harry could only shake his head. *A mountain of weapons, and these guys leave it unlocked.*

Harry looked up and down the road, and the rumbling of tank engines covered his footsteps as he ran back to the chapel and slipped through the doors. No one was in sight, though he'd have been hard pressed to see anyone in the dim light filtering through a handful of stained-glass windows. He stepped to one side and his foot hit something. Metal clattered against the floor.

He looked down. *A rifle.* The soldier who had opened the door must have left it here. Harry set the gun back where he'd found it and pulled a penlight from his pocket, clicking it so its narrow beam of light cut through the chapel darkness. He looked down. A marble floor, undecorated. He looked up. He hesitated. An overhead walkway like some sort of a viewing platform ran the circumference of the room. Standing room only, perhaps? His light went to the walls, flitting over statues, none of them depicting Charlemagne or saints, none of them— *whoa.*

An image of a man had been painted on the wall. A beardless man wearing plain robes and looking forward. A thin circle of gold sat on his head. A golden crown. A crown Harry recognized, because he had found it hidden under the streets of Zurich barely a month ago. The lost crown of Charlemagne.

"It's Charlemagne," Harry said to himself. "Without a beard."

All the imagery of Charlemagne he'd seen thus far had consistently shown him with a beard. Until now. "Found you." Harry tilted his head. "What are you looking at?"

This painting was above the chapel's main entrance. Charlemagne looked directly across the room to the rear wall, to somewhere behind the altar. During worship a priest would stand behind the altar and in front of a beautifully carved, gigantic cross. Harry's gaze narrowed. Was that writing on the cross? He stepped closer and looked past the cross, back to the rear wall. It also had writing on it. Latin letters, carved into the stone. His gut told him to check there first. The Latin letters on the rear wall came into view as he moved to stand beside the cross.

I follow the heavenly path to look down on Agilulph's cross.

His actual name. Not a vague allusion, and left in plain sight. Harry frowned. Why was Agilulph changing tactics now, being more direct? So far, most clues had been left where anyone could find them, but the trick was realizing those images or messages *were* clues.

"He's being direct now. Why?" Maybe it was because this message was on the far edge of Charlemagne's world. Maybe something else. Hard to say. Just follow the clues. Find the treasure.

"What is *Agilulph's cross*?" Harry turned back toward the giant wooden cross and leaned back until he could see the letters on it, also Latin.

For the glory of God. Standard stuff. What came next was not. Agilulph's name was inscribed directly below the phrase. "Agilulph brought the cross here," Harry said to himself. "That's what the message means. Charlemagne is looking at both the rear wall *and* the cross."

The rear wall told him to *look down on Agilulph's cross* by taking *the heavenly path*. He studied the cross. A cross big enough to stand on, come to think of it. Instinct told him to keep looking. To look all the way up to the walkway halfway up the wall, running around the upper reaches of the chapel. A walkway he'd thought was there for overflow seating. "Or for getting to the top of the cross." The central portion of the cross was almost level with the walkway, and it was hardly more than a short step from it to the cross. A cross more than big enough to hold something inside.

A narrow staircase led from the chapel floor to the circular walkway. His footsteps were painfully loud as he banged his way up the wood-and-metal stairs to the upper level, then hurried around until he stood at a point where he could look down on the cross. The top of the middle post looked large enough to stand on. All he had to do was hop the guardrail. Harry stepped over, rested his posterior on the rail for a moment, then stepped across. No more than a normal stride length and he was atop the cross, standing on a square of wood several feet wide.

The distant rumbling of tank engines grew louder. Harry hesitated, half expecting the doors to clang open and the platoon to storm through, guns drawn. Nothing happened. He shuffled his feet and squatted. One boot caught on something in the wood of the cross. He looked down and a deep engraving came to life under his penlight. "It's Charlemagne's signature."

A monogram, four letters in all. *K-R-L-S*. "Karolus," Harry said. In Latin, Charlemagne was called *Carolus Magnus*. "Charles the Great." Harry angled his head. Something wasn't right. The shape and letters were correct, but it was just…odd. He blinked. "It's upside down." The *L* should be at the bottom, not the top. The cross's face was in front of him, and from where Harry stood, the *K* should have been at the top. Only a second later the solution hit him. "Fix the signature."

He knelt and was able to put his fingers well into the letter grooves and get a grip. He put the penlight into a pocket, grabbed hold of the grooves and twisted. Nothing. He scowled, twisting harder. One foot skidded out from beneath him and it took some quick dancing to stay atop the cross. "Focus, Harry." He grabbed hold again, got low, and gave it all he had. Hot pain sliced into his fingers where he gripped the wood.

It moved. An inch at first, then two, until without warning the entire signature spun around until it sat right-side up. Harry's breath fogged the chill air. No hidden compartment opened. Harry frowned. He hooked his fingers into the groove and lifted.

The signature came up without any resistance. It was a cover. He lifted the cover like he was opening a jar and held it to one side. He reached for his penlight and clicked it on. "It's empty."

He set the cover down. He immediately picked it up again. Letters had been inscribed on the interior of it. Harry translated the Latin as he read it aloud. *"Seek the temple of Wodanaz where Charlemagne defeated and converted Widukind."*

Who the heck was *Widukind*? He'd never seen that word. "Now Odin's involved?" Odin, also known as Wodanaz, was *the* god in Germanic paganism. A god the defender of Christianity would likely clash with—and it seemed he had. "I bet things didn't turn out well for those *Widukind*." Whoever they were.

A problem for later. Harry had what he needed—a clue as to the next step on his path. Faint shouting sounded from outside. Harry set the lid upside down and took his phone out, turning the light on to snap a photo. It took a moment for the camera to focus on the image. He waited, then tapped the screen.

A door banged open as the light flashed. Harry twisted to find a soldier standing in the now-open doorframe. A soldier who was staring at him. A soldier without a gun. The guy shouted something in Russian. Harry didn't have to understand to get the gist of it. *What are you doing?* He put the lid back, turning his back to block the soldier from seeing before he stood and waved his arms around. He growled a string of unintelligible nonsense, shouting as though the cross had offended him. The arm-waving and throaty noise continued until he was back on the platform and halfway around the room, at which point the soldier spoke again. This time the shout definitely wasn't a question.

Harry ignored him and kept walking. The soldier shouted again. Harry kept walking, faster now, watching out of the corner of his eye. The soldier picked up his gun, the one he'd left behind, slung it over a shoulder, and reached for his belt. Instead of a sidearm, the soldier aimed a flashlight, the beam illuminating Harry, who by now was walking down the stairs to the chapel floor.

Harry lifted a hand to block the light from his face and walked directly at the soldier, growling to cut off yet another outburst from him. A few more steps and he'd be on the guy, close enough to take him down. He only needed time enough to get out of here and away from the base. A few more—

A bomb exploded. Orange light filled the windows and a blast of noise barreled through the open doors as a massive fireball erupted outside. The ground rattled and Harry went to one knee. He swore loudly. In English.

The soldier's eyes widened.

Harry had no time to react before the soldier dropped his flashlight, grabbing at a radio on his belt and turning for the door. The radio chirped, the soldier shouted into it, and Harry ran. The soldier was fast, nearly to the open door and still shouting into his radio when Harry scooped up the dropped flashlight and hurled it at the running soldier's head. *Direct hit.*

The soldier stumbled and fell forward as the flashlight collided with his cranium, his forehead smacking off the doorframe with a *clang* that made Harry wince. The thud of his body hitting the ground was a bit softer. The door swung shut, stopping when it hit the soldier's arm, and a gust of frigid air set Harry's teeth chattering as he ran over to haul the unconscious soldier inside before anyone spotted him. He grabbed the man's feet and pulled.

Gunfire chattered outside, and Harry looked up to see the smoky ruin that used to be a Russian tank, now only charred metal and broken treads. Several soldiers aimed their weapons skyward and were firing, muzzles flashing in a deadly strobe pattern as the men aimed in every direction. They shouted one word over and over as they fired. *Dron. Dron.*

A drone attack. The Ukrainians had attacked with armed drones. Would have been useful to know this was coming. He leaned back down and continued to drag the soldier inside.

Fire erupted by his ear. The metal door flew open as a second bullet hit it, inches from his head. Harry flew back, pulling the unconscious soldier with him into the chapel before kicking the door shut with his foot. The lock caught an instant before more gunfire sounded and shots ripped through the door, tiny holes of light now streaming in. Harry lay flat, not moving until the barrage ceased.

A high-pitched whine filled the air for a few seconds before another explosion rocked the ground and Harry stumbled as he scrambled to his feet and tried to run for the chapel exit. He was nearly to the door when metal banged on metal, gunfire sounded and bullets whizzed past from behind him before slamming into the exit door ahead. Harry dove beneath a row of pews and watched as first one pair of boots came through the door, then a second and third pair. The men were yelling in Russian as they entered the dark chapel. Harry shook his head. *Sorry about this, Agilulph.*

A prayer book lay on the pew behind him. He picked it up, twisted, and hurled the book over the cross so it banged against the rear wall. One Russian immediately loosed fire toward the noise. Everyone was shouting, pointing toward the noise or yelling at the shooter. Harry reached into his pocket, grabbed the ace hidden up his metaphorical sleeve, took aim, and pulled the pin.

Nobody heard the grenade land. The soldiers were still arguing when it detonated by the rear wall. Harry covered his ears and closed his eyes an instant before the muffled explosion. Light filled the room, and when he looked, all the soldiers had dropped to the floor and covered their heads.

He took off out the door and into the hallway, then veered back toward the main entrance, dim hallway lights flashing past as he raced onward, his boots slapping the marble floors. As he passed the gaping hole in the hallway corridor, he glanced out to see soldiers milling about, many with their rifles aimed at the sky and firing toward the stars. Others were jumping into vehicles or simply taking cover in the instant he could see them before the hole flew by and he turned and continued down the hallway stretching ahead. He sped up when he heard the sound of soldiers giving chase, their footfalls echoing off the walls. *I need another exit. Not the front. They could radio ahead. A different way out.* No exits waited ahead. His throat tightened as a sharp whine sounded and grew quickly louder.

The wall ahead of him exploded.

One moment, the hallway existed. The next, a fireball blew through it to leave a crater in front of him. A Ukrainian missile had been sent from the gods. Harry blinked, then ran through the jagged gap, stopping only to pull a radio from one soldier's belt before he darted outside into utter chaos. Russians were lying on the ground, arms covering their heads, as Harry raced past them. Anti-aircraft guns mounted on the backs of trucks were blasting away, their operators too busy to notice the single soldier zipping past.

A quick check to get his bearings and he discovered the first armory he'd passed was not far ahead, along with a personnel carrier and a row of Jeeps. He ran toward the armory, the one from which he'd stolen the grenades. Engines roared behind him as he approached the big metal box, its lights flashing and washing away the protective darkness. He juked to one side, dove and rolled on the ground, then stopped in time to see a pair of motorcycles fly past, with more coming behind them. The armory door was within arm's reach. He accelerated, ripped the metal door open and jumped inside. The last thing he saw before the door slammed shut was a glimpse of his escape route, a side road that should have been virtually empty. The road was crawling with Russians.

I need a distraction. He turned. Row upon row of weaponry stretched out behind him. One familiar item caught his eye. *That should work.*

The door creaked as he opened it a fraction, just far enough that he could see the row of Jeeps. And one other type of vehicle. A big one. As he turned and went back to a specific row of weaponry, one thought ran through his head. *The keys better be in there.*

He hefted the long metal tube onto a shoulder, walked to the door, and paused. Deep breath, then another. What was the secret of blending in? Act like you belong. He pushed the door open and stepped out.

Pandemonium reigned. Helicopters circled overhead. Jeeps and soldiers on foot were moving fast toward the camp in a line, flashlights lighting up the waving grass and headlights bouncing as vehicles covered rough ground. Another drone firing missiles lit the night sky to his rear. Harry ran straight for a personnel carrier parked alongside a row of Jeeps, lugging his new tool with each step, eyes straight ahead. A flashlight blinded him for a moment. He stood his ground and it moved away.

He made it to the carrier. It was long and shaped like a school bus, and the rear portion had a canvas roof atop metal ribs, with a small enclosed area at the front for a driver and passenger. Eight oversized tires helped it move through all sorts of terrain. He stood beside the driver's door. The vehicle was big enough to hold twenty soldiers. Or to cause one heck of a distraction. He hoped.

Harry spread his legs, distributing his weight equally between his front and back feet, his rear foot braced against one of the big tires. The metal tube went on his shoulder. He couldn't read the Cyrillic writing running across it. He imagined it said something like *Shoulder-Launched Multipurpose Assault Weapon*. A weapon designed for taking out tanks. Most people called them missile launchers. Tonight, Harry called it his ticket out of there.

He closed one eye and took aim at the arms depot. He needed an explosion, the bigger the better. His finger settled on the trigger.

Light blinded him. A helicopter's downdraft sent dirt and snow flying as it moved toward Harry, the brilliant spotlight now trained on him. Russian words blared from the chopper's speaker. The big machine whirled no more than twenty feet overhead. A side door flew open, and one soldier leaned out of the big bird to aim his pistol at Harry. Bullets sparked off the personnel carrier.

Harry dropped the launcher, reached into his pocket, and with a smooth toss threw a live grenade into the chopper's open door. A beat passed as he scooped up the missile launcher and took aim. He touched the trigger as the first man jumped, followed by the rest of the soldiers on board the chopper. They shouted as they fell, landing and rolling on the ground. Harry waited a full breath before he squeezed the trigger.

The rocket launched and Harry flew back. A fireball burst to life on his arm, the missile erupting and streaking away in a fiery display, passing underneath the falling helicopter and across the field before crashing directly into the metal shed. That's the last thing Harry saw before he landed on his backside, thrown by the missile's force.

The concussive blast of who-knows-what exploding was a physical force that blew the unmanned helicopter sideways and down, its spinning blades digging into the earth before the metal bird crumpled on itself, flipped over and was still. Soldiers ran, windows shattered and for a few seconds Harry had a quiet piece of the world to himself—quiet because he'd probably done permanent damage to his hearing, but in that chaos, nobody was looking for him. He saw something spin down from the sky in a burning circle. It was a drone.

Time to go. He jumped up, banged into the side of the personnel carrier and fell down. The second try had better results. Clambering up, he slammed the door shut and reached for the ignition. No keys. They weren't hanging from the dashboard, weren't on the seat, weren't under the mat. No keys in here at all. Only a push-button ignition that was no good without keys. The button just sat there, taunting him. He jabbed his thumb at it.

The engine fired to life.

Harry sat straight up. Apparently military vehicles didn't have keys. Who knew?

Soldiers had started moving outside the windshield as he ripped his coat off and jammed it down onto the accelerator. The thick military fabric was heavy enough to keep the pedal down and the engine roaring as he sat up and threw his door open. One soldier looked at the vehicle's blazing lights, angled his head a bit to listen to the thundering engine, and stared. Harry twisted the wheel. A little more, a little more—*perfect.* He reached for the seat belt and looped it through the top of the steering wheel, then down and around before pulling it back out the bottom and clicking it into the lock. Harry tested the makeshift aiming device by twisting the wheel back and forth. It held steady.

Good enough. He ripped the shifter from *Park* to *Drive* and leapt out. The doorframe clipped his heel as the truck shot forward, churning dirt and snow into a muddy shower that sprayed behind the personnel carrier as it raced directly at the line of cars moving slowly toward camp. A handful of gunshots rang out before the carrier smashed off one Jeep and then another before careening down the line to take out several more.

Harry hunched low and ran toward the parked Jeeps. Everyone was running toward the explosion or the helicopter or shooting at the runaway personnel carrier. Nobody noticed the too-tan not-a-Russian soldier climbing into a Jeep at the very edge of the row. A Jeep parked close to the river. A Jeep, an observant person might notice, that was an amphibious vehicle. Harry knew the moment he spotted it that this relic from past conflicts was his ticket out. Fate smiled on him as he found the keys in the ignition.

The engine sparked to life. Harry kept the lights off, backing slowly toward the river behind him until the rear end dipped down, and then the front end followed, and just like that, he was floating. He pressed the accelerator to activate the screw hidden between the tires. Water churned softly as he spun the wheel and headed downriver, aiming the bow toward his rendezvous point. He turned to look back toward the Russian camp. A crashed helicopter, a burning arms depot, and a personnel carrier now immobilized on bullet-riddled tires.

Harry leaned back and shook his head. *Sara's never gonna believe me.*

Chapter 2

Brooklyn

A soft *ding* sounded in Harry's office. He frowned, looked up from the piece of paper in front of him and pressed a button on his desk phone. "What's up, Scott?"

"She's coming."

"How far?"

"Half a block."

"Thanks for the warning." Harry pressed a button to disconnect the call, then stood from behind his desk. His back let out a series of alarming noises when he stretched this way and that. Scott Marlow had barely been working there for a month. One of the changes his very first employee had made right off the bat was installing security cameras on buildings all around the block. It was a good thing Harry was on friendly terms with all his neighbors. They were the sort of people who didn't mind him putting up surveillance equipment that was probably illegal. Cameras on other shops. On streetlights. On fire hydrants. Cameras covering every inch of the block. His neighbors didn't mind because, of all the residents in this decidedly Italian block in Brooklyn, Harry Fox was the most Italian of them all. In spirit, at least.

"Good morning, Scott."

"Good morning, Sara. Nice to see you."

"I'm sorry your employer has returned."

"As am I."

Harry called out from behind his desk. "I can hear you."

"I certainly hope so," Sara fired back. "How else would you get the message? Scott is far too polite."

Scott chuckled softly. Not so softly Harry couldn't hear it, but the laughter and everything else in his world momentarily vanished when Sara Hamed walked into his office. She made a show of checking her watch. "It's almost noon. I'm surprised you're awake."

"How can I sleep when there's a mystery to unravel?" He tapped the single sheet of paper on his desk. "You're just in time. I might have something."

Sara's eyes narrowed as she picked up the paper, pushing past him without looking up to take his chair. Harry crossed his arms on his chest. "Be my guest," he said.

"I will," she said. Finally, she looked up for the briefest of moments. "Care to tell me where you found this? I asked last night but you fell asleep before I could get an answer."

His mind went back to a haze of airplanes, sleep deprivation, and the aftereffects of nearly getting killed a half-dozen times in thirty minutes. "I was tired."

"Would that be from your escapades with the Ukrainian army, the Russian army, or a different nation's armed forces of which I am unaware?"

"The first two." He frowned his best frown. "Fine," he said. "It started on Evgeny's yacht."

"Were there stewardesses?"

"What do you think?"

"I'll take that as a yes."

One side of his lip curled up. "You worried they might like me?"

"Disappointed they didn't keep you is more like it."

He ignored her jibe and relayed the tale of his Ukrainian adventure. Being smuggled into the Russian operating base, borrowing a Russian uniform, finding Charlemagne's image and the message in Agilulph's cross, and finally the destruction and the waterlogged route of his escape. She listened until he finished. "I didn't know amphibious vehicles were still in use."

"Guess I'm lucky." Harry inclined his head toward a glossy magazine on his desk. He'd left it open to a specific page. The one with Sara's beaming face on it. "Impressive."

Sara spared herself half a glance. "The impressive part will be me surviving this tour. The logistics are already a nightmare."

"That happens when you make the biggest archaeological discovery since King Tut's tomb."

"*We* made the discovery. Not me. We."

True, he had been with her when they found the tomb of Alexander the Great. It had been a team effort, but the media tended to focus on her. "You'll dazzle them."

"I'd rather help unravel Agilulph's message." She set the paper down. "Tell me your thoughts."

Scott appeared in his office doorway before Harry could respond. "You said you wanted this when I was done." Scott lobbed the morning paper onto Harry's desk. A direct hit on top of the printout. "The write-up on your stepfather is nice."

"Thanks, Scott." Harry grabbed the newspaper off Agilulph's message. He held the front page up for Sara to see. "He's moving up in the world."

He was Harry Fox's stepfather, Gary Doyle. A man who, only several months prior, had told Harry he'd never want to be the district attorney. Then the political dominoes fell, ending with Gary Doyle appointed as the interim district attorney. The prior D.A., who had been Gary's boss, had won the special election for mayor.

"The world *is* change," Sara said. "Embrace it. Or be left behind."

"You should write greeting cards."

She aimed a finger loaded with ill-intent. "At least they've moved on from pictures of me."

"You mean pictures of us."

A theatrical sigh. "Yes, of us. I cannot believe they published that photo."

It was a snapshot of Sara and Harry at a museum reception announcing that Sara's exhibition would be making an international tour. As the American Museum of Natural History's curator-in-charge of Asian and African ethnology, and one of the duo who had located Alexander the Great's tomb and the Library of Alexandria, Sara Hamed's face likely sold papers. Harry liked to think he didn't drag the overall aesthetic down too much.

"I like that picture of us," Harry said. "Maybe I'll get it framed and hang it on the wall."

"You will do no such thing."

"Jeez. You've hardly been living there a month and I no longer control what goes on my own walls."

"I control what hangs on our walls. You exist to agree."

"And to pay for overpriced towels."

"Towels and robes. Both are crucial." She lifted her chin. "Your thoughts on the message?"

He reached over his desk and opened a drawer, making a point of bumping her knee before he lifted a tablet from inside and set it on the desk. "Here is Agilulph's message." Harry scrawled an English translation on the pad, angled so Sara could see it. *"Seek the temple of Wodanaz where Charlemagne defeated and converted Widukind."*

"Confusing, isn't it?"

"Allow me to enlighten you." He laughed when she smacked his arm. "Over time, facts can become hazy, subject to change for many reasons, one being that the stories are retold by people, and the people sharing those stories let their personal experiences color what they say."

"The historical record can become a long game of 'Telephone,'" Sara said. "I believe that's how you put it before."

"Excellent description, so I'm sure I did. *Wodanaz* is a god. One we know of. Quite well, in fact."

"Except we know him as Odin," Sara said. "A Germanic deity whose mythological influence touches every person in America even today."

"Odin, or *Woden* or *Wodanaz*—take your pick—is the origin of the fourth day of our week. Wednesday."

Sara gave him a silent golf clap. "Well done."

"Agilulph is telling us to look for a temple of Odin. Seems odd that an abbot for the most fiercely Christian king of the Middle Ages points us to a pagan," Harry said. "Apparently things didn't go well for the *Widukind*. Ever heard of them?"

"Widukind wasn't a tribe. Widukind was a Saxon king."

"Who worshipped Odin."

"And who spent three decades fighting Charlemagne in the Saxon Wars."

"Forget greeting cards. You should have been a professor." He failed to dodge her fist before it whacked his arm. "That war began when a small band of Saxons burned an anonymous church. It ended with Charlemagne forcing the king to be baptized."

"A condition of surrender."

"Imposed by Charlemagne," Harry said. "They were *converted*, but not by choice."

"Any chance their final defeat occurred at a temple dedicated to Odin?"

"That's the rub. It's hard to pin down the *final* final defeat. Widukind and Charlemagne engaged in a series of battles, none of them ending in a complete, lasting surrender."

"None was decisive enough to end the war."

"There would be peace for a time, then the conflict would start up again. It seems Widukind eventually surrendered without a fight, and without losing his kingdom."

Sara grinned. "He agreed to be baptized a Christian in exchange for keeping his crown."

"Shrewd on his part. Yes, Widukind converted to keep his crown. And his head, I expect. Where did all of this happen?" Harry lifted a shoulder. "Hard to say. The records are unclear. It definitely happened in Germany, and most sources agree it was at a site of importance to the Saxons, but there are a few candidates."

Sara leaned forward, reached across the desk and picked up the newspaper. "Do any appear more likely to you?" she asked as she unfolded the paper and looked at the picture of Gary Doyle.

"As a matter of fact, yes." Harry tapped his notebook. "Agilulph left this trail of messages in order to ensure peace after Charlemagne's death. He believed whoever followed it would be Frankish, perhaps even related to Charlemagne. They would have known about Charlemagne's victory over the Saxons. More importantly, they would have known what Charlemagne did to his enemies. While historians can't agree on where Widukind surrendered, it is clear where he was *baptized*."

"Charlemagne would have made a big show of it. In a castle, rather than a humble church."

"Exactly. Big, imposing and impenetrable castles. Widukind's baptism occurred at the biggest, most impressive castle in all of Germany at the time. A castle that's still around today." He paused. "Cochem Imperial Castle."

A look Harry rarely saw on Sara's face crossed it. "I'm not familiar with it."

"You haven't heard of it because Cochem was a big deal in Charlemagne's time, but it's a small place today. Only about five thousand people live there."

He moved around to stand in front of his computer and tapped at the keyboard. A few moments later a castle appeared on-screen. One straight out of a fairy tale. "Impressed?"

Cochem Castle dated to a century before Charlemagne's time and had originally been built by a Frankish duke. Charlemagne's father had taken a liking to the place and decided such a structure was fit for a king. The Frankish duke, understanding what friends in high places could do for him, gave his castle to the king, who then expanded it into a grand palace of pointed spires and imposing towers surrounded by a twenty-foot wall. Any army hoping to breach those walls would soon find themselves running short on soldiers.

"It's pretty," Sara said. "Strategically located, too." She feigned a wide yawn. "You want to impress me? Tell me why Agilulph pointed you here. And do better than 'Widukind surrendered inside.'"

Harry typed on the keyboard again. A new image came up. One of a yellowed, aged book. "This is an account of Charlemagne's conquests. A second-hand account from one of his generals, written in Latin and based on a different first-hand account written in German by a priest in Widukind's court."

"Making it unreliable at best. Charlemagne's man would have taken pains to paint his king in a positive light. A wholly different approach than the one the German cleric would take."

"True, but I'm not looking for historical accuracy." Harry zoomed in on a specific section of the page. "I'm looking for *directions*."

One of Sara's eyebrows went up. "Go on."

"This book mentions a temple in Cochem Castle. One that existed *before* Widukind's surrender and baptism. A temple I cannot find another mention of anywhere else."

"A Germanic pagan temple." She looked at Harry. He didn't respond. He tapped the screen, and she leaned closer, angling her head to one side. "Not merely a temple. One dedicated to the *false pagan god*."

"What false pagan god would a Christian general serving Charlemagne know of?" Harry drew a breath. "Odin."

Sara's lips parted in surprise. "Well done, Harry. You found it."

"Perhaps." He noted the confusion on her face. "Cochem Castle has been in private hands since the first stone was laid."

She sat upright in the chair. "It's privately owned?"

"By different families over the centuries, but the current family has been in residence for over four hundred years."

A fan on the ceiling twirled slowly as Sara looked at nothing, staring through Harry, through the wall behind him. He waited. "That may present a challenge," Sara eventually said. "Is the castle open to the public?"

"No. The Schweinsteiger family is very private. They're wealthy, of course. Cochem Castle is their ancestral home, and they treat it like a fortress in constant danger of being attacked."

"So they're paranoid?"

"Maybe they're just oddballs. Every recent image I've seen of the place shows armed guards on patrol."

"Do older photographs show any details?"

Harry shook his head. "Cameras didn't exist when outsiders could last get inside. There's nothing."

"Written descriptions?"

"There are a few. They're old, and by old, I mean centuries old." He tapped the keyboard until a new image appeared on-screen. "This is a translation of a letter from a Bavarian aristocrat to the King of Bavaria. It's mainly about business involving the Schweinsteigers and the king. The Schweinsteiger family had invited this aristocrat into their home, and the aristocrat wrote the king a detailed description of his tour." Harry touched the monitor. "Which included a description of a chapel inside the castle. A chapel for which he uses a unique turn of phrase."

Sara pushed his hand aside. "A *chapel reclaimed from the pagans to celebrate Charlemagne's glorious victory.*" She looked to Harry. "Charlemagne had more than one victory over pagans."

"Yes, but how many in which he defeated King Widukind?"

"Very few."

"Which tells me any pagan temple inside Cochem Castle is a solid candidate for the site of Widukind's baptism." Harry stepped back and spread his arms out. "What better way to celebrate victory than to baptize the pagan in his own temple? The symbolism is incredible."

"A temple we're pinpointing based on the word of some Bavarian aristocrat from when Abraham Lincoln was president. Hardly conclusive." The look on her face said otherwise.

"This isn't like your world of academia. My world isn't exact. You know this." She'd been on enough adventures with him to understand. "From where I stand, it's a fairly solid lead."

"Solid enough to investigate," Sara said. "I agree. How do you convince the Schweinsteigers to let you in?"

Harry rubbed the stubble on his chin. He pursed his lips, letting air flow out in a stream. "I have no idea."

"Come now, Harry." Sara aimed her finger, the one that made him nervous, at his chest. "Think about what you have to offer. That's what will get you inside. Where do your interests align with the Schweinsteigers' interests? That is where you start."

"They're rich German aristocrats. Not the sort of people you see in this Italian part of Brooklyn. Cultural connections won't work."

"Are you certain?"

"Yes."

"You shouldn't be."

"Why not?"

"Think about what you said. *Cultural.* They live in an ancient castle. What do old castles often contain?"

Of course. "Cultural relics. I know a thing or two about those."

"There you have it." Her teeth flashed again, but when she pulled an errant strand of auburn hair behind her ear, Sara's gaze was slightly unfocused, her tone soft. "Your way inside."

"The family has lived there long enough that they must have German and Bavarian relics stacked to the ceiling. Tapestries, paintings, weaponry." Yes, this could work. "I could inquire about buying some of it."

"I thought you said they are rich."

"I could offer to sell them some of my inventory. Rich people love relics." He would know, given how much money flowed in and out of his store every week. Fox and Son was the hottest private antiquities shop in the city right now, and the more business Harry did with people in high-income brackets, the more they talked to their friends, and the more his business grew. One of his clients might even know the Schweinsteiger family. "There's one problem. People like them go through intermediaries. I almost never meet clients face-to-face." He rubbed his chin again. "I need to get inside the castle. And I need to be left alone to check it out."

"To find the pagan temple."

"Which I can hardly do with the Schweinsteigers and their guards hanging around."

"Baron or Count Schweinsteiger is likely an old man," Sara said. "I'm sure you can convince him to let you explore the grounds."

"Hardly. The old baron died recently. His only son is a young man, around twenty-five years old. It appears the new baron is far more interested in his social circle than in assuming his familial responsibilities. It may still be an opportunity, though. This new baron may not be as protective of any relics gathering dust in corners. I could look to purchase antiquities, not sell them. That might give me a chance to poke around inside the castle as part of my 'acquisition trip.'"

"Perhaps."

Sara's gaze landed on him only briefly before she went back to looking through the wall. Harry counted to five in his head. "Are you okay?" he asked.

"I'm fine."

"I get the feeling there's something you're not saying." Her face said there was, so he barreled on. "You think this is asking for trouble. You think I should let this be, that I don't need what Agilulph left behind to finish what I started."

A mild way to describe his personal vendetta against the man who had stolen everything Harry should have had. A normal life. A family. "Olivier Lloris will be dealt with," Harry said. "Nobody is safe until he's gone."

"You have his trust," Sara said. "Why keep going? Finish it now."

Funny how Sara had changed since she'd met Harry a few years ago. When she was an Egyptologist at a German university, the idea that she would condone a blood feud against a French industrialist would have been laughable. That was before she moved across an ocean to be with Harry. Then moved into his house.

"I promised Olivier the most incredible relic tied to Charlemagne that anyone has ever seen."

"A ruse to get close enough to finish him," Sara said. "You're close enough to him now. The only reason you keep going is for you. Not him."

He hesitated. She was right. Not that he'd admit it. "I'm just being thorough." The derisive noise she made summed up her thoughts. "Agilulph's trail is nearly at its end. Which means Olivier's time is running out as well."

"I hope you are right," Sara said. "Remember to keep an open mind in the castle. Charlemagne was interested in more than gold and wealth. Relics tied to him may be of a completely different variety."

"What are you getting at?"

"The Carolingian Renaissance, mainly."

Faint memories of long-ago textbooks came to mind. "Right," he said without conviction.

Sara sighed. "A revival of learning equal to the European cultural movement five centuries ago?"

"That would be the Renaissance."

"Yes, but it's hardly the only one. The Carolingian Renaissance was arguably as important, if not more so. Charlemagne gave full effort to increasing literacy and preserving knowledge. He followed the example of Emperor Constantine, who did much the same in the fourth century. They both focused on the *trivium* and the *quadrivium*." She noted the lack of response on his face. "Two different courses of study? Not ringing any bells?"

"Remind me."

"Trivium includes the study of grammar, logic and rhetoric. Quadrivium focuses on arithmetic, geometry, music and astronomy." A hint of a smile. "Care to guess which Charlemagne believed to be more valuable?"

"Quadrivium, of course. Romans were mathematicians, scientists. Charlemagne would have held those in higher regard than grammar and rhetoric."

"You would have made a poor Carolingian scholar. Charlemagne valued the trivium more. He considered that study to be more relevant to understanding the meaning of Scripture and the Will of God."

"That's a trick question."

"Perhaps," she said with a toss of her hair. "You are also wrong about one other point."

Harry crossed his arms. "What's that?"

"What I'm not saying." She stood from her chair, pulled Harry past her and deposited his backside into the warm seat. "I do have another matter occupying my thoughts," she said as she half-sat on his desk. "I've received an offer."

Harry nearly shot out of the chair. "A job offer? Is it back in Europe?"

"Not a teaching offer. An offer to participate in a dig."

The nerves that had gone so tight relaxed. "Oh," he said, settling back down. "That's neat. Where?"

She rolled her eyes at the word *neat*. "The Sinai Peninsula. Archaeologists uncovered a temple complex slightly over a month ago. A Greek temple dedicated to Zeus."

Harry's brain caught up with her words. "Hang on. In *Egypt?* Zeus is a Greek god. Egyptians didn't worship him."

Her eyes sparked. "It appears every history book I've studied has been wrong."

"Wow."

"This could upend everything we thought we knew about the evolution of the Grecian belief system." She stood, her arms moving in every direction. "Greeks and Egyptians worshipping Zeus together hundreds or even thousands of years earlier than we believed."

She must have noticed the look on Harry's face, for Sara trailed off quickly.

"Sounds like you're excited," he said. "Good."

Sara, whose well of confidence always appeared bottomless, hesitated. "Do you mean that?"

"Why wouldn't I support this? It's what you do."

"I was worried you might be disappointed."

He *was* disappointed. He also knew to keep his mouth shut. "Because you wouldn't come with me to Germany?"

"Yes."

"Would I love for you to come? Yes." A true statement. "Am I even more excited for you to get back in the field for such a great project? Yes times two." Partially true, at best. "Get back to your field work and remind people who's still the best Egyptologist in the world."

She leaned over and touched his arm. "Despite your many flaws, you can be wonderful."

He nodded. "I try." He pushed aside any personal disappointment at the news. Sara was clearly thrilled at this chance. And he could handle himself in the field, same as he'd done for years before Sara came along. Going it alone would even do him some good, let him sharpen his skills. Yes, that's what it would do. This was good. "Tell me more about the dig."

"It is organized by—" and here she stopped. Harry didn't move, didn't say a word. Not with the look on her face. A look he'd seen before and knew enough to stay far away from. Sara was unhappy about something. "By a professional colleague with whom I've dealt in the past."

"That's an odd way to say *old friend*."

Lines creased her forehead. "No. Ramy Gad is certainly not my friend."

Harry sensed dangerous waters ahead. "Then what is he?"

"Ramy Gad is an arrogant, entitled boor. Ramy Gad would never admit this out loud, because he is far too scheming, but he believes women are better suited for washing dishes and baking bread than conducting scholarly research. Or thinking for themselves."

"Sounds like a nice guy."

"Unfortunately, he is not unique in the world of Egyptian academia. As such, he has friends. One of whom is funding this large-scale dig."

"Does Ramy know you're not a fan?"

"He knows I have nothing but contempt for him."

"Then why would he invite you to join his dig?"

"It's not *his* dig." She gritted her teeth. "He's merely the head Egyptologist."

"Who may realize you're the person to make this dig succeed *and* make him look good."

"Perhaps." Her pocket buzzed. Sara pulled out her phone. "How did Ramy get my phone number?"

"Probably called your office and asked for it. That's what I'd do."

She glared at him. He'd missed the note stating her question was rhetorical. "Listen to this message. 'Looking forward to your support as you join our dig.'" She showed Harry the screen, as though he were foolish enough to doubt her. "Can you believe it? Assuming I will accept any offer from him."

"So you're refusing?"

"Of course not." She sighed the sigh of a woman surrounded by fools. "I can't miss this opportunity."

"Why don't you call him?"

"Why would I do that?"

"To show you're doing this on your terms. Not his." Sara didn't bite his head off, which meant she was considering it. Harry took the opening. "Call and make a demand," Harry continued. "Insist on your own tent. Or a personal trailer. With air conditioning."

"I don't need air conditioning."

"Then demand something else." Harry threw a hand up. "What you ask for isn't the point. Ask for something, and make him give it to you. Be pleasant, and show him he can't boss you around. This may be his dig, but that doesn't mean he's in charge."

"I just told you it's not *his* dig."

"Then whose is it?"

"Whoever signs the checks." She chewed the inside of her lip for a moment. "You're right. It's a good idea to call."

Sara tapped her phone screen as a thought lingered in Harry's mind. *She doesn't know who's paying for the dig?* Odd. Could be this happened all the time. As long as she received credit for her work, and he'd push to confirm she would, then where the money came from probably didn't matter.

"Good morning," Sara said, putting the phone to her ear. "Yes, Ramy. It has been a long time. Yes, I am well." She rolled her eyes at Harry. "I need a moment of your time. Yes, right now."

Harry flashed a thumbs-up gesture and mouthed *You got this*.

"It's about your offer," Sara said. "I'm intrigued. No," she said quicky. "I didn't say I was coming. I said I was intrigued. Why wouldn't I come? I cannot imagine spending that amount of time in the Sinai Peninsula without..." and here she hesitated, her gaze racing across the room. It settled on Harry and he nearly jumped. "The proper office equipment," Sara finished. "I will require a specific working environment."

Ramy clearly didn't like that. "Come now," Sara said. "This is not an unreasonable request." She then rattled off a list of very unreasonable demands. A specific office chair. Multiple computers. Carpeting for her private working area. Plus, and this was Harry's favorite, the working area must be both heated *and* air conditioned.

"I'm certain you will find the funding," Sara said. "Do we have an agreement?"

Judging from the look of pleasure on her face, Ramy was letting her have it. She kept quiet. Eventually, he must have agreed. "Excellent," Sara said. "Then I look forward to this project."

She clicked off without waiting for a reply. "Was that what you had in mind?" she asked.

"Even better," Harry said.

"Thank you." Sara set the phone down. "Now, about your castle visit. I worry that this proposed relic purchase ruse may not be sufficient to give you full access."

"Yeah, I do too. There are a dozen ways they could handle that request without letting me inside, let alone giving me a chance to roam freely."

She leaned against his desk once more, arms across her chest. "I used to give students with thesis proposals this advice: aim high."

"I'm breaking into a castle. How is that not high enough?"

Her ponytail shook. "I don't mean your goal isn't lofty. It's your approach." She stood, tried to begin pacing, and had to settle for a single step. "Consider. You want to get inside the castle, with time to move about undetected. The Schweinsteigers certainly won't take kindly to you wandering around their personal residence, so you must redirect their attention. Make them believe your purpose is not an imposition, but a benefit. Any ideas?"

He considered for a second. "I'd say gain their trust. Or make them think I'm someone I'm not. Someone there to help, not hurt."

"Or someone less important than they realize. A follower, not a leader."

"I could be the trophy assistant to a beautiful Egyptologist interested in the collection."

"Funny, but you're on the right path. The best way is to take the attention off you and onto their interests."

"Okay, I'll bite. I'm the antiquities expert. Allegedly. But my visit can't be about antiquities or relics. It has to make them focus on something else."

"A larger issue."

He puzzled. He puzzled some more. "I'm lost," he finally said. "Tell me."

"I wouldn't ask to buy relics from them. You said the new family head is young, a socialite. Someone who may not appreciate the relics in that castle." One corner of her lip turned up. "What if they're not interested in the history of the castle at all? Perhaps you can offer more modern accommodations, befitting a modern baron."

It hit him. *Aim high.* "You don't think I should buy their antiquities. You think I should offer to buy the *entire castle*. How much does a castle cost?"

"More than you can afford."

"This is a bad plan."

"But not more than your friend Evgeny can afford."

Harry raised his hands, palms out. "I've had it with Evgeny Smolov."

The exiled Russian oligarch was worth more than ten billion dollars. Evgeny Smolov believed the world belonged to him and that everyone in it was at his disposal. The first time they'd crossed paths Harry had been forced to hand over the armor of Achilles. Armor Evgeny now took great pride in displaying in his private museum.

"Why would Evgeny buy a castle?"

"He wouldn't buy the castle. It's a ruse to get you inside. And he owes you." Her face tightened. "Many times over. You can finally use Evgeny for your purposes instead of the other way round. How would that feel?"

"Long overdue." Harry still wasn't sold. "Why would he stick his neck out for me?"

"Because Evgeny Smolov is decent. It's buried beneath a thick shell of arrogance, but it's there."

"He doesn't like me," Harry said. "He likes you."

"Then tell him it's a favor for me." She shrugged. "Or tell him you won't work for him again unless he agrees to help us."

Harry couldn't help but grin. "I like it. But tell me how in the world Evgeny can get us inside."

"His money is your ticket in. Evgeny collects. Jets, paintings, women." Her voice dropped. "And massive homes."

"You want Evgeny to pretend he wants to buy the castle."

"Yes. An offer that requires an inspection, and in this case, an inventory of the contents."

Harry snapped his fingers. "He can say I'm his antiquities expert or whatever. That's my chance to look for the pagan temple without anyone watching." He turned it over in his head. "The baron's guards won't be happy if they find me snooping around."

"Play dumb. You can sell it."

"I choose to ignore your comment." The sound of Scott Marlow's stool creaking from the front sounded. A bell pinged as the front door opened. Scott was walking to the back now, his footsteps soft. "It could work," Harry said. "I'll need someone who knows their way around the finances—how to create a believable offer."

"Evgeny has dozens of people to help."

Harry shook his head. "None of whom I can trust. I need someone I know. Someone who can warn me if things start going wrong. Evgeny's people won't speak up."

A knock sounded on the open office door. Harry looked up to see Scott standing there with a small box in his hands. "Package for you," Scott said.

Harry pointed at Scott. "Any idea where I can find a financial whiz?"

Scott set the box on the floor. "You want my take on where to find someone like that?"

Harry started. "You heard us?"

"Every word. Close the door if you want to keep secrets."

Harry ignored Sara's smirk. "Yes, I'd like your take," he told Scott.

"It's a solid plan. Risky, but solid."

"You ever deal with anything like this?" Harry asked.

"Deceiving someone with the gross domestic product of a small nation, along with putting a neck or two on the line?" Scott winked. "All the time. Count me in."

"Fair enough. Evgeny will be our money man. He just doesn't know it yet."

"That solves half the problem."

Harry and Sara looked at each other. "Half?" they asked in unison.

"All the money in the world isn't useful without a way to move it. For that, you need a bank. Know anybody who runs one?"

"I do." Joey Morello had expanded his criminal operations to include legitimate businesses, including a genuine boutique bank. "Right now, he mainly deals in renewable energy and banking, with a side of legal gambling. Not real estate."

Scott waved a hand. "If it's a legitimate banking operation, it can convince the seller."

"How do we start?" Harry asked.

"First, make sure both Evgeny and Joey are on board." Scott turned and began to walk back to the front counter. "I'll take it from there."

Harry couldn't find his tongue until Scott was out of sight. "What a great hire."

"I believe the word you meant to use is *lucky*," Sara said. "And don't get too excited. Will Joey agree to participate in this charade?"

"He won't say no."

"He's also a"—and here Sara appeared to search for a word—"developing entrepreneur. He may not want to risk his reputation."

Joey Morello ran organized crime in New York. His position as the head of the five families, the *capo dei capi*, made him the most powerful mobster on the east coast. Would he turn down Harry's request to save his reputation? Normally Harry would dismiss this out of hand. Except he'd learned the hard way that Sara was often right where he was wrong. "I'll ask him," Harry said. "In person."

"If he hesitates," Sara said. "Tell him I support the idea."

That meant more to him than she knew. "Sure you don't want to come to Germany?" Harry asked.

"Unless this offer falls through, I leave for Egypt soon."

"You think this Ramy guy would make up a story about a dig to get you there for some reason?"

"No, but I learned long ago to verify everything." She motioned for him to move aside so she could get to his chair again. "I will be making travel arrangements while you talk to Joey."

"You sure?"

"Certain."

Harry told her he'd be back soon as he headed for the exit. A quick text to Joey found his old friend at his new bank, in an actual office, overseeing legitimate banking matters. Harry could only shake his head. No smoke-filled rooms with shady characters for Joey.

A trip across the borough and Harry stood on a street corner as the shade of a two-story office building made the cool breeze feel downright cold. He stuck his hands in his pockets and darted across the street. A brass plaque by the front door told visitors the building housed Morello & Partners. No sign hung above the door. Harry nodded approval. Understated. And the *& Partners*? They didn't exist. Joey just liked the way it sounded, and this was Joey's show. Harry pushed through the front door and walked in.

No tellers stood behind a counter. No receptionist waited to greet him. There was no cash machine here. This wasn't that sort of bank. It was the sort where a single employee sat behind a gleaming wooden desk in the corner. Four rich leather armchairs occupied the room's center. The only sound was Harry's footsteps as he crossed the marble floor. The woman looked up when Harry stopped in front of her large desk.

"Mr. Fox," she said in greeting. "Mr. Morello said to send you directly in."

"Thanks." The woman tapped a button on her desk and a door practically hidden in the wall behind her slid open. She gestured for him to enter. Harry walked through, stopping to look back as the door closed behind him. Doors lined either side of the hallway ahead, the sound of muffled conversation coming from behind each of them, the conversations of market analysts at work. He approached the open door at the hall's end and leaned his head through the frame. "Hello?"

"Yes, I understand." Joey Morello turned from a window and waved one hand at Harry to come in, the other hand holding a phone to his ear. "Good. I'll look for that proposal tonight." He clicked off and dropped the phone on his desk. "Come in, Harry. Come in." He got to his feet.

"Good to see you, Joey." Harry gave his closest friend a hug, replete with a couple of whacks on the back. "Thanks for letting me stop by."

"Letting you?" Joey indicated a table beside a window. "You don't need an appointment. You also don't do anything without a reason, including coming here when a phone call works just as well. Want a drink?"

A shelf filled with bottles and a small refrigerator beside it spoke to Harry. "Sure. I'll take a beer."

Joey pulled two bottles from the fridge and opened the tops.

"Cheers," he said, handing one over before they tapped and each took a long pull. "Sit, please." Harry sat, and Joey did likewise. "You in trouble?"

"When am I ever in trouble?"

"Do you want me to talk about this year only, or go back further than that? Which could take a while."

"Fair enough," Harry said. "You've known me too long. No, I'm not in trouble. Trying to avoid it, in fact."

"Pull the other one, kid. It has bells on."

"Very funny."

Joey set his beer down. "Harry Fox does not avoid trouble. He dives in headfirst, consequences be damned, and by some miracle he comes out alive, usually with an ancient relic in hand."

"Or in the hands of a rich guy who may or may not still want to kill me."

"Uh-oh. Sounds like Evgeny Smolov is back. Be nice to him. He's most of the reason I have"—and here Joey picked his beer bottle up and swept it slowly around—"all of this."

"I know he's your biggest client and I shouldn't cross him," Harry said.

"That's pretty much it."

Harry smiled. Joey frowned. "That's exactly what I'm trying to avoid." Harry sipped his drink. "Remember when I told you about Olivier Lloris?"

"The French guy who ruined your life," Joey said.

"Evgeny despises the man."

"Why?"

"It involves a counterfeit painting."

"Sounds interesting."

"I'll tell you about it later. Evgeny Smolov would like nothing more than to see Olivier ruined. Or worse."

"I thought that's what you were doing."

"I am." Harry hesitated. "For me, and for Evgeny." The first part was true. The second, not so much. "I need your help."

No hesitation. "Anything."

"You sure about that?"

"Your father saved my father." Joey lifted a hand, palm out, to stop Harry's response. "I know, I know. I saved your life, then you saved mine, so we're even. Not in my book. The Morello family wouldn't have survived without the Foxes. Whatever you need, ask."

Harry took a breath. "I need your bank."

Joey's beer paused halfway to his mouth. His eyes opened a bit. "This bank."

"Yes, and here's why." Joey sat quietly as Harry roughed out a plan that brought the word *caper* to mind. Joey said nothing until Harry finished speaking. The silence stretched on as Joey studied the tabletop between them, slowly twirling the now-empty beer bottle in his hand.

"You need Evgeny's buy-in," Joey finally said.

"I'm sure I can get him on board. I've done enough favors for him."

"He also saved your life on Mount Olympus."

"Then he stole my Achilles' armor," Harry grumbled.

A hint of a grin flashed across Joey's face. "If we can make this happen without jeopardizing my business, you know I'm in. Whatever you need."

"All we need is a bank to make them believe we're serious. That we have the funds."

"Evgeny Smolov could buy half the castles in Europe if he felt like it."

"That's a yes?"

"Of course it's a yes. Whatever you need." Joey rose before Harry could thank him. "Now take a ride with me."

If Harry wasn't Joey's closest friend, those words could have felt like a threat. "A ride?"

"I have a meeting with the other family heads."

"That's not my business," Harry said.

"You're part of this family." He walked out, leaving Harry to follow as they moved down the quiet hallway. "Call Evgeny while we drive, iron out the details. I'll get your back if he argues."

A sedan waited outside at the curb, an electric vehicle that made zero noise. The man who loomed beside it, however, was far from quiet. "Aladdin!"

Mack was Joey's bodyguard and driver, only two of many hats he had worn while in the Morello family's employ. He was roughly the same size as the trucks bearing his name. Arms resembling tree trunks spread wide before Harry's world turned to an airless darkness of pain. He kept still until the big man let go. "Hey, Mack." Harry gulped a breath. "Good to see you too."

"You too, pretty boy." Mack whacked Harry on the shoulder. Good-natured, and hard enough to bruise. "You coming for the ride?"

"He is," Joey said as he climbed into the rear seat.

What might have been the only bulletproof electric sedan in the city shot away from the curb once they were all inside. Harry texted and called Evgeny without luck. He kept trying during the short drive through Brooklyn until Mack pulled into the lot behind a nondescript residential building in the Hispanic area of Sunset Park. Construction material could be seen through the uncovered windows, with a building permit on display in one. To anyone walking past, this was just another building being upgraded as rents inexorably rose. There was even a small graffiti tag on the front bricks. One Harry knew Joey would have instructed to be done.

"One of your safe houses?" Harry asked as they got out.

"You like it?" Joey asked. "Don't be fooled. The windows are bulletproof."

"You'se want me to wait outside, boss?"

"Yes," Joey told Mack. "I won't be long."

Mack said he understood before pulling something out of the car that made Harry do a double-take. "Is that a remote-control car?" Harry asked.

"Sure is," Mack said. "Watch this."

Mack's two massive thumbs fiddled with the tiny remote control and sent the small car racing for the building front. It didn't slow on approach; instead, it accelerated until Mack hit another button and the car leapt off the ground, spun in mid-air, then latched onto the brickwork and continued *up* the wall at full speed. "Pretty cool, right?" Mack asked as he steered the device. "Even has a camera on it so I can do corners." He pointed to a screen on the control device. "And a walkie-talkie."

Why anyone would need that for a toy car was beyond him. "Very cool," is what Harry said. "They didn't have those when I was a kid."

"Just decide that you haven't grown up yet," Mack said. "Never too late to have some fun."

Harry followed Joey into the safe house with a newfound respect for Mack. The guy might have looked like a lug, but nothing could have been further from the truth. Joey led Harry into what should have been a large dining room, though now the room held only a single table with several chairs around it. The perfect place for a quiet meeting.

Harry turned to find Joey staring at a wall, worry etched on his face. "Something wrong?" Harry asked.

Lines creased Joey's forehead. "I keep thinking Carmelo Piazza has been too quiet lately."

"You keep people close to him, right?"

"Close enough."

"What are they saying?"

"Nothing."

Harry lifted a shoulder. "Could be that's all it is. Nothing."

Joey shook his head. "There's quiet, and then there's too quiet. Carmelo went from trying to kill me to acting as though I don't exist."

Harry knew one thing about what it was like to be Joey Morello. He knew he had no idea what it was like. "Could be he decided picking a fight with you is a bad idea."

"Or he's waiting until my guard is down."

Harry may have imagined it, but the quick jerk of Joey's head could have been that of a man seeing shadows in every corner. "Sicily is a small island. Very small when you're talking about Carmelo's world. Odds are someone would hear something if he was planning to try again."

"Would you risk your life on *odds are*?"

"You do what you think is right," Harry replied. "Just remember, Carmelo doesn't know you found out he sent a guy to kill you. Carmelo thinks he dodged that bullet. Maybe he's not anxious to risk crossing you again." Harry spread his hands out. "Or maybe he's waiting for a better chance."

"Anybody ever tell you how helpful you are?"

Harry couldn't help but chuckle. "I do my best. Unless one of your sources hears anything concrete, it's all a guessing game."

"It makes me nervous."

"It probably should."

Joey rubbed the back of his neck with one hand. "Maybe I'm letting him get to me when there are other things I should worry about."

That's more like it. "Like what?" Harry asked.

"Gio Sabella invited me to discuss a business opportunity," Joey said. "I mentioned how well my investments are doing, and I think he wants to ask me to invest his money in the same fashion as Evgeny and his associates."

"Because you're generating great returns?"

"Perhaps, though I suspect it's more to do with how he feels about my recent changes."

"Going legit."

"As legit as a semi-reformed gangster can be," Joey said. "The Sabellas should be here in a few minutes. Gio's bringing Raf with him." Joey nodded at Harry's pocket. "Try Evgeny again."

Harry's phone vibrated at the same time. "Speak of the devil," he said as he connected the call on speaker. "I'm with Joey Morello," Harry said. "We need to talk."

"How is my money?" Evgeny asked.

"Growing," Joey said.

"It better be." Evgeny laughed, though his tone was ice cold. "What do you want?"

"I need your help," Harry said. "Do what I ask, and you'll have your revenge on Olivier Lloris."

Indecipherable Russian words came through in reply, probably some serious cursing. "How will it happen?"

"I'll have what I need to get him close. Close enough to take him out."

"Tell me the plan."

"It involves a German aristocrat and his castle, Joey's bank, and your money."

"You cannot have my money."

"I don't want your money," Harry said. "I want the influence it brings. This won't cost you a penny."

"Talk. The truth."

"Here's my plan." Harry recited the same story he'd shared with Joey earlier. Unlike Joey, Evgeny couldn't help but interrupt. "Where is this Cochem Castle?" he asked.

"Germany."

"Why do I want to pretend to buy a German castle?"

"Let me finish. It's guarded, likely because the previous baron was paranoid. Or possibly because they have a massive pile of gold bricks and jewels in the basement. I don't know why and it doesn't matter. What does is the only way I can get past those guards to look for a pagan temple is by deception."

"I say I want to buy it, and that gets you inside. Then you find this temple."

"That's it."

"What is in the temple?" Harry explained how it tied to Agilulph's message and the trail to Charlemagne's relic. "There are no relics for me in this plan?" Evgeny asked.

"You have enough relics from me," Harry said. "Alexander's rolling tomb counts as more than one."

Evgeny growled. "This is true."

"And you get revenge on a guy you detest. Unless you forgave him for that business with the painting?"

Evgeny's desire to see pain inflicted upon Olivier Lloris stemmed from a counterfeit painting the Frenchman had sold to Evgeny. Many people held grudges. Evgeny put them all to shame. His ability to never forgive or forget was world class. "Never," Evgeny said. "I will help you."

"I'll be in touch with what I need," Harry said.

Evgeny signed off with heartfelt words celebrating Olivier's impending demise. Harry pocketed his phone as the safe house's front door opened to reveal a man of roughly the same dimensions as Mack. The man stepped inside, nodded respectfully to Joey, then stepped back out. A moment later two normal-sized humans entered before the door closed behind them. One wore the deeply creased face and silvered hair only a lifetime of experience could bring, and he wore it well. The other soon would.

Joey spread his arms out. "Gio. Thank you for coming."

Gio Sabella moved with the grace of a man far younger. He accepted Joey's embrace. "You as well, Joey."

"Hey, Joey." Rafael Sabella offered his hand. "Good to see you."

Joey pulled the Sabella heir in for a smashing hug. "You too, Raf."

Only once this was done did either newcomer acknowledge Harry, though both did so warmly. How a Pakistani-American had come to be so close with the patriarch and son of a powerful crime family in New York was simple: Vincent Morello. Joey's late father had treated Harry Fox like one of his own, and both Sabella men knew better than to risk offending Vincent. That he was dead mattered not one bit. It was about respect.

After the Sabellas exchanged greetings with Harry, he stepped toward the door. "See you around," he said.

Gio lifted a hand. "Please, Harry. You are welcome here."

"Thank you, but I have business."

"Don't we always?" Gio tapped his son on the shoulder. "Rafael will walk you out."

He would? Harry didn't have a chance to respond before Raf turned and headed for the door. Harry took long strides to catch up. He didn't speak until they were outside. "Everything okay?" Harry asked. Having Raf accompany him could mean nothing, merely a ploy on Gio's part to get time alone with Joey. Except why would Gio exclude his son?

Raf watched Mack racing his remote-control car up the building's side. "It's fine," Raf said. "You know my father. Always has a plan up his sleeve."

Harry's ears didn't exactly perk up, but they were listening. "Is that so?"

"Come on, Harry." Raf cuffed him on the arm. "Go ahead and ask. What's he planning?" Raf went ahead before Harry could ask. "He's planning," Raf said softly, "for when he's not around."

"When you're in charge of the family." Harry paused. "Is your father not well?"

"He's more than well. He's a royal pain in my ass." Raf half-grinned. "Which I appreciate. He's making sure you and I are on good terms."

"Good terms?" Harry stepped back. "We've known each other forever. We grew up together."

Raf made a face that some might interpret as guilty. "Yeah, we did. But I wasn't always the nicest guy to outsiders."

"You mean to people who looked like me even if we lived in the neighborhood?"

Raf kicked at the sidewalk. "That's about right."

Harry laughed as a car rolled past with decades-old pop music blaring from the open windows while a woman older than him shouted along. "You think you were the only one? Heck, Raf. I didn't have many friends for a long time. Real friends, at least. You know who treated me the best out of everyone?" Raf said he didn't. "That guy." Harry pointed at Mack. "Mack was my closest Italian friend for most of my childhood. People tolerated me, sure, but that's only because Vincent Morello stood up for me."

"He loved you."

"And lucky for me he did." Harry considered dwelling on the past for a moment, then decided against it. "But that's in the past. People change.

I know I have."

"Same here. I told my father we've been tight for years now. You're a guy I can trust."

All of it true. "He's not so sure?"

"Oh, he is. He's just hedging his bets, as always. If you ask me, he told me to walk out here for you, not for me."

"To show me he wants us to have trust."

"Something like that." Another kick at the concrete. "My father can be funny. The old ways and all that. Besides"—and now Raf turned to look at Harry—"you're someone who makes things happen. We all know that. Guys like you are good to have in our corner."

Harry found himself at a loss for words. Only for a moment. "Thanks." The moment passed. "I'm here if you need me, Raf. Tell your father I said that."

"And I'm here for you."

Apparently, Harry now had two family heads on his side. Not bad. "Thanks."

An impressively awkward second passed as both men struggled with the vitally masculine question of whether they should hug, high five, or ignore what had just happened. They both chose the third option. "So what's this business you're headed off for?" Raf asked to settle the matter.

"You wouldn't believe me if I told you."

"Try me."

Why not? Raf had his back. "I'm using Joey's bank and a Russian oligarch's money as a front to break into a German castle."

Raf nodded. "Sounds like something you'd get into. Anything I can do to help?" Harry said there was not. "Then good luck," Raf said.

Harry sensed an opportunity and took it. "What are you guys up to here?" he asked, inclining his head to the safe house. "Just a business opportunity?"

"That's what my father said, but I think he really wants to talk about what happens after he dies."

"Oh."

Raf waved a hand. "He's just preparing. He'll be around another twenty years at least. He still has too much to do. Like flip our family's entire business operation upside down." Raf shook his head. "He wants to live in peace. Best way to do that is expand our operations to places outside the city. Work with families from other cities. Boston, Chicago, maybe even London or Paris. More money to be made working together instead of fighting each other. Being a"—and here Raf's voice trailed off for a second before he rallied—"diversified businessman is more challenging every day. We need to adapt to survive. Look at you."

"Me?"

"That shop of yours already has an exclusive clientele. At least from what I hear."

"Business is good," Harry said. "What can I say?"

"You can say you adapted to the times and profited because you made some agile moves."

Harry chuckled. "I'll go with that."

Raf offered his hand. "Maybe we'll work together someday. I know some people who would want to buy relics from you."

"Maybe we will," Harry said as he shook Raf's hand. *After I take care of Olivier Lloris.*

Harry's phone buzzed moments after he turned from Raf to head down the sidewalk. He pulled it out. His mouth tightened. Olivier Lloris wanted to talk.

Chapter 3

Zurich, Switzerland

"What happened in Ukraine?"

Olivier Lloris walked into his private office with a phone pressed to his ear, ignoring the question posed by a guest. He closed the door behind him to cut off the sounds of the string quartet and the fifty guests eating his food and drinking his wine. "You've been gone nearly a week. Why have you not contacted me with an update?"

"None of your concern," Harry Fox replied.

Olivier almost laughed. *The man has backbone.* "I do not appreciate being ignored."

"And I don't appreciate you acting like I work for you," Harry said. "You want to talk? Start talking."

A log in the fireplace crackled as Olivier stood in front of a floor-to-ceiling window. Falling snow glittered under the moonlight, and a Swiss mountain famous for its slopes loomed over the dark lake below. "Where exactly was this church?"

"In Ukraine."

A sharp reply rose in his throat. Olivier bit it off. "Did you find anything useful?"

"Yes."

Olivier kept his voice neutral. Harry Fox would not get a rise out of him. "Agilulph pointed to the church for a reason. What was there?"

Harry let the silence stretch on longer than necessary. "Proof I was correct." Harry detailed finding a giant cross with Agilulph's name on it, along with a hidden compartment marked by Charlemagne's signature. "Inside the cross," Harry finished, "were directions on what to do next."

Olivier's hand tightened on the phone. "What was inside?"

"Nothing I can sell you. Unfortunately." Harry chuckled at his own joke. "Just Agilulph's directions."

"I assume you will not share that information."

"Correct."

"How much longer?"

"Until I finish following this trail, or until I have another artifact to sell?"

"Both."

"No idea. I'll know I'm at the end when I find what Charlemagne left to preserve peace in his empire. As for the second part, that depends on what I find when I get to where I'm going."

"When will you arrive there?"

"A week or so. Maybe a bit longer. These things take time."

Olivier wouldn't admit it, but his heartbeat picked up slightly. "Then I can expect you to be in Paris in shortly over a week."

"No chance."

"What?"

"I said, no chance."

"I am paying you to locate an artifact," Olivier said. "You will deliver it to me."

"You're paying me for an artifact you didn't know existed until I told you about it. If it weren't for me, you'd never know any of this existed. In the past month you acquired an illuminated manuscript tied to Charlemagne, which is nothing compared his *actual crown*, which I just found for you."

"They are nice pieces," Olivier said. "But you promised the greatest Charlemagne artifact the world has ever seen."

"You have his crown. Relax." A moment passed. "Look, Olivier. I like doing business with you. But I can't meet you in Paris in a week. We can meet, but only on neutral ground. Somewhere we're both comfortable."

Olivier walked to the room's bar and poured a glass of water. He drank from it, then adjusted the knot on his tie. "There is no other reason you do not want to meet in Paris?" A reason like the fact Olivier had sent a hit man to kill Harry in Cyprus and steal whatever relic Harry had found.

"Other reason?" Harry asked. "No. This is me being cautious. Nothing more."

Olivier let a breath out. *Thank goodness.* "Fine. Give me some idea of when you expect to deliver the promised relic."

"When I have it. Best guess? Under a month. You know this isn't an exact science. Whatever's waiting has been there for a thousand years. There's a reason no one's found it yet."

"It is well hidden."

"I'll call you when it's done."

Heat flared in Olivier's gut. "Unacceptable. I require regular updates."

"You want to chase this down yourself?"

"That's your role. Mine is paying you."

A sigh meant to be heard sounded in Olivier's ear. "Fine."

Olivier looked out his window at the lights of a small plane coming in for landing at the nearby private airstrip. "Once you acquire the relic, I will have one of my associates meet you for verification and collection."

"Afraid to get it yourself?"

"As you said, caution pays."

"No deal, Olivier. You want the artifact? Meet me in person. That way we both have incentive to play by the rules."

Who did Harry Fox think he was? "Impossible."

"Make it possible. I'll contact you when I have the relic. You don't show, the deal's off," Harry said. "You already have some impressive relics tied to Charlemagne. Not the world's best collection, but impressive. You'll have to be content with that." Harry's voice dropped. "There are plenty of other collectors who will buy my relics in person.

Maybe they'll show it to you sometime."

Olivier's jaw tightened. "Fine," he spat. "I will meet you in person." Harry Fox thought he had the upper hand. Little did he know.

"Good," Harry said. "On neutral turf."

Olivier clicked off. He returned to the bar, choosing a more fortifying drink this time. The muted sound of his guests mingling continued in the background as he sipped wine and walked to an empty display stand. Normally it held a musical instrument, but tonight Olivier's personal Stradivarius violin was being used by one of the musicians playing in his dining hall. He'd doubled the insurance on it yesterday.

A knock sounded on the door. "Who is it?" Olivier called without turning around.

The door opened. Olivier frowned. Only one man would do that. "What is it, Benoit?"

"Your party is a delight."

Olivier turned to see his attorney walk to the fireplace and stand in front of it, but only for a moment before he stepped back from the heat and went to the bar. Benoit Lafont's colorful scarf may have been a bit much, Olivier reflected wryly. "Why are you bothering me?" Olivier asked. "It's peaceful in here."

"You being alone during such an event makes me wonder." Benoit picked up the bottle of white wine Olivier had just opened and poured himself a glass. "Excellent," he said after drinking.

"Of course it's excellent."

"Of course." Benoit moved to stand by Olivier's desk. "I wonder, what is keeping you in here?"

"Business."

"Perhaps you should ask for my assistance."

"I'll ask for your assistance when I need it." Olivier took a sip of his wine. "As you're here, give me an update on my insurance project."

"The private insurance?" Benoit asked. Olivier nodded. "It is proceeding as planned," Benoit said, then hesitated. "You understand, this is not my area of expertise."

"Nor is it mine," Olivier said. "Which is why I employ professionals. Who report to you. What are they telling you?"

"That all is well," Benoit said. "The goal is now in place."

Olivier nodded. He sipped his drink again and turned from the empty display stand. "What oversight team do you have in place?"

"A capable one. I hired a man with extensive experience in the field. He also has a wide network of contacts, developed over decades."

"And those include the contacts we need."

"It appears so. Everything will be in position within forty-eight hours."

Olivier lifted his glass. "To success. And to fate." Benoit touched his glass to Olivier's, and both men drank. "The first counterfeit painting I ever sold was to a collector who had more money than sense," Olivier said. "His cousin was a curator in a major gallery. He thought no one could deceive him. The collector told me his cousin wanted to see the painting after I delivered it to him. I was nervous. My painting was excellent, but good enough to fool an expert?" The memory brought light to Olivier's face. "As luck would have it, the curator had a heart attack shortly before his planned visit."

"How fortuitous for you."

"If you are implying I had anything to do with it, you are mistaken." Benoit merely shrugged. "Though I admit I was not saddened by his death," Olivier said. "Fortunes can change quickly."

A folded newspaper on the desk caught his eye for a moment before Olivier's head snapped up. "You're certain that everything is in order for the insurance project?"

"Yes," Benoit said hesitantly, as though caught off guard. "I am certain."

"I want you to supervise this personally." Olivier picked up the folded newspaper, an old copy of the *New York Times*. "A month ago, I would never have considered spending my money on such an"—and here his face brightened—"*insurance* project. But that was before my fortunes changed. Or fate, in this case. Fate can change in a moment." He leafed through the paper, then paused at a photograph beside a small article buried in the cultural section. "Or in the flash of a camera bulb."

Olivier looked at the image. Two people looked back, a man and a woman, the former looking slightly uncomfortable in a tuxedo, the latter quite attractive in a black dress. The caption told readers the woman was the guest of honor at an event hosted by the American Museum of Natural History in Manhattan. The woman's smiling face was one Olivier Lloris had never seen, and on any other day, wouldn't have given a second glance. Except this woman had her arm around a man Olivier knew quite well.

Harry Fox. And the woman with him? The museum's Egyptologist, Dr. Sara Hamed.

Chapter 4

Sinai, Egypt

Sand shifted under Sara's boots as she stepped out of the dusty Land Rover. The sun's top edge was barely visible above the horizon, and a welcome morning breeze blew. The sun would soon dominate the sky, bringing unforgiving heat to this dry and sandy peninsula. Distant mountains still showed snow at their peaks, but Sara didn't have time to admire the view. She closed her eyes and breathed deeply.

It's good to be back.

Egypt held a special place in her heart. All of it, even this nondescript portion of the Sinai Peninsula, located several hundred miles and a lifetime away from where Sara had grown up. She'd left Egypt as a newly minted Egyptologist, ready to make her mark on the world. First Germany, then New York. Now she had returned, but in an unfamiliar role. She was a guest at this dig, the guest of a man she considered a professional antagonist.

Ramy Gad had also been born in Egypt. He'd made a name for himself in the world of academia, earning tenure at a prestigious Egyptian university where he became known more for his extravagant rhetoric than for anything he'd recovered from the desert. Ramy was a masterful wordsmith, using allusion and insinuation to drum up public interest in the most mundane of finds. Once he had reported that a newly discovered tablet seemed to be written in code and might reveal the truth behind a major battle between the ancient Egyptians and the Nubians.

Ramy had very publicly employed a team of cryptologists and linguists to decipher the hidden message.

One of those linguists had finally succeeded when they'd recognized it wasn't a code at all. The writer hadn't been trying to conceal anything. He simply couldn't spell. The secret code turned out to be the inventory list of a merchant who was impressively bad at writing. Despite this, Ramy's reputation remained.

"*Mrhbaann!*"

A shouted greeting swept across the sandy plain. Sara looked across the vehicle's hood to see Ramy himself striding toward her, arms open and an alarmingly wide smile on his face. The last time Sara had encountered Ramy Gad there had been few smiles. Mostly, it had been an exchange of stern words and contemptuous looks when Sara openly questioned his implausible assertions regarding his archaeological work. Few things irritated Ramy more than a truth that didn't match his story.

Sara returned Ramy's greeting in Arabic, their shared language. "A fine morning for a dig," she said. May as well try to play nice.

"I am so happy to see you," Ramy said. "How was your journey?"

His opening statement was a lie if Sara had ever heard one. At least Ramy had the sense not to try and hug her like some sort of long-lost friend. The tips of his oversized mustache quivered when he stopped just short of reaching her. Ramy opened his mouth, so Sara beat him to the punch. "Fine, thank you." She hurried on to put this charade out of its misery. "Having a chance to prove Zeus's reach extended farther and faster than ever expected is one I could not miss. Where will I work?"

Ramy's eyes narrowed and deep lines creased his forehead as he stepped back. "Follow me. Your workstation is this way."

A short walk across the sand led to a row of tents erected on a flat area between several sloping desert hills. Men and women in all manner of field dress moved about with purpose, some carrying shovels and shaker screens, others carrying brushes and buckets. She saw someone carrying a compact metal box she recognized as a new style of ground-penetrating radar. The familiar, reserved movements of an active dig site put a bounce in Sara's step, and she had to slow her pace before she overtook Ramy en route to her quarters. Heads turned as she passed; one or two of the researchers tapped colleagues on the shoulder and pointed to the slightly famous Sara Hamed, the Egyptologist who'd found Alexander's tomb. Ramy couldn't help but notice. Sara couldn't help but grin.

Ramy stopped in front of a large tent. "Your team will be based here."

The tent was long enough to host a medium-sized wedding. Sturdy tables with assorted tools both technological and time-tested waited inside. Computers, shovels, field lights and even a small wash station had been set up and were clearly waiting for her arrival.

"Very nice," Sara said. "Your funding is impressive."

"We will have whatever is needed."

"I've not heard of the organization sponsoring this dig," Sara said. "The paperwork listed our funding source as *Poe N.A.* I had no luck identifying the benefactor."

"It is a recently formed entity supported by one generous benefactor," Ramy said. "Who wishes to remain anonymous."

"I see." She waited. Ramy did not fill the silence. "In that case, I hope their generosity continues."

It wouldn't be the first time a rich person had decided they wanted to sponsor some worthwhile cause but didn't want their name to be known. If someone wanted to spend their money on expanding humanity's understanding of Zeus, far be it from Sara to turn it down. "I'll inspect the site and then meet with my team to organize our work." She turned to look across the dig site, which stretched out before them in all directions. "Which area is under my supervision?"

"You will work under my direction," Ramy said. "I haven't yet determined where."

She didn't blink as he pulled first at one side of his mustache, then the other. "I see." Sara inspected a solitary cloud hanging in the brightening sky. "Where were the first relics found?"

"In the northeast quadrant of the site." Ramy angled his head in that direction. "Beside my tent."

Of course. "The summary of the initial find suggests the most likely direction to extend the site is toward the northwest section," Sara said. "I would like to have oversight of that area."

Now the mustache edged upward to reveal Ramy's teeth. "That area is also under my supervision."

"Why?"

The directness seemed to knock him back. "As the lead archaeologist, assignments are at my discretion."

"Then assign me to the northwest section."

"I cannot."

"You mean you *will* not." Her words rang clear in the warming air. A few people turned their heads to look. Sara ignored them. "You may choose not to assign me there, but don't imply it's out of your control. Unless you don't really have control of this dig." She paused to let that sink in. The heat coming from Ramy's face was almost palpable. "Do you?"

"This is my—"

"Am I interrupting?"

Those three words were in English. Sara turned to find a man in a linen suit who looked as if he had stepped off a fashion show runway. The brilliantly white scarf was borderline ridiculous. Did he think it would get cold here?

"Not at all," Sara said before Ramy could gather himself. "I just arrived."

"You must be Dr. Hamed." Sara accepted the hand of a man who did not spend his days in the field. "My name is Benoit."

Ramy had, in a minor miracle, fallen silent. "Nice to meet you," Sara said. "Will we be working together?"

"It is I who will be working for you. Whatever is required, I will do my very best to see you have it."

She took her chance. "I would like to have the northwest section of the dig site as my assigned location."

Ramy made a noise of disapproval, but he did not say a word.

Benoit's eyebrows rose a fraction of an inch. "I don't see why that would be a problem. Do you?" The last words were directed to Ramy.

"The northwest section is in my area," Ramy said.

"I believe you indicated the north*east* section is under your purview," Benoit said.

"As is the northwest."

"Come now, Ramy. Dr. Hamed is here to maximize the success of this effort. Her credentials are impeccable. Unmatched, some would say." Ramy's face turned a color Sara couldn't identify. "Not assigning her the location of her choice would be a mistake, given you already have plenty to focus on. Our goal is a successful dig." Benoit's voice changed slightly, and only so the three of them could tell. "That's what you want, isn't it?"

Ramy stood in silence for several long beats. "Of course it is," he eventually said. "Dr. Hamed, my excitement at what is to come clouded my judgment." What came next nearly sent Sara tumbling to her backside. "I apologize."

Ramy Gad never apologized for anything. "None needed," Sara said. *At least someone recognizes my abilities.* "And the excitement is infectious."

"Excellent." Benoit gestured toward Sara's tent. "Please, do not let me detain you. And remember. Should you require anything, please ask."

Sara thanked him and headed for the shade of her tent; the day was quickly going from warm to hot. Benoit's people had even thought to put a coffee machine inside. She was searching for water and ground beans when her cell phone buzzed with a text from Harry. *How's it going?*

Great, she replied. *Seems like Ramy Gad is a changed man.* She described his apology. Harry's response was *Don't trust him.* She was in the middle of replying when he called. "Why are you up this early?" she asked. It's the middle of the night in New York."

"Someone's gotta keep an eye on you," he said. "Can't have you trusting shady characters the moment you land in Egypt."

"Ramy Gad is not shady. He's a somewhat-respected Egyptologist.

He's also a horrible person to work with. Or at least he was, until several minutes ago."

"From what you told me there's no way that apology is genuine."

"I suspect the man controlling the money had something to do with it." She relayed Benoit's intervention. "He's interested in results, not bickering."

"Maybe. Maybe not. Don't trust either of them."

"I'll keep that in mind." Sara found the coffee grounds and attempted, using one hand, to get a pot going.

"Find anything yet?"

"I have been on site for under an hour," Sara said. "Even I'm not that good."

"What do you think is under the sand?"

"At minimum I expect to find evidence showing the worship of Zeus extended into Egypt earlier than we believe. Perhaps we can uncover the methods by which this expansion occurred, whether through expanded trade, migration, or some other means."

"That would be cool."

Sara shook her head. "Yes. It would be *cool*. What we don't know is what *else* there is to find. How large is the temple? We have no idea. Was it built to worship multiple deities? What evidence is intact and recoverable?" She found her grip on the phone had tightened. "The spread of Zeus's worship could be only the start." She made progress with the coffee battle. "Do you have any updates on your castle invasion?"

"I do." Harry detailed how Evgeny Smolov had confirmed he would supply money provided Harry didn't actually spend it, with Joey Morello's bank serving as the front. "Scott dug around online into the new Baron Schweinsteiger, and from what he found, the new baron—he's not much more than a kid—doesn't much care about the castle. He only uses it to host lavish parties."

"So he may be open to your offer."

"I'm hoping he's not around when we inspect the property. Joey found a law firm experienced in global property acquisitions to coordinate the visit. We should be inside that castle within the week."

"Don't get ahead of yourself," Sara said. "Think of what your father would do." Fred Fox had taught his son everything he knew about relic-chasing, and he'd had a saying for every situation. "He would say to watch your back," she hazarded.

"He said a lot of things." She could practically see Harry's face when he said it. "That was one of them. I'll be careful."

Before she clicked off Sara asked that he keep her in the loop. The coffee pot burbled a moment later, and within seconds she had in hand a hot beverage not meant for this hot climate. She stood sipping as her gaze ran around the tent. Everything she might need sat ready. The place even had a cot in one corner in case she needed a nap during her workday. *Perfect.*

"Dr. Hamed?"

Her head whipped around toward the tent entrance. A man stood under one upraised flap. He held a plastic bag in one hand. "Yes?" she replied.

"My name is John. I am part of the security team."

"Good morning, John."

"Good morning." He gestured toward her. "May I come in?"

"Of course."

"We are pleased to have you here," he said as he walked toward her. "I read about your recent discovery. Amazing."

"It was a team effort."

John held up the small bag. "A piece of equipment for your phone."

"My phone?"

"Dr. Gad is concerned others may try to tap into our communications," John said. "Steal our information to learn what we know."

Sara put her coffee down. "Ramy thinks someone might eavesdrop?"

"Yes." John opened the bag and removed a manila folder. "These are jamming devices. They attach to your phone to prevent anyone from accessing the line remotely."

"I have an iPhone," Sara said. "Aren't those already secure?"

John pointed at her phone. "Your device is secure." Now he pointed through the tent wall and into the distance. "But the tower it uses for a signal is not. This device prevents anyone from intercepting your signal through a cellular tower." He opened the folder to reveal a plastic sheet with what resembled tiny buttons on it. "I'll place one on the back of the phone. Once I activate it, your phone is secure from that risk."

"Interesting."

"We have satellite phones arriving soon. Once we have those, you can get rid of the dots."

"And make all calls to team members using the satellite phone."

"Yes."

"We wouldn't want anyone listening in on our conversations." Sara held out her phone. "Here you go."

In a few seconds John peeled the paper-thin button from the plastic sheet and stuck it on her device near the microphone. She noticed tiny metallic lines running through the clear button. "All set," John said as he handed the phone back. "If you have any concerns, find me and I'll take care of them."

Sara thanked him as he walked out. The tent flap rustled when his head bumped it. Sara studied the nearly invisible security device on her phone, a thought springing to mind. A thought that sounded like Harry's advice. *Don't trust anyone.*

Sara shook her head. "Stop it," she told herself. The chances of anyone trying to eavesdrop on her discussions were remote. Remote, but not impossible.

Her concern was forgotten as she turned to planning how to divide the dig area now under her control. Outside her tent, John made his way to his car, which was parked alongside several Land Rovers close to the entrance. John walked past his car and opened a rear door on one of the Land Rovers, which had its engine running. Benoit sat in the rear seat.

"Is it done?" Benoit asked. John said it was. "Is it working now?"

John removed a rather bulky cell phone from his pocket. He tapped the screen a few times, then turned it so Benoit could see. "This is a mirror image of Dr. Hamed's phone," John said. "Anything she does, anyone she calls, we can see and hear it."

"There is no way for her to know?"

"None."

Benoit nodded. "Excellent."

Chapter 5

Brooklyn

The sign on the front door of Fox and Son flipped from *Open* to *Closed*. Harry walked back to the counter to where Scott sat and leaned on the display case. "Cameras outside working?"

"You wanted me to install cameras?"

"Funny. I don't want to be disturbed."

"We won't be," Scott said. "Not with that bulletproof front façade you installed."

The glass and walls of his storefront appeared to be nothing unusual, though they were designed to withstand anything short of a full-on military assault.

"Good," Harry said. "Now, what do you need to know?"

"How you plan to get inside the castle."

"With stealth."

Scott's eyebrows came together. "Do better than that."

"By using the information the Schweinsteigers provided to us," Harry said. "I need to avoid any guards, have a plausible excuse if they do spot me, and have multiple routes to get where I'm going. That detailed enough?"

"It's a start. Look at this." Scott turned his computer monitor so Harry could see a three-dimensional schematic. "I turned the written descriptions and photographs into a building blueprint of the castle and grounds. I can't guarantee it's entirely accurate, but it should be useful.

This shows the courtyard and main entrance." A rendering composed of colorful lines came up, the entire image rotating as Scott dragged his finger across the screen. It looked like an X-ray of the building and grounds. "You should arrive here." He indicated the expansive, circular courtyard. "The front entrance is the most impressive way to bring guests inside, and if they're serious about selling, they'll pull out all the stops."

"Like Cinderella coming to the ball."

"She knew a lady with better magic." Scott touched the screen. "You let Evgeny's moneyman take the lead here. I read his bio, and the guy knows his way around high-end real estate deals. He'll know what to ask and how to be sufficiently arrogant. That'll keep people from noticing you."

"I'm the antiquities expert."

"Who would be wise to appear unthreatening, perhaps even bumbling." Scott paused. "Sara told me you'd be good at it." Harry did not dignify that with a response. "You'll go up the steps," Scott continued, "into this enormous reception area."

The diagram flowed as Scott talked, taking the point of view from outside the see-through walls, looking into an open room featuring a grand staircase, huge hallways on either side and suits of armor everywhere.

"Impressive," Harry said.

"The owner's representative should take the lead," Scott said. "They'll show you the main areas, including the formal dining room, the ballroom, and I'm sure the exterior grounds with its surrounding views. My suggestion is to show mild interest in some of the artifacts. Start with this one." Scott hit a button and the digital schematic was replaced with an actual image. "This is a sword given to one of the baron's ancestors over a thousand years ago by Otto the Great, who was the Holy Roman Emperor. The hallway beside it leads to the chapel."

"Show interest in that and maybe I can slip off on my own."

"Have Evgeny's moneyman demand you be free to roam where you please," Scott said. "It should work."

"Good call," Harry said. "I'll figure something out if it doesn't work."

"Take the hallway by the sword." The image went back to its prior three-dimensional line structure as Scott walked virtually down the hallway. "You will pass four doors to your left, and then take the branching hallway on the left. Watch for guards once you turn. They'll definitely be on patrol in the area."

Harry lifted a hand. "Hang on. Even if a guard stops me, I'll have a valid reason for being there. I'm more worried about getting rid of anyone following me around."

"Ask questions," Scott said. "You're on site to evaluate the historical contents. Ask enough detailed questions and eventually you'll hit on one the person doesn't know. They'll leave to find an answer and that's your opening."

"I like it." Harry nodded to the screen. "Where do I go once I turn into the northern hallway?"

"Not far." Scott took Harry on the virtual journey down the hall, past a cavernous dining hall, and then to the eastern edge of the castle. "The chapel is here. It faces east."

The three-dimensional rendering of the layout was replaced with actual images. "It's not as large as you might expect," Scott said.

"Good."

"Why's that?"

"If this really was a pagan temple, it wouldn't be massive. Their temple would be smaller, built for functions. Christians built for show."

"Show me around the chapel," Harry said.

Scott pulled up a different image that revealed two rows of pews with a modest altar at the front, behind which were a pair of stained-glass windows depicting Jesus's birth in Bethlehem and his crucifixion. A large wooden cross had been planted in the floor to one side of the altar.

Harry pointed at the screen. "Zoom in on the cross."

"Looks like a wooden cross to me."

"It's not the cross." Harry leaned closer to the screen. "The wall behind it looks funny. You see it?"

"I do. Looks like the wall isn't flat. Is it an alcove, or another doorway?"

"Could be. I can't say for certain from this picture," Harry said. "But there's a recessed area back there." Harry filed that away. "Walk me through the rest of the castle."

Half an hour later the virtual tour ended, and Harry had his plan. "I get inside, distract anyone with me by asking questions about the relics, and then get into the chapel by myself. It won't take long to go through the entire room."

"That's the best we can do for now," Scott said. "It's still risky."

"Everything is a risk." Harry looked at Scott. "What haven't I thought of?"

Scott stood from his stool. Arms crossed, he tapped the fingers of one hand on his opposite shoulder. "You've focused on the internal threats. The guards, the baron's staff. What about external threats?"

"Such as?"

"The local authorities. The townspeople."

Harry smirked. "Should I be worried about a mob with torches and pitchforks?"

"I'd at least think about it. Minus the theatrics."

"I'm listening."

"What's the biggest draw to outsiders in a rural town like this one?"

"A famous castle."

"If the barons have any sense, they've gone to some trouble over the years to be friends with people in town, particularly people in positions of power."

"Including the police."

"The point is, don't think anyone there is going to help you if you have to make a quick getaway."

Sounds like advice my dad would give me. Harry's phone buzzed. "We'll find out soon enough if this plan can work." He set the phone down. "Joey just talked to Evgeny's moneyman. The meeting is tomorrow."

"You'd better get a plane ticket."

Harry shook his head. "This is Evgeny Smolov we're talking about. He doesn't do anything halfway. He's letting us borrow his plane. We'll arrive in style."

Chapter 6

Rhineland-Palatinate, Germany

Cochem Castle's walls presided over the quaint German town as three Bavarian sedans motored through the streets. Harry's nose almost touched the tinted window of the first car as he studied his destination. Each tower cast long shadows down the hillside on which the castle sat, the sun coming and going behind the stone walls as the cars made their final approach. The two men in the car with Harry spoke quietly in their native Russian.

"Are you nervous?" The question came from Evgeny Smolov's acquisitions attorney. Tamerlan Prutsev's impeccably tailored suit and coiffed hair went well with the whitest set of teeth modern dentistry could provide. While Tamerlan's smile seemed genuine, his eyes were empty. The eyes of a man who knew exactly what Evgeny Smolov was capable of and still served him without question.

"I'm good," Harry said.

"It would be normal." Tamerlan waved a hand toward the castle without bothering to look at it. "Do not worry. You are with me. I never lose."

Harry believed him. People who worked for Evgeny were usually too scared to fail. "Our plan is solid. We can handle these guys."

Another smile without feeling again. "You are the relic hunter who always finds what he seeks. Evgeny told me so. You will be fine."

"I know." Harry's reply came and went without a response. Tamerlan's gaze was on the paperwork in his lap as their small motorcade ascended the entrance road. Stone walls blocked their view on either side as the world shrank to nothing but the gray sky overhead and gray stone walls to the left and right. The world quickly returned when they entered the castle's courtyard.

Water sparkled as it shot from an ornate fountain in the courtyard's center. A man waited at the foot of a short staircase leading to the massive front doors as Harry and Evgeny's men stepped out of the sedan into a brisk wind. *Here we go.*

"Welcome to Cochem Castle." The suited man inclined his head toward Tamerlan. "Mads Undav, at your service."

"A pleasure to meet you." Tamerlan and Mads shook hands before Tamerlan introduced everyone in his party, ending with Harry. "This is Dr. Brady Leinart, our antiquities expert."

Mads shook Harry's hand before turning to the stairs and leading them inside. Exactly as Harry hoped, he was able to trail behind as the group moved up the stairs. Harry was the last man through the heavy wood doors before they stopped in the front hall, a room that felt oddly familiar. The oversized chandelier, the wide staircase leading to the upper levels, and the hallways stretching in multiple directions—all just as shown in Scott's schematic. Suits of armor and one very ornate sword were displayed along one wall.

A butler approached the group of visitors as they stood beneath the chandelier, and Harry couldn't help but step clear of the giant crystal fixture above. "Would anyone care for refreshments?" the butler asked the assembled group. They all declined, so the butler bowed lower than was necessary and retreated to the closest wall.

"Our tour begins here in the reception area," Tamerlan said, and launched into a description of the room and its medieval history. Harry listened for under a minute before he wandered around the room to inspect the armored suits. He soon sensed a presence behind him, but he did not turn around.

"Good morning, Dr. Leinart." A decidedly German voice spoke in friendly tones. "I see this suit of armor has your attention." It took a few seconds, but finally the unknown woman spoke in more pointed tones. "Why has this caught your eye?"

Harry turned. "I appreciate exceptional artifacts." Harry stuck a hand toward the woman who stood before him. "Brady Leinart."

"Victoria Hurley." Her loose brunette curls bounced softly when he shook her extended hand. "I am the castle archivist."

He recalled mention of such a role in the documentation he'd reviewed. The materials had not included a photograph of Ms. Hurley. "The baron's people speak highly of you," Harry said, making it up on the fly. "Though I'm afraid I'm a bit short on details about your specific role." He inclined his head toward the gleaming metal suit. "A nice piece."

"It has a fascinating story to tell."

Harry looked at the armor. "Fifteenth century?"

"Correct." She indicated a symbol on the arm. "The coat of arms shows this belonged to a Schweinsteiger, one who was an earl at the time, not a baron. The gold filigree was created by the French court's personal goldsmith."

"Very nice," Harry said. "This sword is what truly catches my attention." He walked slowly toward the sword displayed near the hallway that led to the castle's eastern side.

"A royal sword, Dr. Leinart." Victoria followed him to stand in front of the weapon. "Presented to one of the baron's ancestors by Otto the Great, Holy Roman Emperor."

"Brady, please."

"Brady." Victoria studied him with a gaze he suspected missed little, then shared the story of how the sword had come to be here. It had only just concluded when footsteps sounded from inside the hallway. Harry peered around the sword with feigned interest as a guard came into view. *Right on time.*

The guard gave them a brief look as he passed. "This tapestry looks familiar," Harry said as he pointed to a tapestry hanging just inside the eastern hallway, one he'd studied in detail from Scott's diagram. "The

Battle of Grunwald, I believe."

"Yes. There is glory even in defeat," Victoria said. "Our German Teutonic Order fought valiantly against the Poles and Lithuanians."

"They did," Harry said.

"Perhaps the tapestry contains more than you realize, Brady. Legend says there are hidden passages in this castle. It further suggests that tapestries and paintings were used to conceal secret doors that allowed the baron to move about unseen."

"Legend? I assume you would know if there are such passages in his castle."

"Some secrets are forgotten over time," Victoria said. "The truth about our past can be difficult to know"—and here she inclined her head toward the Grunwald tapestry—"including the truth about secret passages."

So the passages are only a myth. Harry moved further down the eastern hallway, this time professing interest in a knight's shield hanging on the wall. Victoria commended Harry's knowledge of the castle's artifacts.

"The baron has an impressive collection of cultural relics," Harry said.

"He does indeed." She looked back toward the main hall. "Perhaps we would like to rejoin the main group?"

He ignored her and moved to the next object farther down the hall. "This painting deserves better lighting." A canvas taller than Harry and wider than he could reach displayed a knight in armor astride a horse, a magnificent sword in one hand pointing toward the sky as the horse reared back as though to charge. "Another of the current baron's ancestors, I presume?" Harry asked.

Victoria detailed the warrior's name and a few facts, but Harry was already walking, counting doors as he moved down the hall. "Impressive." He stopped, acting as though the displayed statue caught him by surprise. "Is this Loki?"

"You know your Germanic pagan deities," Victoria said. She no longer seemed concerned about rejoining the group. "It is Loki. Most people would recognize this only as an elderly woman."

"Elderly women don't have beards concealed beneath their shawls." Harry leaned forward to peer down the next hallway. One that led to the chapel. "Is that a longbow?" Harry asked. He went down the hallway without waiting for a response and heard Victoria set off after him. Approaching footsteps sounded as he stopped in front of the longbow. Harry glanced at his watch. Another guard, right on time. "It's English," Harry said as the guard came into view. "Why does the baron have an English longbow?"

She hesitated. "I don't know," she finally said. "I'm not certain about that."

Harry lifted his chin ever so slightly. "You should know."

"I would be happy to locate the information," Victoria replied.

"Could you find out now? I will use that information for my report. That's why I'm here."

"Is it urgent?"

"It is. I don't mind waiting. I'll be here when you get back."

With that, he turned and walked toward his true destination. He didn't look back, instead listening for the sound of her receding footsteps, which he soon heard.

Harry checked his watch. He had ten minutes at most. Pausing at the nearest painting, he waited until she turned the corner at the end of the hallway and vanished from sight. Then he took off, running due east at full speed past the massive dining hall on a direct line for the chapel.

The hallway seemed to stretch on forever, though it couldn't have been more than a few hundred feet until he approached the open chapel doors. They were twice as tall as Harry, nearly reaching the ceiling. He slowed only as he crossed the threshold and stepped into the chapel, going still as he listened for any footsteps or voices. Nothing. A moment was all it took to confirm his suspicions. This structure had been built on top of an older one. A pagan temple.

Yes, it had the pews for worshippers, an altar behind which a preacher stood, and stained-glass windows depicting Christian scenes. All that along with a tall wooden cross behind the altar plus an odd, slender metal cross hanging in shadow by the door.

Harry walked directly down the nave, past the rows of pews, and approached the section of this chapel that had caught his eye before—a recessed area behind the cross. This was an old doorway, repurposed as an alcove. A now-empty alcove. He angled his head. There was a cross carved into a stone on the wall directly above the alcove.

He stepped into the carveout, then reached up and touched the rounded upper section barely a foot above his head. His fingers brushed the stone and the hair on his arms rose slightly. The stonework had been painted back here, but over time, the paint had worn away to leave a mottled pattern on the gray stones.

The sunlight filtering through the stained-glass windows did little to illuminate this rear portion of the room, so Harry pulled out a penlight and flicked it on. He first checked the upper part of the recessed ceiling, running his hands over the stones as he studied each stone and the mortar in detail, though the stones held firm and revealed nothing but a slight dampness.

His gaze went to the floor. The alcove was set back about two stone lengths, no more than a stride, and the mortar and stonework underfoot appeared to be solid. Solid, but different. While the stones on either side of the floor were rough, the middle portion directly beneath his feet was smooth and flatter.

Why? If this had truly been a door at some point, it could be due to people walking over it, but it would have had to have been a highly trafficked area for the stones to be worn down. Plus, the exterior wall was directly behind this alcove. There was no evidence of an additional room, no hillside to walk into, nothing to suggest this had once been a pathway leading someplace else.

He frowned. *Maybe I'm looking at this from the wrong angle.* If this was once a pagan chapel, and all the signs indicated it had been, it had changed over time. What if the changes weren't limited to the interior? A glance at his watch showed the earliest a guard should arrive would be in eight minutes, though Victoria could return sooner. He needed to test his theory quickly.

The stained-glass windows on either side rose above his head at their tops, but they were closer to chest height on the sides. He found a clear pane and pressed his face against it to get a view of the ground directly behind the alcove. Lush grass stretched in either direction before sloping down the hillside and out of sight. Grass everywhere, except one spot. Directly behind the alcove. No grass existed there at all. Nothing but a patch of dirt twice as long as it was wide. A barren spot in an otherwise lush lawn. Why did nothing grow there?

He backed up and his gaze went to the metal cross. An odd place for one.

The rounded archway of the recessed alcove was rough when he touched it, as were the stones on either side of the cross—not worn down. His fingertips moved to the middle stone and the cross it held. The cross had been embedded into the rock. The edges of the cuts were smooth, same as the rest of the stone face. When he touched the stone immediately around the cross it was also smooth, slightly bumpy in spots, but not rough at all. Nothing like the stonework everywhere else. Why was this section different?

"They ground it down." The stone had been smoothed down, all of it except for the cross cut into the center. He touched the smoothed stone again. It was smooth, but not entirely *flat*. "Of course."

He spun and darted back toward the pews. Bibles were tucked into holders on the rear of each long pew, and with a silent apology to any deities who happened to be watching, he found a blank page at the end of one book and tore the wafer-thin sheet loose. "Pencil," he said. "I need a pencil."

None presented themselves, so he ran as quietly as he could back to the empty ballroom, slipped inside and headed straight for a fireplace. There were four of them, and thankfully the baron must have had a recent party, for when he reached into the back corner of one fireplace, he found a small piece of charred wood. It would do. Back in the chapel, he stopped in front of the carved cross and placed the translucent page on it so the stone was completely covered, then used the burnt piece of wood like a pencil and started rubbing.

An image appeared on the paper. The ghost of an image erased centuries earlier by Christians intent on eradicating a pagan religion. "That's Odin," Harry said when he finished rubbing. "The Norse god."

The impression showed a man with a thick beard, a man of power, a being beyond this world that Harry knew could only be Odin. How? The image only had one eye. That had been Odin's punishment for drinking from the waters of cosmic knowledge.

"This must have been erased after Charlemagne's time." Harry held the rubbing up to the light. Odin's face with a cross carved on top of him. Harry rubbed the stubble on his chin. "I'm missing something."

Agilulph only obscured his directions; he didn't fail to leave them. Harry couldn't see the next step, but it had to be here, somewhere right in front of him.

The rubbing went into his pocket as he checked the alcove again. Nothing else to see. He turned and went to the tall wooden cross, though even as he gave the beams a once-over, his inner voice was shouting that the large cross wasn't the key. His gut clamored for attention, trying to jog his memory. He closed his eyes and listened.

An image appeared on the backs of his eyelids, and it remained there when they snapped open. "The metal cross." It looked unlike any he'd seen before. He moved back toward the chapel entrance, toward the shadows where sunlight never reached. The metal cross didn't gleam under the beam of Harry's penlight when he flicked it on. The light reflected dully, the hallmark of iron. The cross was tall enough to reach to Harry's waist, and half as wide. The vertical iron section tapered to a rounded point at the bottom, much like a cane, while the end of the upper portion was much wider—as wide as his hand. That section also curved outward at the very top, almost like a handle. He reached out to touch the top of the cross, and in doing so his penlight beam went above the cross and illuminated the wall above.

Harry's mouth opened slightly. "I knew it."

A message had been carved into the wall above the cross. In Latin. Harry read it aloud. *"Here Karolus placed his cross below the head of the pagan god."*

Karolus was Charlemagne, who had defeated the German pagans and baptized their king in this very castle, near this temple. A temple Agilulph said held the next step on this mysterious path. Harry slowly removed the rubbing from his pocket. "The head of *the* pagan god." That could only refer to Odin, chief god of the Germanic tribes. "Placed his cross below the head?" Harry asked the cool air. "What—*of course.*"

It all came together in a rush. The metal cross. The image of Odin's head. Harry spun and went to stand beneath the faint image of Odin in the alcove. He didn't look up. He looked down. "It's a circle."

The gray flagstones that comprised the chapel floor were rectangular, all the same dull gray color. Except for the stone directly below Odin's image. That stone had a circle carved into it. Harry knelt and touched the stone. "There's no mortar between the circle and the rest of the stone." The best part? The circle looked to be the same size as the bottom of the slender cross.

A cross Harry now ripped from the wall. After a few heaves, the iron cross came loose and he carried it back to the alcove. The rounded bottom aligned perfectly with the odd stone circle. He grunted as he lifted the iron cross up, ready to smash it down, then he hesitated. This wouldn't require an act of brute strength. This was a key, not a hammer. He lowered the cross until its circular bottom sat on the stone circle, took a breath, and leaned on it.

Nothing happened. He pushed again. Still nothing. The second hand on his watch seemed to tick audibly as he pressed without result. "I don't have time for this." The smooth metal handle of the cross's upper portion cooled his hands when he grabbed it, raised it slightly, took not-very-close aim, and smashed it down.

Direct hit. The circle disappeared, crushed into the floor as the cross broke through centuries of grime and debris to force the stone circle into the ground before jamming to a halt. Harry barely stopped his chin from smashing into the iron point. He tensed, his hands tight on the crossbar, breath caught in his lungs.

The ground shook. Harry's knuckles whitened as he clenched the iron cross. Dust blew out of the floor in a stream as the stones in front of him cracked along a seam, one section retracting to reveal a large, dark hole.

Harry stood still, aiming his penlight into the dusty cloud. A million specks of diamond reflected as the dust settled on the chapel floor. Harry's jaw ached, and he realized he'd been clenching it tight. His breath sent the falling dust motes swirling again until his view cleared and the beam from his penlight revealed what had been hiding beneath his feet.

Narrow stairs that descended out of sight.

I was right. He'd cracked the next part of Agilulph's code. A look at his watch revealed Harry might not be the only one to find the staircase. The guard would pass by any moment, and Victoria had already been away longer than he could have hoped.

He returned the metal cross to its wall hanging, got down on one knee in front of the hole in the floor, and inspected the first step. Stone, no pressure triggers, nothing to suggest the stairway was a trap. One foot tested the first step. It held. Same with the second. "Get on with it," Harry told himself.

His penlight beam pushed back some of the darkness as the rough stone walls on either side of the stairs rose up around him. Ten steps down and he reached the bottom. Harry lifted a hand and could nearly touch the ceiling overhead. The underside of the chapel floor flagstones. He looked left. Nothing. He looked right. "Thought so."

The Germanic pagan lord who had built this castle knew safety mattered above all. He had included this underground hideaway, a place to escape if enemies overran the castle walls. Agilulph must have learned of this safe room and made it part of his quest. Both Agilulph and the king had planned ahead. Far ahead. How did Harry know? The lever to his right, sticking out of the wall and pointing toward the ceiling. Harry reached over and pulled it down to the floor.

The secret access panel above him closed, hiding the stairs and turning

Harry's world into the beam of a penlight. Harry aimed it ahead and moved on. Only two steps, because what he saw next made him draw a quick breath. "Hello, there."

Chapter 7

Cochem Castle

The chamber stretched perhaps ten paces ahead before it stopped at a stone wall. Another stone wall to his right was almost close enough to touch. A dark passage opened to the left, though he gave it only a brief glance before he turned back to face the wall just ahead of him. Three items attached to the wall took his full attention.

He first looked at the small hourglass hanging at eye level, its dull iron and gleaming glass unmoving. All the sand lay in the bottom half. What possible use did it serve here?

A creaking sound sent tiny lightning bolts through Harry's teeth and as he watched, the hourglass slowly rotated. *This isn't good.*

The second feature that had grabbed his eye were the Latin words running across the wall beside the hourglass. Two more sentences were engraved just above it. One of them was contained inside a larger square outline that Harry strongly suspected concealed something. Harry's voice sounded above the grating metal of the hourglass, which turned slowly as he translated the Latin. "*In this palace was our Empire born. Find it before the sand has fallen.*"

There were two images under the writing, side by side: two castles. The left one had several tall spires, while the other was squatter and had a drawbridge in front of it. He moved closer to each image as the sand began falling from the hourglass. "These castles both stick out of the wall." He leaned closer. The drawing of each castle was completely contained within the confines of its own stone, and each of those stones stuck out from the wall. *Like buttons.* Did he need to press one before the sand ran out?

He shook his head. Not yet. A button would be pushed, but right now he had a problem: he had no clue about the riddle. "Okay, Harry. Focus. Where was Charlemagne's empire born? In a castle, apparently." But he had no idea which one of these castles to choose. Which must have been Agilulph's purpose. The abbot meant to conceal this path from anyone not loyal to Charlemagne.

The hourglass stopped turning and the sand began to run from the top receptacle to the bottom. Harry swallowed, his throat dry. "Come on, Harry. Don't mess this up."

He stared at each image in turn, searching for clues. The castle with a drawbridge must have a moat. Was that the giveaway? He didn't recall any mention of a moat in all the literature he'd read or the research he'd conducted on Charlemagne. Nor did anything about massive towers with pointed spires come to mind. He looked back and forth, then glanced nervously at the hourglass. The sand had nearly emptied. "Agilulph thought Charlemagne walked on water. He'd make a bigger castle." Harry pressed a hand on the castle with the tall spires and shoved it.

The stone slid into the wall as the final grains fell. The stone made a *click*. He leaned on it, eyes wide. *Am I right?*

Stone ground on stone and a section of wall above the question he'd just answered slid back to reveal a new Latin directive. "*Look down to where Widukind ran from the Great One.*"

"Paderborn. Charlemagne first defeated Widukind in Paderborn." He knew that. He'd read about it a dozen times while researching what to do at this castle. "It's Paderborn. I know it is. What can—*look down.*" Harry went to one knee to find the wall had changed. Two stones on the floor near the wall's base, which definitely didn't have anything on them a moment ago, had changed. Each stone now sported a word on it. A word written in a language Harry couldn't read.

Old High German. He didn't understand it, didn't read a bit of it, but he'd seen enough of it in his research to know whatever was written on these stones was in the language of Charlemagne. The spoken language, not the written one. Charlemagne wrote in Latin, but he'd spoken Old High German. This was Agilulph's second test. Anyone who had made it this far on the trail would know the language. All they had to do was find which of these stones said *Paderborn*.

Which Harry couldn't do. Neither word looked anything like the modern German language, thus there was no clue to give him an idea of what either one said. They had the same number of letters, both texts were written in all capitals, and most of their letters were the same. Nothing to tell them apart.

These two new words weren't the only changes in the wall, he realized with surprise. A hole had opened below each of the Old High German stones. Empty holes inviting him to look inside. No, not look. Reach.

He reached for the left opening. Something flashed as his fingers slipped inside. *That's metal.* He pulled his hand back. *Sharp metal.*

Secreted a finger-length inside the dark opening were pointed metal teeth. He risked a touch and found a row of teeth on the upper and lower sections of the stone. A hand could go in, but never come out.

He checked for metal in the right opening and found none, so he reached inside. Nothing. He stuck his arm in as far as he could.

Pain bloomed when his fingers smashed into stone. But it wasn't a wall. He grasped a handle and pulled. The handle moved, so he pulled it back. It shot forward again and the chamber rattled loud enough to shake his teeth loose as he whipped his arm back to safety.

"What's that?"

The wall with the sentence on it had moved to reveal a recessed opening. An opening that was not empty. Harry rose to his feet and took a cautious step toward it.

"That's a book." A single volume stood upright on a pedestal with golden letters in block script on its dark, rough leather cover. "In *Arabic*?"

What was an Arabic book doing in a German castle? No one in Charlemagne's court communicated in Arabic, least of all Charlemagne or Agilulph. Charlemagne wouldn't have needed the language except for diplomacy, and he had scholars to translate for him. Was the book a gift, perhaps a symbol of peace between the two empires?

The cover read *One Thousand and One Nights*. "Arabic folktales?" *Aladdin and the Wonderful Lamp. Ali Baba and the Forty Thieves*. Why would a book of Arabian stories be hidden here? Harry carefully picked up the book and opened it to the first page.

A Latin inscription ran across the inside cover. Agilulph's handwriting.

"Retrieve St. Patrick's Cross from where he began his studies. It is stored beneath the thoughts of Ireland's saint."

Harry closed the book. The riddle of this message wouldn't be solved right now. Victoria was certainly looking for the artifact expert who had vanished.

He tucked the book under his shirt and moved to stand beneath the stairs. He reached for the wall lever to open them. He didn't pull it. Instead, his gaze and penlight beam went to the gloomy opening on one side. Another passageway.

"Time to find out where this leads." An unlit torch hung on the wall. A tangle of spiderwebs crisscrossed the pathway ahead. Even with his penlight he could see only a few feet in front of him. He knelt to get a better look at the floor ahead. Nothing suggested this passageway meant him harm.

That's the problem. His head told him to play it safe, but his gut said the fun had ended and this passage led back to safety. He walked on until the passage made a hard left, a route that took him back toward the castle entrance. He was now moving under the center of the castle, the ground beneath his feet smooth and sturdy, the stone walls cool to the touch. His footsteps quickened when a dark spot appeared ahead. A branch off the main path with rough stone steps leading upward.

Tiny dust clouds bloomed under his feet as he ran up the stairs. Nobody had used these steps for centuries. His penlight beam revealed a stone wall at the top. A dead end. Harry grinned. *Thought so.* He looked for and immediately found a familiar feature on the side wall. He reached out and pulled the short lever. The stone wall in front of Harry retracted to one side to reveal a set of steps leading upward. He took them quickly, though his trip ended abruptly at a rocky wall. Harry touched the rocks. They looked awfully familiar. The tightly mortared blocks were stacked neatly together and constructed in exactly the same fashion as the castle's exterior wall. Harry put his cheek against the wall and held his breath. *That's a breeze.*

Another lever was in the wall beside him. He pulled it down. Debris fell from above, pebbles bouncing all around as the wall in front of him swung open on invisible hinges to reveal a brightly lit open area.

The castle's exterior grounds. Manicured grass stretched to either side, while a crenellated perimeter wall stood ahead. Nobody could be seen in either direction. Harry lifted the lever as he stepped out beneath gray skies, and the hidden door closed silently behind him. If he hadn't watched it close, he'd never have known it existed. The stones were perfectly cut to obscure the fact that an entrance had been secreted in the stout castle wall.

"It's a perfect place to escape." A small, closed doorway was in the exterior wall ahead, and beyond that lay a short, sloping hillside that would take him into town. A panicked baron could make his getaway with ease if the worst befell this castle. "Victoria's going to love this."

He walked alongside the castle wall until he reached the front, where he turned the corner and gave a friendly nod to the Russian driver leaning against one of their vehicles as he had a smoke. The man nodded back. Harry walked inside.

"Mr. Fox?"

Victoria Hurley stood below the giant chandelier. "Why did you go outside?"

"The legends were true. I found a hidden passage. It took me outside."

He gave her a bare-bones overview that sent her racing for the chapel. Exactly the distraction he needed.

Apparently, Victoria hadn't alerted anyone about Harry's vanishing act, as neither of the attendants in sight gave him a second look when he turned and walked back outside to their waiting vehicles. Harry pulled open the door of the closest one and slid into the rear seat before grabbing his phone and dialing.

Joey Morello answered. "How's it going?"

"Don't talk," Harry said. "Just listen. Is anyone else with you?"

"I'm alone. Most of the guys are at a big festival across town. Only Mack and a couple others stayed behind."

The annual Italian heritage festival in a neighborhood near Joey's had first attracted the senior Morello's generation with its food, music and old-world atmosphere. "I hope you didn't actually buy that castle," Joey said.

"Better. I found what I came for." Harry detailed locating and recovering the book. "I'll text Evgeny's man as soon as we hang up," Harry said. "Tell him to wrap it up so we can get out of here. This book is the key to whatever is next."

"A book of Middle Eastern folktales? The only connection to Charlemagne would be his peace accord with the Caliphate."

"My thoughts exactly," Harry said. "I only had a quick look, but I can't rule out that this is an original copy." He drew a breath. "Maybe even *the* original copy." Which meant he had a fortune on his hands.

"Better get moving," Joey said. "Figure out what's next."

"I recognized Agilulph's handwriting. That means—"

"Get outta here!"

Harry heard the sound of shouting from Joey's end of the phone. A voice Harry knew. "Joey?" Harry yelled. "Is that Mack? What's wrong?"

A gunshot boomed in response and the line went dead.

Chapter 8

Brooklyn

Mack burst through the door of Joey's office with a pistol in one outstretched hand. "Get outta here!" The massive bodyguard slammed the door shut behind him, then ran at Joey and grabbed hold of his boss's shoulder with an iron grip.

Joey's phone went flying. He grabbed for it, missed, and then his office door crumbled as bullets ripped through it before Mack threw Joey to the ground. He crashed down, bounced off the floor and got back to his feet in one motion to find Mack had made his way back to stand beside the door, taking cover behind an oversized chair.

Mack stuffed the pistol in a pocket and lifted a finger to his lips. His other hand held a shotgun. The gun Mack had insisted on stashing behind that oversized, beautiful chair.

More bullets tore through the door before it flew inward. Joey ducked down as a squat man with an olive complexion, dark eyes and a rough beard burst through it. Joey didn't recognize him. A second man shouted in accented French behind the first man, who looked around, his gun up, the barrel moving left and right in search of a target. The second man followed, doing much the same. Neither man saw Mack crouched behind the large chair.

Thunk.

Both men turned and opened fire at a closet door. A door with a cell phone now lying in front of it. Mack's phone, tossed low at the door.

Mack stood and fired. Two blasts and the intruders were down. "Boss?" Mack shouted and moved to Joey faster than a man his size should be able to move. He grabbed Joey's arm. "Get up. There're at least three more outside."

Joey stumbled as Mack dragged him up. "Who are these guys?"

"I was outside when they pulled up." Mack kept one hand on Joey as he moved them both to the door. "They came in a delivery truck. I was inside the front door and I saw them all get out. Five of them." Mack described the intruders gunning down two Morello men in seconds. "They knew the boys left for the festival," Mack said. "That's why they came now."

Nobody was crazy enough to attack him in the heart of Morello turf. This was his city. He ran these streets. He was known as a good guy who took care of people and protected them "Who are they?"

"French? I dunno." Mack poked his head out the splintered remains of the doorway. "Never seen them before. You?" Joey said he hadn't. "Worry about it later. You gotta get outta here. Come on."

"Who else is alive?" Joey asked.

"Me and you. That's it. Everybody else went to the festival."

Joey only realized his hands were clenched into fists when they started aching. "We need to get out back to the armored SUV."

Mack stuck his head out again. "Follow me. And take this."

Joey fell back a step when Mack shoved the pistol into his hand. "Thanks," Joey said. He checked it was loaded and flicked the safety off as he followed Mack through the doorway. "Mack, they're Corsican." His voice was low, the words barely audible. "And I know who sent them."

"Let's get outta here first," Mack rumbled. "Then worry about—"

A gunshot cut him off. Wood splinters erupted as a bullet slammed into the wall inches above Joey's head. Mack shoved Joey toward the back of the house and shouted at him to run before turning to fill the air with buckshot. Joey took off through the open door. He did not get far before Mack shouted in pain.

Joey fought the urge to turn back and help as a lesson his father had drilled into him since Joey was a young man filled his head. *It is not about you. It is about the family. Protect the family.* Mack knew it too. That's why he'd thrown himself in the line of fire. The family had to survive.

Joey raced down a rear hallway toward the armored electric SUV waiting out back. Once in it, the only way these French punks would get him would be with a rocket launcher. He pushed the rear door open and leaned out to look outside.

A pistol looked back. Joey launched himself back as the gun jerked and a bullet flew past his ear. Two more shots rang out as he hit the floor and rolled. This guy had circled around back in case Joey did exactly what he tried to do. Joey crawled full-speed back down the hallway and around a corner, where he stopped and carefully stood up. He hugged a wall, aiming the pistol in his hand with a steady bead on the doorway. Joey took a breath and the shooter came through, firing.

Joey managed to get a shot off before an incoming barrage sent him ducking for cover again. When it stopped, Joey stood once more, planted his feet, and raised the pistol. A beat later the assailant flew around the corner. Joey pulled the trigger, and he kept pulling. The intruder groaned, fell to one knee and rolled out of sight. *Got him.* Joey lowered his gun.

Joey ran back into his office and went to his desk, reaching for a drawer. A pistol barked and splinters erupted from the desktop. "Freeze."

Joey went still. His hand stayed in place, a foot from the drawer handle. The intruder now stood in the doorway, one hand clenching his shoulder, the other holding a gun. The shoulder he covered had a dark stain on it. "You shot me," the man said in a familiar accent. "But I am still here."

"You know who I am," Joey said. "Shoot me and you never get out of this city alive."

The man tensed, turned to look quickly down the hall, then turned back to Joey with a sneer. "We leave together."

A shadow flashed outside the office window. "I'm not going anywhere," Joey said.

The window exploded as a round of buckshot came through and hit the gunman square in the chest, sending him to the floor. He did not get up.

Joey turned to find Mack clambering through the destroyed window. "Good shot," Joey said.

Mack brushed broken glass off his shoulder. "That's the last of them. You're right. They're Corsicans."

"And who hires Corsicans to do their dirty work?" Joey asked.

Storm clouds crossed Mack's face. "The Sicilians."

Sicilians had been outsourcing their dirty work to Corsican hired guns for centuries. The geographic proximity of the two islands offered the opportunity for recruiting low-level criminals to carry out enforcement. In work such as this, it didn't matter who pulled the trigger. It was who paid for the bullet.

"Carmelo Piazza sent these guys." Joey sighed. "I have to take care of this. Now."

"Send me after 'em." Mack scowled. "I'll finish it."

"No," Joey said. "I don't want a war." He pointed a finger at Mack. "You don't say anything. To anyone. Understood?" Mack nodded, grimacing as he put a hand over what looked like a flesh wound. "I need to think. Then we act."

"What are you gonna do?" Mack asked.

"I have no idea."

Chapter 9

Paris, France

Evening sunlight turned the sky a burnt orange, a warm umbrella above Olivier as he sat beneath it on his back patio, paintbrush in hand while he contemplated a half-finished canvas. A scene of the Seine on a spring day; so far it showed pedestrians crossing a bridge beneath soft clouds and a blue sky. The cityscape had yet to appear. A horse-drawn carriage moved past a black motorized vehicle on the bridge. Anyone familiar with Impressionist art might compare it favorably to a Renoir.

Which was exactly his intent. Olivier Lloris had made his first real money creating forged works and selling them to collectors as the real thing. The canvas he used today had once held the work of a little-known painter from Renoir's time. Olivier had purchased it only for the canvas. Once scraped clean, the canvas became a blank sheet from the correct timeframe on which to create a fake masterpiece. The brush he used was over a century old, and the paints had been created in the exact same way as paints from Renoir's time. If someone ever tested his finished work, it would pass muster. Or at least he hoped it would. The damned authenticators were getting better every year.

Olivier smirked as he put brush to canvas. *I'm still better.*

He dipped the brush into a tin of blue pigment, then moved it toward the canvas. It hadn't touched yet when the phone beside him vibrated. Benoit Lafont was calling. Olivier set his brush aside. "What is it?"

"We must speak."

An alarm bell dinged at the back of Olivier's mind. "I'm listening."

"We must speak in person. I am at your front door."

The ding exploded to a roar. "You're here? Why?"

"There has been an incident."

Olivier shot from his chair and hurried through the patio door to the sitting area and past the massive entry room with its towering ceilings. One thought ran through his head. *I told him not to do it.*

The attorney stood outside Olivier's front door. "What do you know?" Olivier asked.

Benoit lifted his chin a fraction. "Perhaps we should speak in private."

Olivier grabbed Benoit by the arm and pulled him inside. "Out back." He shut the door and left Benoit to trail behind him as he retraced his steps back to the patio. A wall of shrubs surrounded them on three sides, while Olivier's mansion penned in the fourth. "This is private," Olivier said. "Talk."

"There was an incident in New York today," Benoit said. "In a Brooklyn neighborhood. An incident involving Joseph Morello. Gunfire was reported at the primary Morello residence. The headquarters, for lack of a better term, for the Morello operation."

"Did they get him?"

"I cannot say who *they* are," Benoit said. "Though I understand Joseph is still alive."

Olivier swore in colorful French. "It was him, wasn't it? That foolish Sicilian."

"I cannot say for certain." Benoit removed a phone from his pocket. "I do have a direct line to our Sicilian associate."

"Call him now."

Benoit dialed a number and put the call on speaker. The gentle tone of a call waiting to connect sounded off and on. A rough voice cut it off. "What is it?"

"Good day, Mr. Piazza." Benoit's gaze flicked to Olivier. "I am here with a mutual friend. He wants to speak with you."

Olivier jabbed at the air with an upraised finger. "Carmelo, if you did this, I swear you're done. You hear me? Done."

"Are you threatening me?" Carmelo Piazza laughed without humor. "Do not make threats unless you intend to act."

"Put me in danger again and you'll regret it," Olivier said. "What did you do to the Morellos?"

"I don't know what happened yet. I am waiting for a call."

Olivier looked at Benoit, who chose that moment to find Olivier's half-finished forgery interesting. "You failed, Carmelo. Joey Morello is still alive."

"Impossible."

Olivier ran a hand over his face. "Whoever you sent made a mess of it."

"I hired men to address a problem," Carmelo said. "Hired them anonymously. No names, no meetings. Nothing to connect me to them."

"You mean us to them."

"Tell me what you know and I will tell you why it is not a problem."

"There was an attack on the Morello headquarters in Brooklyn. Joey Morello survived. That's all I know."

Carmelo said something in Italian that couldn't be good. "It's not possible," he finally said in English. "The men I hired are professionals."

"You think Joey Morello is a fool? He runs New York. Nobody who does that is a fool, and you just tried to kill him."

"Nobody knows it was me. Or you," Carmelo added quickly.

"Joey will know you were behind this." Which wasn't his biggest problem. He still had the Charlemagne relic to worry about, and if Harry Fox ever learned Olivier was anywhere near this attack, those Charlemagne relics were gone forever. "I have an interest in this beyond what you know," Olivier said. "You may have undercut an entirely separate operation."

"Nothing has been undercut," Carmelo said. "This will never be tied to us."

"Who did you send?"

"Corsicans."

"That was a mistake." Olivier kneaded his forehead. "Listen to me.

Back off Joey Morello, for good. Understand?"

"Now is not the time to hide. It is a time to strengthen relationships."

"You won't have many friends when they find out who you tried to kill."

"Settling scores is a way of life on my island. Memories are long. Revenge can be generations in coming. My concern is strengthening the relationships I need to survive. The same as every other day."

"I see," Olivier said. "Do you believe the Morello family will seek their revenge?"

Carmelo considered. "Joey Morello doesn't want trouble with me. He only recently consolidated his rule over New York. Engaging in a war with Sicilians is not in his best interests."

"He could hire someone to do the job."

"Perhaps. But I have eyes and ears in many places. To prepare for what is to come."

The fool better not interfere. "Do not do anything to jeopardize me or my interests," Olivier said. "There's more going on here than you know. I won't tolerate your interference again."

"Be careful. You do not want to offend me."

The line went dead. Olivier growled, looking up to find Benoit's interest in the painting ongoing. "This could derail my agreement with Harry Fox," Olivier said.

"I think it unlikely." Benoit turned from the canvas, hands clasped behind his back, eyes inscrutable behind yellow-tinted sunglasses. "Carmelo blusters, but he is a cautious man. Could Joseph Morello suspect the Piazza clan is behind the attack? Yes. Could he prove it? I think not. That may keep both the Piazza clan and you from becoming involved any further."

"*May* doesn't cut it for me," Olivier said. "I need assurance that the Morellos and Harry Fox have no reason to suspect I'm involved."

"You have taken the necessary steps in that regard."

"I have. Time to increase my coverage level." He picked up his phone and dialed a number. Soft tones ensued.

"*Mrhban.*"

"Professor Gad."

"Mr. Lloris." Ramy Gad had the charm on full blast. "It is wonderful to hear from you. I have incredible news to sh—"

"Stop talking and listen. Where is Dr. Hamed?"

"I believe she is working in her tent." The veneer of professional kowtowing slipped. "Is something wrong?"

"Are you certain she is on site?"

"I saw her less than an hour ago."

"What is her assignment?"

A note of what Olivier could only call disdain crept into Ramy's answer. "Whatever she wishes. You requested she be assigned her own area."

"Every artifact of note related to Greeks and Egyptians worshipping Zeus simultaneously has come from your area of the dig," Olivier said. "This suggests the most likely place to locate additional relics is where you are in control."

Ramy knew better than to argue with the man who signed his checks. "It does."

"You will ask Dr. Hamed to assist you with excavating your assigned area."

"What?" Ramy sputtered and spat more protests. "That is illogical. She has her own area."

"You will do it," Olivier said. "And you will do it now. Do you understand?"

"There is no need for two supervisors in one area. Even she will agree with that."

"I don't care what you have her do as long as she becomes more involved. You agreed to follow orders when I funded this dig. There were other, less controversial dig leaders available. I chose you. Even though you couldn't provide me with a single positive reference from any prior colleague."

"I cannot stop the jealousy of others."

"You are a terrible colleague," Olivier said. "That's why. However," he said to cut off any protests, "you are qualified to oversee this dig, and you understand how the world works. Ask Dr. Hamed to assist you with a desirable task. Make her feel valued. Make her want to remain at the dig as long as possible."

A silence ensued. "Fine," Ramy finally said. "There has been a discovery."

"I'm listening."

The hesitation in Ramy's tone was noticeable. "We uncovered a temple. The entrance was hidden by fallen rocks from the nearby cliff. It could be an incredible site."

"A site you will now assign to Dr. Hamed," Olivier said. "Do you understand me?"

"I will have it done today."

Olivier clicked off. "When did you last speak with him?" he asked Benoit. "About Dr. Hamed's state of mind."

"This morning," Benoit said. "By all accounts, she is excited to be involved, grateful for having her own section to lead, and suspects nothing."

"You're certain?"

"I took the precaution of hacking into her phone. We listen to her calls, read her text messages and emails. She suspects nothing."

"One call or text may be all it takes to change her mind."

"We will cut off her access if necessary," Benoit said. "One of our men implied to Dr. Hamed that the situation on the ground is somewhat precarious. That is how we obtained access to her phone. Should we need to cut her communication with anyone, we can blame the disruption on the need for enhanced security."

Olivier sensed opportunity. "That's a start."

Benoit raised a manicured eyebrow. "A start?"

"Plan to create an emergency. One in which Sara Hamed is injured."

Benoit didn't blink. "How serious an injury?"

"Not fatal. Serious enough that Harry Fox will drop what it is he's doing and come to her."

"Why would you want him to stop pursuing the relics?"

"Three reasons. One, he gets close enough to the end that I can pick up the path and get it myself, which means I won't pay him. Two, if that incompetent Sicilian's attack is tied back to me, her injury will distract Harry from anything Joey Morello is doing." Olivier's mouth tightened. "Three, if the worst comes to pass and I'm truly in danger, Sara Hamed is my bargaining chip." Olivier shrugged. "Not that it will come to any of that."

"Consider it done." Benoit turned to go.

Olivier picked up his paintbrush and turned back to the half-finished canvas.

"There is another option," Benoit said.

Olivier's brush hung halfway to the canvas. "Which is?" Olivier asked.

"Remind Dr. Hamed she is not secure. Perhaps a 'close call' is in order. Should we decide to rid ourselves of her, having two unfortunate incidents close to each other would make both seem natural."

Olivier considered it. "Agreed."

Chapter 10

Cochem Castle

Cursing erupted from the rear seat of a vehicle parked outside Cochem Castle.

Harry dialed Joey's number for what had to be the tenth time since their call had ended in Mack's shouting and the sound of gunfire. The previous nine times his call had rung through unanswered. This time it went immediately to voicemail.

Either Joey's phone had died, or someone had sent the call to voicemail. Harry tried the call again, but his jittery fingers lost hold of his phone and the device went spinning across the floor. It took him a moment to get the thing unlocked before he could try to call Joey again. Come on, Joey. Answer. He reached for the screen.

A message popped up. *I'm safe. Don't tell anyone what you heard. Call you later.*

"He's alive." Harry fell back into the seat and blew a gale-force breath from his lungs.

Someone had come for Joey and had failed. Joey was alive, which was all that mattered, and if Joey needed him to sit tight for a while, so be it. Harry rubbed a hand over his face. He sat there for a long minute, perhaps two, then sat up so fast he nearly lost hold of his phone again. Joey had been attacked. Was it tied to Harry's hunt for Charlemagne's relics? Could be Carmelo Piazza coming to finish what he'd started, or a friend of Altin Cana's, if that miserable turd had any friends. Or maybe Harry was totally off-base and this involved a grudge from a conflict

Harry didn't know existed.

He had no idea. For now, the only useful course he could follow was the book lying on the seat beside him. Unraveling the mystery of Agilulph's scrawled message inside this book of fables. He picked up the book and flipped the cover open.

Movement caught Harry's eye. He closed the book and slid it out of sight as Tamerlan Prutsev walked out of the castle with Mads Undav by his side and the retinue of Russian moneymen trailing behind. Tamerlan blinked when Harry exited the vehicle and walked toward him. The Russian spoke before anyone else.

"Are you satisfied with your review, Dr. Leinart?"

"I am," Harry said. He offered Mads Undav his hand. "Thank you for your hospitality."

"Leaving now?" Mads didn't seem like the sort of man who allowed life to surprise him. "Dr. Hurley informed me you uncovered an entrance to our mythical hidden passages."

"No myth," Harry said. "And it wasn't difficult. I'm certain you'll find them interesting. Remind Victoria to be careful."

Mads had no idea how to respond. Harry turned and slid back into the car holding the book of fables while Tamerlan said whatever rich bankers said to rich landowners before getting into the car as well and directing the driver to get them out of there. Tamerlan had a hand on his chin, gazing through the window as their vehicle motored past the defensive walls, around a lazy curve and the down the long, sloping entrance road leading to town. Only once their tires shuddered over those cobblestone streets did Tamerlan speak.

"Did you find what you sought?" The Russian still hadn't looked at Harry.

"I did," Harry said.

"Do you wish to update Mr. Smolov?"

"No. Not now."

Only now did Tamerlan look over. His face revealed nothing as he studied in the thick book Harry held. "Where do you wish to go now?"

"The hotel," Harry said. "I have work to do."

The remainder of the drive passed in silence. Once Harry was back in his hotel room with the door deadbolted he opened the book atop his room desk. He immediately closed it. "Start at the beginning," he reminded himself.

He angled his desk lamp so that its soft yellow light would better catch the cover. Block Arabic script of hammered gold ran across the deeply aged leather. *One Thousand and One Nights*. He consulted his phone to confirm what he already knew. This collection of Middle Eastern folktales had been cultivated during the Islamic Golden Age, a period of literary, scientific and monetary achievement in the Muslim world. The period began around 700 A.D. and lasted for five hundred years. A written compilation of these tales hadn't appeared in English until the early 1700s.

He flipped past Agilulph's message to find a title running across the top of the next page. The first story in the collection, one well known to children around the world thanks to Disney's movie adaptation. *Aladdin and his Wonderful Lamp*. He laughed. "Mack will never let me hear the end of this."

The tale following *Aladdin* was also familiar. *Ali Baba and the Forty Thieves*. As he scanned the remaining stories his thoughts kept returning to the handwritten message on the front cover. The only handwritten message in the entire book.

"Retrieve St. Patrick's Cross from where he began his studies. It is stored beneath the thoughts of Ireland's saint."

Agilulph never said what he meant. His purpose in using obscure directions had almost certainly been to ensure Charlemagne's empire remained at peace, steered by a man wise enough to decipher the messages and strong enough to keep the peace. Agilulph wanted the right person to follow this trail. Turns out that person was Harry.

"St. Patrick," Harry said. "The patron saint of Ireland." Patrick was an Irish bishop centuries before Charlemagne's time, and the man history credited with bringing Christianity to Ireland. Charlemagne would have revered him as the man who converted a pagan society. Harry frowned. He recalled nothing about a cross belonging to St. Patrick. Did Patrick have a specific type of cross?

Patrick was believed to have been an animal herder. This suggested a staff as Patrick's likeliest accessory, not a cross. Harry shook his head. "Worry about that later."

Next came a more concrete message. *Where he began his studies.* "Let's see about that." Harry pulled his laptop out and fired it up.

His phone vibrated. Harry snatched it up and connected the incoming call. "Joey?"

"Hey, buddy."

"Are you okay?" The words spilled out. "Who was it?"

"I'm fine." Dark clouds seemed to accompany his words.

"Is Mack okay?"

"He's the only one of us who is." Joey rattled off several familiar names. "They're all dead."

"What?" Harry ran a hand over his face. "How?"

"Shot in my house." Joey recounted the ordeal, from Mack's shouted warnings to the final confrontation in his office. "Mack saved my life," Joey said. "They gave him a flesh wound, but he managed to take the last two down from outside the window."

Names swirled through Harry's head. Only one stood out as crazy enough to attack Joey in his own neighborhood. "The only person dumb enough to do this is in jail," he said. "Altin Cana must have sent someone."

"It wasn't Altin Cana. Someone else sent these guys. Someone you know."

It hit him a breath later. "Carmelo Piazza."

"That Sicilian chump sent Corsicans to do his dirty work." Joey muttered a few words Harry couldn't catch. More noises than words. "I thought Carmelo was smart enough to let it go. I was wrong."

"What are you going to do?"

"I have an obligation to my men, to the city. An obligation to keep the peace."

Harry hesitated before speaking. "What would your father do?"

Joey had no such hesitation. "He would make the right decision. For everyone, not just for himself."

"Which is?"

"I have no idea."

Fine. They had to start somewhere. "Consider the options."

"My father would remind me emotional reactions are for weak men. Wise men use logic, not anger. I'll need to consider the other families."

"The other families will support you striking back."

"They'll demand it. Or else I look weak."

"This isn't their fight. It's yours. Dragging them into your fight is bad for their business. The families make money in New York, not Sicily. What is there to gain by fighting across an ocean?"

"It's about more than money," Joey said quietly. "I need to think."

"Want me to come back and help? Whatever's here isn't going anywhere."

"You're a good friend," Joey said.

"You'd do the same."

"I would. Let me think about this. I'll be in touch."

Joey's voice had barely faded from his ear when a new worry came to life. Joey could handle himself and so could the people close to him. This was their world. Other people weren't as well-suited for the danger this could bring. People like Sara. Joey taking revenge might be only the opening act in a deadly play for power or revenge. Other people could get hurt. People like Harry. Or Sara.

Harry rubbed his chin with force. He'd learned how fine a line existed between caution and paranoia. Preparation saved your life. Obsession could steal it. Focus too much on what might happen and he'd miss what was actually playing out. Was he jumping at shadows?

"French Corsicans attacked Joey." Might as well talk to himself about it. Nobody else was around. "Maybe there's a French connection." Maybe. More likely not. "Olivier's French. Could be he's involved."

Harry considered it. He nearly laughed. French Corsicans and a French industrialist? That was a stretch.

Except his gut said no. It wasn't a stretch at all. His gut was the reason he was here to have these crazy thoughts. His dad had told him to trust his instincts. Trust, but verify. "Find the evidence, Harry. Then act." He turned back to Agilulph's message and his laptop.

"Saint Patrick's studies. Where did he first study?"

Sometimes the past hid a treasure so well it was never found. Other times that treasure was out in the open for anyone to find it, if only they knew where to look. Harry read through Patrick's biography once, then once more. Nothing. He grumbled and started again.

"Hold on." One word grabbed his eye. A word he'd passed over twice before. "Tonsure. He received the *tonsure*."

Priests in Patrick's time demonstrated their humility by getting a rather awful haircut known as tonsure, basically shaving the top of their head to leave a horseshoe of hair slightly above the ears, running from one side to the other. Harry closed his eyes, digging through the recesses of his memory for a fact he'd learned long ago, one he had no use for. Until now.

His eyes snapped open. "Graduation. Priests could get the tonsure when they *graduated*. That's what Patrick did. He finished studying and received the tonsure." Harry read on. "At Lérins Abbey."

Keys clicked and an image of an ancient monastery on the French Riviera appeared. A sprawling compound hugged the Mediterranean coastline, blue waters only steps away from the monastery walls. It was still an active monastery even fifteen hundred years after its founding.

One spot on the photo grabbed Harry's eye. A remnant from the past situated across the blue waters beside the current abbey. The community's former home, it seemed. At some point the brothers had relocated to the current site on an adjacent island. It took him only a few seconds to unravel why they had chosen the now-abandoned island first. The decrepit structure was closer to deeper waters, but also close enough to the mainland that they could cross a short bridge, burn it, then get on their horses and hightail it out of there. In short, a defensible location from which they could escape via land or sea. It took him a few minutes to confirm the newer building dated to 1073 A.D.

After Agilulph's time. Agilulph could only have visited the older building. His laptop keys clicked and his brow furrowed as he dug for any connection between Agilulph, this old monastery and an Irish saint.

He nearly missed it. The bottom line of a paragraph in a story about the abbey's history referenced a holy relic. What relic? "St. Patrick's skull."

His actual skull, or so they claimed, a relic to draw visitors from far and wide. And what did a skull contain? "His thoughts." Harry smacked the desktop. "That's what he means. Patrick's skull held his thoughts."

He read on. "They moved the skull from the original building, placing it in a replica coffin." Harry read the words aloud. "It used to be on the other island, in the original building."

The monks carried their holy relic to this new building and placed it in a new coffin. Why? He had no idea. All he knew for certain was the answer lay to the south alongside blue Mediterranean waters. That's where he would find the truth behind Agilulph's message.

In the skull of a dead man.

Chapter 11

Sinai Peninsula, Egypt

"Dr. Hamed?"

Sara looked up from the examination table. She did not set her brush down as Ramy Gad stepped under the tent flap, wiping his brow as he moved through the gigantic interior toward her. It took a moment for his eyes to adjust. When he stopped blinking and came closer to where Sara stood, he stopped cold. The exam lamp on the table cast strong light on a pottery fragment. Sara lifted an eyebrow. She did not speak.

"I have news." The words tumbled out of Ramy's mouth before he could stop them. He caught himself, straightened his back and spoke again, more softly this time. "I have a request."

"A request?" She frowned. Ramy Gad wasn't the sort of man to request anything. He gave orders.

"Yes," Ramy said. "I ask that you change assignments."

Her hand tightened on the brush and her throat grew tight. "Why?"

Ramy put his hands up, then quickly lowered them. "We have located a new building not far from the main dig site," he said.

Sara dropped the brush onto the table. "Where?"

Ramy extended a finger toward the tent walls. "In the only hill of any significance on the site."

"The hillside?" He was referencing a large hill, whose sides were too vertical to climb.

"It is not a hill," Ramy said. "A new building has been located inside of it." He put his hands behind his back. "A large building." She opened her mouth to loose a barrage of questions, but stopped herself. Ramy Gad was many things. Benevolent or considerate was not among them. "Why are you telling me?"

"I want you to lead the excavation."

Internal alarms blared. Ramy wouldn't give her the chance to find anything of value, not if he could take the lead first. "Tell me more," she said.

"The initial report suggests the building is twice the size of any found so far."

Really? She kept that question to herself. "What type of structure?"

"We think it could be an abandoned temple."

She couldn't contain herself. "Is it a temple to Zeus? That would be incredible." Sara's legs took over and she stepped toward Ramy, touching his arm with her hand as she spoke. "There's no record of any temple." She pulled her hand away and stepped back. "You want me to lead this excavation?"

She had to strain to catch his reply. "Yes."

"Why me?"

Ramy appeared to chew on his lower lip. "You are well qualified."

"This could be the biggest find on the dig and you're offering me the lead on it. Why?"

"As I said, you are qualified."

"So are you."

"I already have an assigned section."

"So do I."

Ramy's gaze went left. It went right. Finally, it returned to her. "You think I have a personal reason?"

"It makes no sense, Ramy. I just joined the team. Why would you step aside on this?"

His heavy sigh nearly knocked her back a step. "I can be difficult. I know. Having you lead this new portion of the dig while I focus on my area is the best decision for the project, and I want the project to succeed."

"I see." Sara rubbed the fingers of one hand together. Maybe Ramy Gad truly could act like a professional. "Of course. When do I begin?"

Ramy seemed almost relieved. "Immediately. Come with me."

"Who found the new entrance?" Sara asked as she followed Ramy's brisk pace.

"A worker. I have been thinking," Ramy said before she could ask anything else. "My demeanor toward you has, possibly, not been as it should."

Sara refrained from rolling her eyes. "I'm not one to hold a grudge." *At least not one I'll tell you about.*

"Your experience is invaluable to our effort. You did find Alexander's tomb." He paused. "Which is impressive."

"Thank you," she said.

"I admit I was jealous of your success," he said. "It is hard to see what others have done and not think I should have done more."

"We're human. Don't worry about it."

"I am sorry for anything I have done in the past that was not considerate."

She, and pretty much every other Egyptologist who'd ever crossed Ramy's path, could make a list. But now wasn't the time. "That's kind of you," Sara said. "And forget about it. It's time to look ahead."

"I agree." Ramy stopped beside a roped-off section of the dig that hadn't been marked last night. "I am glad we agree."

Sara didn't recall agreeing with anything, but she went with it. Her thoughts had already turned to what came next. "Incredible," she said, craning her neck to look up. "Sitting beside us the entire time."

The dig site was situated on a flat plain amid several larger hills, the level ground having only scrubby vegetation and an occasional haggard tree. Very different from the hill in front of her. The largest hill, with a face too steep to ascend.

"No trees or shrubs." Sara could have kicked herself. "The only hill with no vegetation at all. I should have noticed."

"The temple entrance was buried over time," Ramy said.

The hill in front of them rose nearly vertically for a hundred feet. "This temple could be quite large," Sara said before she stopped and pointed. "Those are steps."

"Found by accident," Ramy said. "A worker hit the hillside with a forklift. It uncovered the steps."

The forklift's prongs would have been driven into the hillside and pierced what looked to be solid ground. Broken clumps of dirt and chunks of rock were cast to one side, showing an opening in the slope. Sara walked close to the revealed steps, which descended into darkness. "The steps are marble. At least this top portion we can see."

"I had a small section excavated so I could check the interior air quality. It is safe. I did not check to see what is inside."

Two columns twenty feet apart framed a series of dusty marble steps leading into the hillside. Smooth depressions in the steps testified to heavy foot traffic over time. "This temple was used for many years, or repurposed." Sara moved closer to get a better look. "When will it be deemed safe to go inside?"

"Our engineers are coming to confirm the structural integrity." Again she sensed a hesitation in Ramy's words. "I will find you as soon we know it is safe to enter," he said.

Sara began walking back to her tent. She had so much to do. Share the news with her team. Prep for the initial excavation. Her mind churned and she reached for her tent flap just as her phone vibrated. Harry. "You will not believe this," she said as she connected the call. "We found a building. Likely a temple." The words poured out. "Once the engineers clear it for entry, guess who is leading the excavation? I am."

"Wow," Harry said. "That's fantastic."

She'd known him long enough now to understand Harry wasn't the most expressive of men. It was all about reading between the lines with him and noticing subtle clues. "What is it?" she asked. "Something is going on."

"Agilulph's path leads to the French Riviera."

"You found a message in the castle." She instinctively looked around.

Nobody in sight. "Where did you find it and what does it say?"

"In a chamber beneath the pagan temple." He detailed using an iron cross to reveal the subterranean chamber. "He left a book. One you know."

"An Egyptian text? An early German one?"

"*A Thousand and One Nights.*"

It took her a second. "Arabic folktales?"

"It's old. First-edition old."

Her knowledge of folktales was limited. "You are certain that's the book?" Harry said he was. "Describe it," she said. Harry rattled off details that made sense. Not only that, the details gave her an idea. "Are there any pearls on it?"

"How'd you know?"

"Harun al-Rashid adored pearls. Quite a few of the caliph's artifacts are decorated with them. What language is used?"

"Mostly Arabic."

"Which makes sense…" She paused. "One moment. 'Mostly'?"

"All except a handwritten message inside the front cover. Handwriting I recognize."

"Agilulph's. What did he write?"

"'*Retrieve St. Patrick's Cross from where he began his studies. It is stored beneath the thoughts of Ireland's saint.*'"

Dates and facts raced through her mind. "Patrick lived in the fifth century, three hundred years before Agilulph, so that fits. But why would Agilulph have the book of fables and leave it in the temple?"

"I'm working on that part. I found a record of where Patrick completed his studies. Lérins Abbey, which is on an island in the French Riviera."

"Is there a cross associated with Patrick in the abbey?"

"Hard to say, considering it's been abandoned for over nine hundred years."

She heard the important part in that sentence. "Which means it's still standing."

"'Standing' is a stretch. 'Not entirely collapsed' is more like it."

"It could contain nearly anything."

"Or nothing. That's a long time for looters to sneak inside. Lucky for us, I think what I'm after can't be carried away very easily." Harry told her about the new abbey's prized relic.

"His skull," Sara said, and the words came out in a high pitch. "That's the link, Harry."

"Agreed. It's where thoughts are stored. I'm hoping whatever is left of the original coffin is somewhere in the old abbey building."

The familiar thrill of discovering untold treasures fluttered in her stomach. A thrill Harry seemed to create every few months. "I assume your exploration of the castle went undiscovered. Otherwise, you would be in jail. When are you leaving for Lérins Abbey?"

"Shortly. But that's not why I called."

"What is it?"

"It's about you and your safety."

She laughed. "I'm perfectly safe. Ramy Gad is loathsome, not dangerous. He's a bully and a coward. Ramy backs down when anyone stands up to him."

"Someone like you."

"Yes."

"I have another reason. Someone tried to kill Joey."

Sara drew in a breath. "Is he hurt?"

"No, but a lot of his men were." Harry recapped a deadly attack on the Morello headquarters.

"How did it end?" she asked.

"The guys who attacked him are currently residents of the city morgue."

"How could an attack on Joey have repercussions for me?"

"Joey said those guys were Corsicans. French Corsicans."

"I'm nowhere near Corsica. I'm in Egypt."

"The relic I'm chasing is meant to lure Olivier Lloris. Who is French."

"That's a stretch. What makes you think the fact someone hired criminals to attack Joey in New York puts me in danger?" Sara didn't give him a chance to respond. "I worry more about them coming after you."

"I'm in Germany. My gut tells me you could be in danger. I learned to trust it a long time ago."

"Your concern is duly noted," she said. "Luckily, I'm perfectly safe at this dig site."

Sara looked up as a head appeared through the tent opening. "May I help you?"

"I'm with the engineering team," the man said. "The entrance to the new location is ready for you."

"Thank you." She waited for the man to step out. "Harry, I have to go. The new site has been declared stable."

"Call me when you're done. I want to know what you find."

"I will." She clicked off and walked out of her tent, forcing herself to slow down as she crossed the site to this new hillside entrance, her feet seeming to never quite touch the ground. Several men surrounded the entrance. Ramy Gad stood at the front of them all with a hardhat on and another in his hands. He extended it to her.

"Ready?" he asked.

"Of course." She put the hat on and activated the attached headlamp. "What do we know so far?"

"Little," Ramy said. "I estimate the interior to be a hundred feet deep and almost as wide, though that is approximate."

"Could be a natural cavern or cave system," Sara said. "Perhaps it's a geologic anomaly."

He pulled at the collar of his shirt. "I suspect this began as a cave before being expanded by hand."

"That would serve two purposes," Sara said. "The worship of Zeus, and concealment in times of danger." She frowned. "How far did you go inside?"

"I did not even reach the top step. What we will find remains a mystery."

Sara turned slowly to look around the site, taking in each of the smaller hills around them. A single digger worked atop a hill directly behind her. Was he searching for other entrances? She blinked and the shadow atop the far hill dropped from her sight. Odd.

She looked at the dark opening ahead. "Are we ready?" No response. "Is something wrong?"

"No, of course not." Ramy spoke so quickly Sara had trouble understanding. "Why do you ask? Everything is ready. You are safe."

A closer look at Ramy showed he was shifting his weight from foot to foot. Nerves? One hand was clenched tight around something that flashed metallic in the light. "This is your section," he said. "You should go first."

Sara dipped her chin in acknowledgment, turned to the opening, and moved to the first marble step. Had she believed in the gods, now is when she would have sent a hopeful word or two skyward. However, she believed in herself, so ahead she went. Dust motes floated through her headlamp beam as she slowly descended the stairs. When she got to the bottom she looked around. The natural stone walls had been carved into an elegant, awe-inspiring house of worship. Decorative columns had been placed on either side, the walls carved back to resemble half-circles of smooth stone.

Outlines on either side called to her, though she resisted and kept moving forward, her eyes on the ground. Another of Harry's lessons. Everything could be dangerous, even the floor, and woe unto the explorer who lost sight of where they stepped. Smooth stone passed beneath her, unremarkable and steady. Sara stopped in this now large, open space.

Ramy's footsteps sounded in the darkness behind her. Her headlamp flickered as he stepped to her side, his breathing rapid. "There are columns on both sides," he said.

"There are more along the wall."

Sara's headlamp flickered again as its bulb winked off and on. "This is not helpful." She tapped the light, hard, and as it flickered off and on once before holding steady, she noted a green tinge on the floor below her. *Where did that come from?*

"Inventory," Sara said to herself. "Take inventory." She turned to Ramy and spoke up. "There are columns and relief carvings cut into the cave walls. Decorative, not structural. I see ten in all, five on each side and equally spaced. The steps leading down were marble, but the columns are stone, as is the floor." She peered intently into the darkness ahead. "What's that?"

She stepped forward. Her headlamp flickered and a red glow seemed to cover the wall. *Crack.*

The ceiling began to break loose. She whirled around to see huge chunks of rock falling back by the entrance. A terrible rumbling told her this was only getting started.

She grabbed Ramy's arm, pulling him back toward the entrance with her as she accelerated toward the sunlight. "Move!" Sara shouted as they ran for the entrance. Three steps out, a rock bigger than her head broke loose from the ceiling and crashed directly in front of her. Sara dodged and they were almost there.

She looked up. Dust billowed around a piece of the ceiling directly atop the entrance. If it fell, they'd be trapped under the collapsing rocks. She planted a foot on the floor and whirled around to throw Ramy headfirst through the entrance. The billowing dust threw a hazy cloud across the exit as she leapt after Ramy and into the light. A deafening *boom* followed her out as she hit the ground and rolled, then kept rolling right over top of the prone Ramy before hopping to her feet and turning.

Half the entranceway had collapsed. Sara gulped a full breath of air that had an odd smell. Almost like almonds. People surrounded her. "Are you injured?" one man asked in English. The question came again in French as a flurry of hands reached toward her.

"I'm fine." She pushed the hands away. "Give me space." She turned back toward the temple entrance. "I can see inside," she said. "Only the roof by the steps collapsed."

"I cannot believe it." One of the engineers stood by her. "It was secure. I was certain."

It was clear this had been less of a collapse and more of a small rockslide. With at least one falling rock the size of her torso. Big enough to kill anyone it fell on. "It's fine," Sara said. "You can't be certain of anything."

"It does not make sense," the engineer said.

It could have been worse. Much worse. "It won't take long to clear the opening," she said. "We can build reinforcements around it to be sure it holds."

"That should not have happened." Ramy Gad appeared beside her, one hand in a pocket, the other on his chest. "It was supposed to be safe." His voice shook.

"We're alive." Sara pointed at the entrance, now jagged at the top where it had been rounded before. "That must have been the weakest part of the ceiling. We need to be careful next time."

Ramy's eyes widened as he turned to look at her. "You intend to go back inside?"

She raised an eyebrow. "You don't?"

The Egyptologist was unable to muster a reply. Sara turned to the engineer. "That flashlight on your belt. May I borrow it?" The man handed over what turned out to be a very serious flashlight. "I saw something inside," Sara said. "At the temple's far end."

"You cannot go back inside," the engineer said.

"I'm not going in. I'm looking from here." She used the light to first inspect the damage at the entrance. The slide and roof collapse were concentrated in one corner of the entranceway, along the ceiling on the right.

"What did you see?" Ramy asked.

"I'm not sure," she said. One more step closer was all she would risk. "An outline. Of what, I can't say. Not yet."

She risked another step. The powerful beam carved a path of light to the rear wall a hundred feet distant, to an outline that looked familiar. An outline that was far more than a shadow.

She couldn't help but grin. "I knew it."

Chapter 12

Brooklyn

A streetlight flickered as the armored SUV rolled to a stop at the curb. A jogger leapt aside when the silent vehicle stopped beside him. Had he known who was inside, he may have run faster to make his getaway.

Mack got out of the driver's seat and opened the rear door. Joey Morello exited, hesitating behind the protection of the bulletproof door for a beat to look left and right. His shadow stretched in front of him on the short walk to a nondescript office building in this nondescript part of town. He walked with purpose until he made it through the front door.

"Good evening, Joseph."

Joey offered his hand as Mack took his customary post by the door. The hand that grasped Joey's may have been wrinkled, but it remained strong as ever. "Good evening, Mr. Sabella. Thank you for agreeing to see me."

The *capo dei capi* of the New York crime families didn't have to work around another man's schedule very often. However, Gio had been a close friend of Joey's father. Gio was one of the very few men in this city Joey Morello could trust with any concern he had. Including the question of how to save his empire.

"In troubled times, a wise man seeks counsel beyond his own."

"Is Rafael here?" Joey asked.

Gio used the cane he carried to point at a nearby door. "In the conference room. I believed it best for us to discuss this matter privately before the other family heads arrive."

The ease with which Gio lifted the cane only reinforced Joey's suspicion the old man used it as much for show as for support. The conference room door opened and his old friend Raf Sabella walked out, his casual workout gear proof that his father had given everyone little notice about this meeting.

"Hey, Joey." The Sabella heir embraced Joey and gave him a solid thump on the back, a gesture Joey returned. "Good to see you. Those Corsican chumps didn't know who they were messing with."

"I'm still standing." Joey shook his head. "But too many good men gone."

Each man crossed himself. "May they rest in peace," Raf said. "Come in."

Joey found two of Gio's bodyguards inside the room, one big like Mack, the other wiry and short. Joey nodded to them as they exited the room and joined Mack. Raf indicated a bottle of wine on the table. "Care for a drink?"

"After today? Yes."

Gio spoke after the wine was poured and each man had taken a seat around the long table. "Tell us what happened."

Joey recounted the attack on his compound and his narrow escape. He named each of his dead men in turn. He did not swear vengeance, did not curse the attackers. Such emotions were not helpful, and if his father had been watching, Vincent Morello would have approved. "I have suspicions as to who ordered the attack," Joey finished. "Though little proof."

"You inspected the attackers' bodies?" Gio asked.

"I did. No identification, no tattoos, nothing to tell me who they were. Only one person has a strong enough motive to send men after me in my neighborhood. Carmelo Piazza."

"No one who survives as a Sicilian clan leader is to be underestimated," Gio said. "Your response must be decisive."

There it was: the reason for this meeting, the looming decision that would chart the course of Joey Morello's reign, and the question Joey couldn't answer. How to respond? An enemy had invaded Joey's home. That enemy had killed Joey's friends and tried to destroy Joey's reputation as the man who controlled the New York families. Everyone who'd ever sat on the throne Joey now occupied would have immediately moved to erase their adversary from the world. An approach Joey was sorely tempted to follow. However, a part of him believed that wasn't the way, that more men didn't have to die.

Raf tapped a finger on the table. "Tell me what you need. You'll have it."

"I need time to confirm who did this."

Raf scoffed. "You already know. Carmelo Piazza."

"I *think* he is behind this. If I'm right, there's a battle on the horizon. I won't risk more lives unless I'm certain."

Gio spoke in flat tones. "The men who follow you do so because they choose to." Gio tapped the cane to his chest. "I am one of those men. I have seen leaders who are kind, and leaders who are tyrants, and leaders who are many other things. Each of them knew a challenge requires a response."

"What type of response does this require?" Joey asked.

Gio answered with a story. "Many years ago, your father and I were collecting tickets for the weekly number." One way the mob generated cash in Vincent's and Gio's day had been through illegal gambling, which included running their own version of the state lottery's daily numbers in the neighborhood. People paid a dime to buy into the daily drawing, receiving a payout if their number hit. Hundreds of dollars, most of the time—a welcome sum for neighborhood families at the time.

"We were near the edge of our territory," Gio said. "Near a different family's turf. A few teenagers with ties to the different family came after us. We ran. We did not escape, so Vincent took the money we had collected and held it up in his fist." Here Gio lifted a clenched hand in the air. "Vincent pointed at the biggest of them. He said 'If you want this money, come take it from me.'" The memory sent laughter dancing across Gio's lined face. "Vincent put the money on the ground and he told me to stay back. I knew your father well enough to listen. And I am grateful I did."

Joey had heard quite a few stories about his father. Never this one. "What happened?"

"The big one Vincent challenged had a gold chain. Vincent told him to put it on the ground beside the money. He said they would box, and whoever won kept the money and the chain. The big one laughed at your father and accepted." Gio tapped his cane on the floor. "He was a fool."

Joey noted that both he and Raf were now leaning forward. "And then?" Joey asked.

"Your father waited for the boy to charge, then he hit him in the chin." They all flinched when Gio whacked the table. "Boom, one punch. Down. Your father then went after the other two, who had more sense than their friend. They ran." Gio chuckled. "We took the money and the chain and we left. That was the day I knew your father would be our *capo dei capi*. He handled it, and he did it alone." Gio coughed into a closed fist. "You asked what I believe this situation requires." He aimed a gnarled finger at Joey. "It requires the same strength your father had."

A knock on the conference room door stopped Joey from responding. A Sabella bodyguard poked his head in. "The others are here, sir."

Gio waved at his man to show them in. One by one the other family heads filed in, three men in all, all of them men Joey had known his entire life. Men who had followed his father, and who now followed him. Whether they liked it or not.

Joey may have been the current boss, but everyone knew who to respect.

"Welcome," Gio said once the conference room door had closed. "Join us at my table."

Only then did they sit. Gio gave the briefest of nods in Joey's direction.

"I believe the man responsible for today's attack is in Sicily," Joey said. "Carmelo Piazza."

The impressively overweight Albert Zurilli spoke up. "I know guys over there. Give me the word. We'll take care of him."

"Thank you," Joey said. "But it's not their fight. It's mine."

"He may as well have attacked all of us." Zurilli poked a thick finger against the table. "We must hit back. Hard." Murmured responses indicated agreement.

"I understand," Joey said. "And we will respond soon."

Zurilli didn't give up. "How long do we wait? The longer it takes us, the worse it looks." A half-second passed. "For all of us."

The message was clear. Zurilli expected Joey to act quickly. Calling out his hesitation in front of the other family heads was no surprise, considering Zurilli had not-so-quietly pushed for his son to lead the families after Vincent Morello's death. Joey had outmaneuvered Zurilli, in no small part thanks to Gio Sabella's backing.

"I hear your concern," Joey said in a level tone. He knew what would come next, so he pre-empted it. "Reputation isn't the only thing we stand to lose. The longer this goes on, the more of a chance our finances take a hit. People won't want to do business with me if I let others push me around. We will respond. When I decide." Joey didn't raise his voice. He didn't do anything except look at the Zurilli family head.

"Of course," Zurilli said. "You're the boss."

And with that, it hit him. A solution to handle this *his* way. "The code."

"The what?" Raf asked.

"*Il Codice.*" Joey looked to the wisest pair of eyes at the table. The eyes of a man who knew the history of their families, and of the families before them. Lines formed at the edge of Gio Sabella's eyes. The old man winked.

This time Joey's voice filled the room. "The code our fathers spoke of. A code of honor." A bit of a stretch. "Generations have lived by these rules. Never talk to the police." A relic of a bygone era, that one. "Never betray your family." Still in effect, thank goodness. "Honor your father and mother. And if there is a dispute between families, the heads of those families are responsible for resolving it."

Recognition dawned on Raf's face. "Individually, if they agree."

Joey tapped the table. "Carmelo Piazza is a clan head. The leader of his family. His actions are intolerable, and he must answer for them. By facing me."

"You're going to challenge Carmelo?" Al Zurilli asked.

"I am. No matter what happens, the matter will be settled. No retaliation, no more bloodshed."

"We have ten times the manpower he does," Raf said. "And more resources. We can crush him. You don't need to risk your neck."

"That's exactly what I need to do. I know some of you don't agree with the new direction of our enterprises. My investments in banking, renewable energy and other"—here he searched for the proper phrase—"less traditional methods of generating revenue." He didn't have to look at Al Zurilli. Everyone at the table knew who had fomented the quiet discontent. "I stand by those decisions. We adapt, or we perish. But this calls for a return to the old days. To show we haven't lost our way. To show the world we are still strong."

"People are watching not only from the old country," Gio said. "They are watching from around the world."

"You'd have to go to Carmelo to issue a challenge," Raf said. "Fight on his turf. That's a bad idea."

"I can take care of myself." The look on Joey's face did not invite further questions. "I'm the *capo*. I'll end this."

"We will face problems if you do not return," Gio said. "Your seat growing cold will not bode well for any of us. The decision to appoint you as leader did not come easily. Who is to say what will happen the next time." He pointedly did not look at Albert Zurilli. "However"—and here he rapped his cane once on the floor—"the decision is yours. We will support you."

"Then it is decided."

One by one, each man came to embrace Joey, then departed. Soon only Gio and Raf remained. Gio put a hand on Joey's shoulder. "Well done. Your father would be proud." Gio's next words were so low Joey barely caught them. "You will not lose."

Thanks, Gio. No pressure at all.

Chapter 13

French Riviera

Church bells tolled afternoon's arrival as Harry pulled into a town he'd long heard of, but never visited. An engine's guttural roar made him look back as he slowed for a stop sign. A Lamborghini zipped around him, so low to the ground it nearly disappeared below his own car's hood as it went by. It wasn't the first one he'd seen around the French seaside resort of Cannes. Harry took the turn with extra caution lest another sportscar happen past. The insurance on his rental car wouldn't hold up to the repair bill.

The Bay of Cannes sparkled as Harry parked his car near the docks, grabbed a pack from the trunk, and headed for the boat rental where he'd booked a small craft for the short trip to the island of Saint-Honorat. He did not tell the manager he might head over to an adjacent island. He did take a complimentary map of the surrounding islands, and he did pay for the fee in case of a late return. Just in case.

Harry easily piloted the craft the short distance from the mainland to Saint-Honorat. His new copy of *A Thousand and One Nights* was safely locked in the trunk of his rental, though Agilulph's message ran through his mind, over and over, as he considered any possible meaning that had not yet been revealed. *Retrieve St. Patrick's Cross from where he began his studies. It is stored beneath the thoughts of Ireland's saint.*

Agilulph used misdirection and obscure references to hide his more precious secrets. This didn't seem to be one of those, but that didn't mean this part of the quest was safe. His lips turned up at the corners.

Risking his life on playing the odds could get him in trouble, and missteps here could be fatal.

With that pleasant thought in his head, he looked up as he reached the newer abbey. Harry glanced toward the older structure on a neighboring island, close enough that he could swim to it if necessary. A voice calling out pulled his attention back to the abbey's dock.

"*Bonjour!*"

Harry returned the greeting in French. His reply must have been accented enough that the small, trim man with a full head of blond hair switched to English. "Welcome," the man said. "Throw me your rope." He caught the rope Harry threw and expertly secured Harry's craft to the dock. "You are Mr. Fox?"

"That's me." Harry jumped from the small boat onto the dock. He'd called the abbey en route from Germany, identifying himself as a novelist who wished to write about the abbey in an upcoming book. The priest Harry had spoken with didn't seem thrilled with the idea of allowing a writer to access areas of the abbey not normally open to the public. Then Harry had mentioned the generous donation he'd bring. That changed everything.

"We are pleased to host you," the blond man said. He offered his hand. "Wes Barcola. I will be your guide."

Harry felt rough calluses on the man's palm as he shook. Wes didn't spend his days behind a desk. "Appreciate your time," Harry said. "When can we get started?"

"Now. Follow me." Wes led Harry past a small group of tourists in line not at the chapel entrance, but at the front door of a restaurant adjacent to the abbey. Wes saw Harry take note.

"That door leads to both the restaurant and our winery." Wes pointed to rows of grapevines stretching from one side of the island to the other.

"You make wine here?" Harry said. He must have missed that in his research.

"Our wine is quite popular with visitors," Wes said, then he winked. "And profitable."

"Maybe I'll grab a bottle on my way out," Harry said. "Is it okay if we start in the chapel?"

Wes nodded and led Harry down a paved pathway into the abbey proper. The abbey was laid out in a large U, with three sides of equal length enclosing the main church and the bell tower. Several smaller outbuildings were spaced on either side. Trees dotted the grounds, and two rows of them led to the chapel. There was a cemetery located along one side of the building, its tombstones too numerous to count.

"Welcome to our chapel," Wes said as they entered the building.

Harry showed interest in the interior for an appropriate amount of time. The stone statues along one wall. The intricately carved reliefs on another. All very nice, and none interesting. He saved his true attention for last. "Is that St. Patrick's tomb?" Harry asked as he pointed to the lustrous marble coffin set hard against a far corner.

"It is. It holds the saint's skull," Wes said. "The rest of his holy remains are not here."

Harry moved toward it without waiting for Wes to lead him. "How long has it been here?" he asked. The coffin sat atop a rectangular stone. Harry leaned over to find a marble lid covered all but the uppermost portion of the coffin. A clear protective cover allowed visitors to inspect a very ordinary-looking skull, as far as skulls went. "Patrick lived over fifteen hundred years ago."

"The skull has been in our care since the fifth century, first in our original abbey across the water, and now here."

"Has it been anywhere else?"

"No," Wes said with pride. "We have cared for his remains all those years."

"Fascinating." Harry paused, a thought striking him. "Have you ever been to the original abbey?"

"Never."

"Does anyone still visit it? I imagine it's still an interesting place."

"No one goes there now. It is too dangerous."

Something in his voice made Harry take note. "Dangerous?"

"The wolves."

"The what?"

"Wolves. The island is home to a population of wild wolves."

Harry's boot squeaked as he turned to face Wes directly. "There are wolves over there?"

"They have adapted to eat fish and birds, and some even swim to the mainland for food."

Harry pointed at the array of floating fortresses along the Cannes shoreline. "I'm surprised all those yacht owners tolerate wolves swimming around."

"The wolves who go to shore can be eliminated," Wes said. "They are protected while on the island. The French government has decreed it."

Lucky me. "Interesting," Harry said. "May I get closer to the tomb here in the chapel? I'd like to take a few photos for my research."

"Normally we ask visitors not to touch the tomb." Wes winked like a bad actor. "But for your book, why not?"

"Thanks," is all Harry said before moving to the tomb. He snapped a photo of the skull with his phone camera, then leaned closer. Everything seemed normal. No etchings or markings to suggest Agilulph had left a message on the poor guy's head.

Nothing else to find here. "I appreciate your time," Harry said as he stepped back from the marble coffin. "The abbey is a busy place. I'd be happy to wander the remaining grounds on my own."

"Impossible." Wes's wide grin made Harry nervous. "You are our honored guest. It is my privilege to show you our island."

A writer interested in learning about the abbey and grounds would never turn down a guided tour, not unless he wasn't a writer and he wanted to blow his cover story apart. "Thank you," Harry said.

Wes was a talker. An intelligent one, with an encyclopedic knowledge of the abbey, the history of the island, and seemingly every person who had ever lived on it. One hour stretched into two, then to a full three hours as they walked through the buildings and vineyard, across the cemetery and along the shoreline. The sun was low in the sky when Wes finally ran out of steam.

"Are you certain you have enough material?" Wes asked.

They were standing at the dock. Harry nearly had one foot in his boat. "Plenty," he said. "I do appreciate your time. It's been very helpful."

"Be careful on your journey home," Wes said as he tossed Harry's mooring line aboard.

"I will." Harry fired up the engine and aimed for the mainland. He did not move quickly, instead idling not far from the dock as he pretended to check his phone. When he was sure that Wes had vanished back inside the abbey, he moved the boat on, this time more quickly, and not toward the mainland. He took a winding path along the coastline of Saint-Honorat until the terrain hid him from view, then he gunned it across the narrow stretch of water separating the islands, looping around to the far side of the island on which the first abbey ruins sat. The island with wolves on it, which Wes had told him was imaginatively named *Ile de Saint Patrick*. Saint Patrick's island, which had once held the saint's skull.

Any docks on this island had rotted long ago, so he chose a narrow strip of water leading slightly inland to a circular pool. This particular pool had several gigantic trees tall and wide enough to obscure his boat from view. Not perfect, and he'd have to get wet to get on shore, but it would do.

He took out his pack, then grabbed the boat's flare gun along with an extra flare and stowed them in the pack. That and his trusty knuckledusters were the only defense he had against any adversary, human or otherwise.

A check on his phone revealed Sara hadn't called. She had texted a few hours ago that she would ring later with an update on her dig. He shook his head. *She's fine.* He let the boat drift as close to the shoreline as caution allowed before it slowed to a halt and he dropped anchor. Harry pulled out a flashlight and played its beam over the shoreline, pushing back the gloom to reveal barren trees and large rocks. Nothing moved.

Harry looked up at the bright moon. *I should have been here hours ago.* He fastened a headlamp around his forehead, flicked the beam to life, then grabbed his pack and lowered himself into the chilly water, which reached his waist. Trying not to shiver, he made for shore, holding his pack above his head until sand crunched beneath his boots and the adventure was truly on.

He moved out of the water toward a thick tree that had been bent by the wind, its trunk going from vertical to nearly horizontal so that the tree's uppermost branches were almost low enough to touch. He passed the bent tree to reach sparse shrubbery and jogged up the gently sloped hillside, his shadow chasing him until he crested the hill and stopped to scan the island now spread out before him.

The remains of an abandoned abbey lay a few hundred yards ahead. Its exterior walls looked to be twice as tall as Harry in some places, though in other spots they had collapsed. A pair of lookout towers at opposite corners of the rectangular structure had holes as though cannonballs had blasted through them, leaving what remained of their interior staircases visible. Any roof was long gone.

Here the shrubbery was denser than near the water. A narrow path led through mostly leafless bushes and trees toward the abbey. He started off along it, then stopped. This was no path. It was a game trail, made over time by the island's apex predators.

Harry moved fast, his boots pounding the dirt as he closed in on the abbey, now only a hundred yards away. His distance from shore and his positioning kept his headlamp from being seen across the water. He should be able to complete his search undisturbed. The abbey came up quickly and he flicked the headlamp downwards before stepping over a break in the wall onto the old abbey grounds.

His research showed St. Patrick's tomb had been adjacent to the watchtower overlooking the ocean, the highest point on the island. Foundation stones showed where interior buildings had stood. He headed for the watchtower ruins, climbing the natural slope of the land with quick steps and chasing his headlamp beam across the ground. He barely noticed the patch of shadow in the ground just ahead, dark as midnight. His boots left streaks in the dirt as he skidded, his toes coming to a stop at the edge of a steep drop. The ground had collapsed into the cavern. He leaned over the edge and gulped. One more step and he would have fallen fifteen feet down to broken, rocky ground. Close, but that was how it went in the field. Sometimes you were good. Other times you were lucky. His gaze went to the nearby tower remnants. All he needed to do was reach the front entrance, jump down to the lower level, and that should put him near the location of Patrick's original coffin. Nothing to—

A howl filled the night.

The cold fingers of primitive fear tightened on his throat. Where did that come from? He looked left, then right, but his headlamp beam was too weak to reveal anything beyond the ruined walls. Nothing moved, and the sound did not return. He shook his head and cool air filled his lungs. That had been the howl of a predator. A big one.

Did wolves hunt at night? He had no idea.

It took more effort than usual to get his feet moving again. He stepped around the hole in the ground, slipped between a pair of hardy trees that had sprouted from an ancient stone floor, and walked until he stood in front of the lookout tower and the remains of a chapel. A chapel of which nothing remained beyond a single wall that reached his knees. The floor inside had collapsed, completely exposing the staircase leading down. That's where St. Patrick's coffin should be.

He moved carefully over to the stone staircase and let his headlamp beam wash over the steps. Time and the elements had left them rounded at the edges. One step at a time brought him halfway down, where he paused, his eyes at ground level. A sweep of the island found no wolves looking back.

Down he went to the lower level, where he found three tunnels. Two on his right went back toward the middle of the chapel. He took one of them and went that way first, passing several alcoves filled with rocks and debris before the tunnel curved around and he found himself coming back the way he'd entered. A larger alcove along the curving passage gave him pause as his light reflected off dull white sticks within. Not sticks.

Bones. He stepped closer.

Animal bones. Dozens of them. A bone near his boot was nearly the length of his forearm. Gouges ran the length of it. The types of gouges a canine tooth would make. Something powerful had chewed on it. Harry turned back to the tunnel, moving faster until he'd circled back to the open area where he'd started. His shadow led him across the moonlit floor, past the staircase and toward the other entrance. Remnants of what had once been metal door hinges clung to either side of the doorway on the second tunnel. Double doors had once covered this entrance.

It wasn't a long tunnel. Two sconces below smoke stains on either side wall showed where torches used to light the way. Ten steps later Harry stood in front of a wider opening, leading to an open space. A large, rectangular box sat in the center. A box with no lid—a coffin. He moved to the side of it, put both hands on the edge, and looked in.

The coffin was empty. Dirt had built up in the corners, and nests of twigs and branches indicated something other than St. Patrick's skull had called this home over time. Harry ran his hand around the inside surface of the empty coffin, then touched the bottom where a head may have rested. His fingers bumped up and down. He stopped, going over that part again. "There's a carving on the bottom," he said to himself.

He scrubbed at the coffin's bottom to reveal the carving—a square outline containing a symbol. "A Celtic cross." He traced the standard cross, then the ring connecting the cross's arm and stem. "Patrick's symbol."

But why wouldn't the monks use Patrick's cross symbol in other ways around the abbey? None had been visible in the newer abbey, and he hadn't seen any others during his short time here. Something was off. Why was such a meaningful symbol ignored here, in the place where Patrick was revered even today? That absence carried meaning.

"There's another cross somewhere." Harry stood back from the coffin and looked around. "Somewhere close." Then it hit him. The monks wouldn't have carved more Celtic crosses because the monks hadn't carved this one. Agilulph had. It was a marker telling Harry to find the corresponding image, one that wouldn't have any meaning if viewed alone. An image that could hide in plain sight, recognizable only by one following Agilulph's path. Harry aimed his headlamp into each dark corner of the room where he stood.

"Got you."

Chapter 14

French Riviera

Harry walked to the cavern's corner. He reached a hand out, his fingers tracing an image carved into the rock. A Celtic cross, identical to the one in Patrick's original tomb, this one also surrounded by a square carved into the rock. Harry touched the uppermost line of the square.

A chunk of it fell to the ground. "Oops." He pulled his hand back, then hesitated, angling his head. The square around this cross looked off. Crooked, almost. This time, when he reached out and brushed his fingers across the stone wall, another chunk broke free, this one about the size of a quarter, and it rattled on the floor by his boot. Harry leaned closer and then he realized what he was looking at. "It's not a square. It's a cutout, and it's falling apart."

What he'd taken to be a square decorative carving in the wall was nothing of the sort. The square image around this Celtic cross was only visible because the wall had deteriorated over time. "Why is this square the only section that's falling apart?"

He poked again. More rock fell. He leaned closer to the wall and it hit him. "It's not part of the wall." Small cracks in the rock ran inside this square, even cutting through the Celtic cross, but none extended beyond the square outline. The square section of rock on which the cross was carved had been cut out of the wall at some point and then placed back in, slotted into an opening. Why?

Agilulph had cut this section out of the wall, marked it with the Celtic cross, then put it back in place. Harry reached out and pulled at the cracked stone. The cross crumbled as he ripped at it, particulate filling the air to block his headlamp beam. He waved it away.

A handle stood inside the opening. Harry reached in, sent out a silent prayer to Patrick, and pulled.

The lever moved toward him, held fast for a moment, then flew all the way back with a loud crack. He crouched, ready to spring for the stairs. One breath, then another. Nothing. He frowned, and that did it.

The floor vibrated and a rumbling sound filled the air. Patrick's coffin moved like a sliding door. Harry stepped closer to look at what had been hidden beneath it.

A set of steps leading down into darkness. Harry found a baseball-sized hunk of broken rock and tossed it down the steps. No fireballs erupted. The stone bounced on a few steps and then disappeared. Harry grabbed a second rock and threw it down, harder this time. It hit something solid. There was a landing down there.

"There must be a wall down there too." The steps looked sturdy enough, though he tested each one as he descended to a flat landing below. At that level there was a natural open space like a small room, and a choice.

Two options faced him. Two openings in the wall ahead. Each opening led to a passageway, and the two passageways appeared to run parallel to each other. Harry aimed his headlamp between them. A wooden board was attached to the wall, a board with Latin letters carved into it. Letters the size of Harry's hand. Why were they so big?

His headlamp beam caught a dull white object off to his left side. Harry turned to it. What he saw made the hair on his arms go up.

A human skeleton lay against the wall to his left. Or half a skeleton. Two legs, hips, and nothing else. He turned another few feet and found the rest of the skeleton. A person had been cut in half. "You didn't read the sign," Harry said to the skeleton. "Why were you down here?"

Harry read the Latin inscription aloud. *Face as the Caliphate does five times daily.* "The Abbasid Caliphate." They had forged an alliance with Charlemagne. "They were Muslims," Harry said. "Muslims pray five times daily." Where did they face when praying? "Mecca."

"I'm in France," Harry said. He closed his eyes and visualized a map. "Mecca is in Saudi Arabia. That's southeast of here. Which means"—and here he bit his tongue while pointing his finger—"I'm facing northeast. Mecca is to my right."

His gaze went to the skeleton, to the piece lying on his *left* side. That could matter. Harry filed that away as he spotted notches carved into either side of the left-most doorway, each about three feet up from the floor. He looked at the halved skeleton. He looked back to the notches, then took one tiny step closer to get a better view, pulling a penlight from his pocket and aiming it into the adjacent passageway.

Metal flashed as his light moved, rusted metal that had been used with deadly effect. A hidden blade tucked inside the wall, no doubt activated when anyone entered the incorrect tunnel. He stepped back to the right-hand tunnel, moving slowly forward as he examined the rough walls on either side of him and found nothing alarming. His gaze then stayed on the ground as he followed the headlamp beam, looking for any sign of danger. He paused, turning one ear back the way he'd come. What was that?

He waited. It sounded again, a low noise at the edge of hearing. His breath stopped short. "Growls."

His pace quickened until the passageway ended in a *T*, one path leading left, the other right. The wall had no markings or any sort of clue as to which way to go. "Maybe Agilulph already told me what to do."

Muslims prayed five times each day. Would it take five right turns to solve this puzzle? Harry stood still as a memory of his father came to him, and an echo of advice Fred Fox had offered. *It's not always certain in the field. Be decisive.*

"I hope you're right, Dad." Harry stood and moved ahead. Thick spiderwebs laced with debris hung from the tunnel ceiling to block any view of what lay ahead. The passageway ended in a wall of hard rock. The wall had a recessed area with a carving. A carving of a very familiar shape.

"A Celtic cross." Harry reached out but didn't touch the carving in the wall. The recessed area held an actual Celtic cross, the vertical portion a foot tall, with the horizontal crossbeam half that long. A cross made of a stone Harry had never seen. The Irish-green cross sparkled as his headlamp moved across it, throwing off brilliant red specks under the light. Harry brushed a finger across its smooth green surface.

"It's one stone." He found no grooves, no indication this had been pieced together. It was a single solid rock that had been cut into the shape of a Celtic cross. The bottommost portion was wrapped in dried-out leather. Harry touched the leather. "It's a *scroll*."

A scroll wrapped around the base. He carefully pulled it away from the base of the cross. Did the cross come off the wall as well? His gut said go for it, so he pulled. A rumbling sounded as he struggled with the cross before it came free. He hefted the stone cross with both hands. "It's heavy."

As he stood there cradling it, a memory came back, a trivial reference from one of the historical texts he'd read about Saint Patrick. "Bloodstone," Harry said. "This is made of bloodstone." The green stone flecked with red specks had been favored by Patrick. Many of the saint's devotees today had amulets and charms honoring Patrick made from the stone. "This is where it all started," he said as he angled the cross for a better look. "The original Celtic cross. Saint Patrick's cross."

Harry carefully put the stone cross down before taking hold of the rolled scroll in both hands, finding one edge and unrolling it. He aimed his headlamp at it and a line of writing came into view. "Agilulph's handwriting." He'd know that script anywhere. Latin writing, as expected, but what did Agilulph have to say now? Harry blew a cobweb off the first word so he could translate it.

Grrrrr.

The noise came from behind him. Not just any noise. *Growling.*

Harry looked up from the scroll. Two glowing dots reflected his headlamp. Two dots at waist height. The dots moved, coming closer, and the wolf came into view. A pair of white fangs appeared. Harry gulped.

The wolf's shoulders came up to his waist; the beast was wide enough to block any attempt at escape. The guttural noises touched a primeval fear inside him.

The growling stopped. Harry blinked and the wolf leapt. Saliva hung from one fang as deadly claws flashed out. He fell back, twisting so the wolf's outstretched claws skidded across his sturdy pack, the wolf's hairy body sliding across it as he fell. The wolf overshot his mark and smashed into the wall, whimpering as it fell. Harry leapt up, tucked the scroll under his arm, grabbed the cross and raced down the tunnel to the intersection, then toward the main room.

The passageway brought him to the room with two doors and the halved skeleton as the wolf howled. He followed his bouncing headlamp as he ran up the stairs to where he'd found the first Celtic cross marker.

Another wolf stood in front of him. Harry stopped, turning to keep his back to a wall and the second wolf in front of him. The first wolf came bounding up the stairs, but it didn't attack, instead lowering its head as it joined the other animal. Only then did both approach, side by side, one slow step at a time.

Out of options, he played the only card left. The stone cross and scroll disappeared into his bag and the flare gun came out. He leveled it and pulled the trigger.

Night turned to day as the flare erupted to send the wolves scrambling for safety. Cursing and half-blind, Harry ran up the stairs to ground level while reloading.

He cleared the last step and promptly tripped on a rock. Harry spun, twisted until he managed to find his feet, and kept running downhill toward the cove and the safety of his boat. He followed the game trail that was really a wolf trail through the brush.

Snarls sounded behind him. His boat sat anchored where he'd left it out in the water—almost directly beneath that overhanging tree that he now realized stretched nearly to his boat. *Can wolves swim?* If not, he should dive in the water and he'd be home free. But if they could, then this water would be the death of him. His feet pounded, propelling him forward, as another option presented itself. A bad option. Harry grinned. *It could work.*

Harry accelerated, aiming for the tree at the shoreline. He took one last step on solid ground and leaped onto the bent tree trunk without stopping, barreling ahead with only water below him. Thick leaves bounced as he jumped for his boat, arms swinging and feet kicking as he flew over empty air before crashing into his waiting vessel.

I made it.

The wolves howled from shore. Only once the engine fired and the anchor was on board could he slam the throttle forward. Water plumed and the bow jumped as his craft raced across the cove. His eyes narrowed as a shiver he couldn't suppress wracked his body. *Too close, Harry. That was too close.*

He gave Saint-Honorat a wide berth, though all that looked back at him as he motored past were a handful of twinkling lights. He kept his own running lights off, flicking them on only after he was closer to the Cannes shoreline. Harry tied up at the same slip he'd left hours ago, jumped on the dock and headed straight to his car. Only once he was inside with the engine running and he was certain nobody was interested in a late-night boater returning to shore did he remove the bloodstone Celtic cross and the scroll from his pack. He set the cross carefully on the seat beside him, before unrolling the scroll and starting to read.

Chapter 15

Sinai Peninsula

A blaring car horn ripped Sara from her sleep. For a moment she fought to understand the world through a thick gauze of sleep, blinking rapidly in the dim light as she looked left and right, not seeing anything. *I'm in a tent?*

Precious metal glinted on the tabletop near her and it all came rushing back. *The riches.*

"Zeus's hoard."

Silver jugs, golden ornaments, staffs and symbolic pieces decorated with precious jewels. An ornately engraved plate the size of a hubcap rested on the desk in front of her, while a six-foot spear of silver with gold plating and rubies on the handle had been placed on a long table.

"The statues." She rubbed her eyes and turned the coffee pot on. "The equal of any in our museum." Not that anything from this dig would make its way to the Museum of Natural History anytime soon. Not unless Ramy agreed to a traveling exhibit.

She poured a cup of coffee, drinking as she walked back to the table to find her personal items scattered about. She'd fallen asleep here last night, never even making it to her cot, her head resting atop a stack of paper. Not the best pillow. Her phone sat beside her computer.

"Harry." She started, nearly spilling her coffee. "I have to tell Harry." She tapped the screen. Nothing. "I didn't charge it." She groaned, searching for a charger. The last time she'd spoken with Harry he was headed to the French Riviera. That was only a half-day ago, but it seemed like much more. He didn't know about the entrance collapse or the treasures she'd uncovered inside. She grinned. Harry wasn't the only person who could think on their toes.

A buzzing made her turn back to the phone. She picked it up. The screen displayed a full battery, though it had only been charging for a minute. Sara tapped at the screen and tried to call Harry. The connection failed. Sara tried a second time. The call wouldn't go through, and as she looked at the screen it lost the signal. She muttered at the device, unplugged it and headed for the tent flap, pushing through into the warming air. She narrowed her eyes at the sun, which had just come fully into view above the horizon.

No amount of fiddling with the device made it connect before she made it to the operations tent and passed one of Ramy's men. "Are you having any issues with your phone?" she asked him.

A phone came out of the man's pocket. "No." He showed her the screen. "You are?"

"I can't get a signal."

"Would you like another phone?"

She looked up at him. "You have one?"

"We have many. One moment." The man stepped to a cabinet, opened a drawer and then held a phone toward her. "Keep it as long as you need," he said.

This time when she dialed Harry's number the call went through. "Harry," she said when he picked up.

"I thought you forgot about me."

"Stop joking and listen," Sara said, cutting off his levity. "You won't believe what I found."

"I could say the same."

That made an alarm bell ding in her head. She ignored it. "We found an untouched temple."

"I'm listening."

Sara described the treasures they'd uncovered, and was rewarded with silence from Harry. "Impressed?"

"I am," Harry said. "Have any trouble?"

"A little." She summarized the cave-in and her escape.

"You nearly died."

"It wasn't that bad."

"Tell me exactly how it happened," he said.

"I already did. We were just inside the temple entrance."

"You and Ramy."

"Ramy and I were there."

"Did anything strange happen? Think before you say no. What did you see right before the collapse?"

What *did* happen right before the collapse? She and Ramy were inside. Ramy was nervous, which was to be expected, and they checked the entrance. An image popped to mind. Of faint red and green light in the chamber. Ramy hadn't seen the lights. She had.

Harry's voice pulled her back. "You're hesitating."

Her mouth hung open a fraction longer. "I'm not." She buried the idea. The light might not have even been real. Why would flashing lights be in an ancient temple? It made no sense. It must have been reflected sunlight. That's it. "Stop interrogating me. I can handle myself." She changed the subject. "Are you still near Cannes?"

"Nope."

"Where are you?" He started to answer. She cut him off. "Hold on. You left for a reason. You left because you found something. What did you find?"

"Patrick's tomb."

"Saint Patrick?"

"You got it."

Sara's grip on the phone tightened as Harry detailed uncovering a hidden staircase beneath the original tomb, a test of Islamic prayer knowledge and a mesmerizing find. "Bloodstone was considered holy by Irish Christians," Sara said.

"I'm thinking this may be his cross."

"That is possible," she said. "Regardless, your trip was eventful."

"I didn't tell you about the wolves."

"Wolves?" He recapped his narrow escape. "Wolves run faster than they swim," she said. "You should have gone in the water."

"It worked out. I still haven't told you the best part. Agilulph left a message wrapped around the bottom of the cross."

"What did the message say?"

"He left two messages, one rolled inside another. The first said *Press the southernmost red star*. The bloodstone cross is green flecked with red. Guess what I found on the very bottom?"

"A star-shaped fleck."

"Bingo. A fleck that is actually a button, and when I pressed it, the top vertical portion popped off."

"What was inside?"

"A key."

"To what?"

"No idea. But I bet the second message is trying to tell me. It says *Time is counted behind the flowing life where Bertrada learned to be a fish. Here you will secure Charlemagne's empire. Use what unlocks the earthly kingdom of heaven. Follow the righteous path toward God.*"

"Bertrada." Sara closed her eyes. "Why do I know that name?"

"She was Charlemagne's mother."

"Perhaps the key you found *unlocks* something related to the *earthly kingdom of heaven*. As to what that is I have no idea."

"What about the *time* that's counted?"

She considered. "It's vague. Agilulph's prior messages were more specific. I don't know at this point."

"These could be metaphors tied in some way to his mother."

"*Charlemagne's empire* makes me think of security, of a continuance."

"Of his power. Or it could be tied to the Abbasid Caliphate."

"Perhaps." Sara agreed more than that, but she'd learned not to get ahead of herself. "Perhaps not."

"What about *the righteous path toward God*? My gut says those are directions or instructions."

"My thoughts as well." Sara looked at her arm to find the hair on it had risen. "Well done, Harry. Well done."

"Well done? We don't understand any of this."

"Take the compliment." Noise came from outside Sara's tent, the sounds of people getting to work. "I have to go," Sara said. "Excavations are starting again."

"Be careful."

"I appreciate your healthy skepticism of everyone here."

"I'll call you when I have more on this message," Harry said. "Let me know what you find down there."

Sara promised she would and clicked off. The phone went into her pocket, a hat went on her unruly hair, and she moved at speed back to the site.

"He's lying to me."

Olivier Lloris clenched the phone in his hand. "Harry Fox knows more than he's saying."

Benoit Lafont's voice was cool as ever. "Perhaps," he said. "Perhaps not."

Olivier scowled from behind his desk. The man's reasonableness was infuriating. "Can you see her now?"

"Not at the moment," Benoit said. "I'm parked away from the site."

Olivier laughed. "No tent for you, eh?"

"Certainly not."

Benoit was in Egypt to keep an eye on Sara Hamed. Olivier took a calming sip of his drink. Why would Harry Fox withhold information on his relic hunt? It could be Harry only wanted to contact Olivier when he had the full picture. Or Harry might want to complete his search and return to Olivier when he had the final prize in hand.

But why not call with an update? Finding the Celtic cross was an achievement. If Harry was in this for the money, for pure profit, he should have jumped at the chance to call Olivier about this artifact. An uneasy feeling called for attention in his head—concern that something he'd done was coming back to haunt him. "How could Harry know?"

"What did you say?" Benoit asked. Olivier ignored him.

A few weeks earlier Olivier had sent a man to kill Harry Fox. He'd contracted a mercenary to take out his own relic hunter and secure the prize Harry chased. Why? Harry Fox's promise to deliver a relic tied to Charlemagne was taking too long, so Olivier had decided to speed things up. Unfortunately, the mercenary had failed.

Had Harry Fox somehow discovered Olivier was behind the attempt on his life? Olivier took a deep breath. Harry could know who paid the men who came after him and be waiting for the right time to take his revenge.

"That's why you have the insurance plan in place," Olivier told himself.

"What did you say?" Benoit asked.

Olivier ignored the question. "Why would Harry not contact me with an update on his search?"

"It is hard to say. Speculation as to his motive is pointless. Why worry? You have insurance."

So be it. "Benoit, go talk with Dr. Hamed. Tell me if you think she suspects anything."

"I will be in contact," Benoit said.

"That's not all. Make certain all of our men are in place. We must act quickly if the need arises."

"The men I hired are in place," Benoit said. "I will have them posted as guards or assistants to Professor Gad's team."

Olivier told Benoit to call him with any developments and clicked off. He looked up as a helicopter whirred past, then came slowly down to rest on the helipad of a neighbor Olivier particularly despised.

"Wait until I invite him to see the new pieces in my collection." That lifted his spirits. "That will put him in his place."

"Dr. Hamed?"

A voice cut through the musty air of Zeus's temple. Sara looked up from the wall inscription she was cleaning to find one of the new dig assistants standing at the temple entrance. "Yes?"

"Dr. Gad would like to speak with you."

Sara could think of fewer things she's rather do at this moment than leave her work to deal with Ramy Gad. She shook her head and bit off a quick retort. *You're on the same team now*, she reminded herself. "Let me put my tools away and I'll be out."

The well-muscled assistant bowed his head in acknowledgment and disappeared. Sara tidied her workspace for a minute before following the man outside. She lowered the brim of her hat against the sun and looked around. Ramy stood a short distance away, having taken refuge from the sun beneath a temporary awning. Parked adjacent to the awning was a clean sport utility vehicle. A well-dressed man stood close to Ramy, speaking quickly.

"Sara." Ramy called out and waved a hand to her. "Please, over here."

Her boots crunched on the dry dirt as she crossed over to join them. "Is everything alright?" she asked as she stopped in the awning's shade.

"Of course," Ramy said quickly. "Why do you ask?"

"I know you are as excited as I am to continue our exploration of the temple," she said. "That's what I was doing."

"I certainly am," he said. "This interruption will be brief." Ramy gestured to the slim and compact man, who Sara now realized was Benoit.

"Hello, Benoit." Sara offered her hand.

"Please call me Ben." If Ben had noticed her less-than-thrilled demeanor, he didn't comment. "I know you by reputation as a world-class Egyptologist, but your success here exceeds even those superlatives."

His French accent caught her ear. Everyone around here seemed to have them now. "Call me Sara," she said. "What brings you to the site today?"

"Ramy updated me on your progress. I wished to see it for myself."

"Would you like to see the temple?" she asked.

"I would love to," Ben said. He turned to Ramy. "You'll see to it that the new employees are properly oriented and assigned where needed?"

"I will," Ramy said.

The words slipped out of her mouth before Sara could stop them. "New employees?"

"Additional staff," Ben said. "For what appears to be a growing project."

"I've noticed several new faces," she said.

"All well qualified, I assure you," Ben said. "We must be even more cautious now, given what you uncovered." Ben's thin mustache flattened as he smiled. "However, if you have any suggestions as to how we can better operate the site, I would love to hear them."

Ben seemed genuinely open to her thoughts on the matter. However, something made her hold back. "Everyone has been thoroughly professional," Sara said. "I'm certain we are well prepared."

"Excellent." Ben took a step toward the temple entrance, then stopped. "If you'll lead the way, Sara? Your thoughts on what has been found so far would be appreciated."

Sara led Ben and Ramy toward the temple, giving her own summary of what they'd seen and what might lie ahead. Ben asked questions, complimented her work, and paid attention as she led them into the temple. If all people who funded digs were like Ben and cared about site safety and security the way he did, her job would be easier.

Chapter 16

Cannes, France

The sound of squeaking wheels rolling by pulled his eyelids open.

A foggy world fluttered to life as he awoke. *What's that noise?* quickly became *Where am I?* and the thought sent Harry shooting up in his chair, his nervous system firing on all cylinders.

He banged his knee on the tabletop and cursed.

"Shh."

He looked toward the sound to find a middle-aged woman glaring at him from behind her glasses, a finger pressed to her lips, her other hand pushing a cart loaded with library books. Books she was returning to shelves in this dark corner of the public library.

I'm in Cannes. Harry lifted a hand to the woman in apology, but didn't speak. Harry rubbed his eyes. He'd taken refuge in a branch of the Cannes public library after speaking with Sara a few hours before. Libraries were the one of the few places he always felt safe in the field, though he hadn't intended to doze off.

"Where was I?"

A book lay open in front of him. What was I looking at? He flipped it closed to reveal the cover. Oh, right. A history of the Frankish empire. Harry checked his watch and did a double-take. He'd been asleep for nearly two hours.

The open book called for his attention. "Bertrada," Harry said to himself. He closed his eyes and pictured Agilulph's message from Saint

Patrick's Celtic cross. *"Time is counted behind the flowing life where Bertrada learned to be a fish. Here you will secure Charlemagne's empire. Use what unlocks the earthly kingdom of heaven. Follow the righteous path toward God."*

What did Agilulph mean when he said someone learned to be a fish? Ah, yes. "He's talking about swimming." Fish swam. Swimming wasn't a common skill in those days, though nobles would have had the leisure time to do it. Where would Bertrada have learned to swim?

Most people learned to swim as children. Bertrada was born in what was now northern France to a noble family with significant wealth. Her father was born in the northern regions of modern-day France, and her mother came from the eastern regions of the empire, in what was now Austria.

He'd pulled several books to review, including a general history of medieval royalty. Bertrada was mentioned briefly in the section discussing her husband's reign as king of the Franks. Pepin the Short was described as a man who defended his people and whose actions benefited the empire. No small part of Pepin's legacy was that his son grew to be known as the Father of Europe.

All of which led to only a few mentions of Bertrada. As fate would have it, one of those mentions included a picture, an engraving showing the ancestral homeland where Bertrada was shown picnicking with a very young Charlemagne. The picnic scene depicted a flat patch of grass alongside one of Austria's incredible lakes, with a waterfall in the background tumbling from a sharp mountain peak. It could only be Lake Altaussee, possibly the most picturesque lake in all of Austria. Why did this matter?

Bertrada and her children weren't sitting alongside the lake. They were swimming in it. He translated the text below the picture. *Queen Bertrada teaching the future king to swim in the same waters she played in as a girl.*

He had a starting point. Bertrada had learned to be a fish at Lake Altaussee in Austria. He snapped a photo of the engraving with his phone then closed the book, stacking it with the others on his table before hurrying out of the library and heading to the nearest café. His gut told him the next answers to Agilulph's puzzle would be found due east. In Austria.

Harry stood at the café counter and ordered an espresso. The scent of brewing coffee and warm scones filled the air, and he stood quietly savoring it until his drink arrived. Harry balanced the cup in one hand while he tapped at his phone with the other until a call rang through to Joey Morello. Joey's voicemail picked up. Harry re-dialed. Same result. "He's probably busy."

Joey could take care of himself, so he pivoted to the other person he needed to check in on. By now he was leaning against a tall tree outside the café. He tried Sara's new phone number. Espresso warmed his throat and kicked his mind into gear as the call rang through.

"Harry?"

An unexpected warmth flowed through his veins. "You expecting someone else?" he quipped.

"Unfortunately, no."

"Good one," Harry said. "I have news."

"As do I."

"Can't you ever give me the limelight?"

"Do something impressive and I might," she said. "Me first. The man funding this dig arrived today. I showed him the temple and told him about our progress."

"What did you think of the moneyman?" Harry asked when she finished updating him on her progress.

"He appears genuinely interested in not only the findings, but the process."

"Where's he from?"

"He spoke impeccable English. If I had to guess, I'd say France."

She hesitated. He noticed. "What else is there?" Harry asked.

"Our staff keeps growing and changing," Sara said. "It's unusual. I believe the sponsor is bringing more of his people on board. All of them seem to be French, too."

Harry's gut spoke up. He did not. "If I was spending that kind of money I'd want my people on site." She agreed with him. Too bad his gut didn't. "Anything else strange going on?" he asked. "Other than you nearly getting killed."

"I was not nearly killed. It was an accident. We've been through this."

Sara carried on before he could respond. "The only strange happening is discovering this temple," Sara said. "Other Egyptologists would kill for a chance to discover this site."

"Maybe that's what they plan to do," he said softly.

"Enough with that." Her tone brooked no dissent. "If you insist on feeding your conspiracy theory, you could say my phone has been acting oddly."

"Hence the new number."

"Yes. It's possible others are having this sort of issue. They were ready with extra phones for me to use. Secure ones."

"You really think someone would hack into your phone to hear what's going on?"

"It seems like a stretch," she said. "And it's not as though they could learn much of value."

"Keep your eyes open."

"Enough about my dig site. You said you have news."

"I think I understand Agilulph's message. Bertrada's father came from northern France."

"Part of the Frankish empire."

"And Bertrada's mother came from the eastern part of the empire. What is now Austria."

"I'm listening."

"A book I found in Cannes included an engraving with Bertrada and Charlemagne by a lake with a waterfall. The caption said"—here he consulted his picture—"'Bertrada is *teaching the future king to swim in the same waters she played in as a girl.*'"

"What lake is it?"

"Lake Altaussee. The waterfall in this engraving is placed in a specific location among several unique peaks. I'm certain."

"Now what?"

"I'm going to Austria. I figure the rest of the answer is there."

"It sounds as though you're getting close."

"I sure hope so." His jaw tightened. "I have other business to take care of when this is done."

"Olivier."

"That's what this is all about."

"Have you told him about Austria?"

"No. The last thing I'd do is be straight with him. It's taken me a long time to get close to him, and the best way to keep him close is to dangle the prize. Do that, and he'll come running."

"What if he doesn't?"

Harry almost laughed. "Olivier Lloris will never let this relic go to anyone else. He'll come running, so that I can"—and here he hesitated—"conclude our business."

"I hope that's true," she said. "Hold one moment." The distant sound of a man's voice filtered through from her end of the call. "Harry, I have to go. The dig sponsor is here and he wants to discuss the temple."

"I'll call you once I know my plans," he said.

"Stay safe."

She clicked off before he had a chance to respond. He held the phone to his ear for a second, as though she might come back, might give him a chance to remind her to do the same. She did not, so he shook his head and stuck the phone in his pocket. The empty espresso cup went into a trash can as he walked toward his car. Why did his gut keep telling him something was off? He couldn't pinpoint it. Not as he approached his car, not as he got behind the wheel and fired up the engine, not as he drove off with little idea of how to get to Austria. The feeling persisted, never going away, never letting him forget. It sat there, waiting.

He lasted all of two minutes before picking up the phone.

"Mr. Fox."

Those two words in that experienced voice brought the smell of expensive tobacco and the sound of ice in fine crystal to mind.

"Hello, Rose."

Rose Leroux was unlike any other woman in New York. She was the city's premier fence for illicit goods and, more than anyone, represented not only the beating heart of the city's thriving black market, but the brains of that system. Nothing happened in the world of illegal antiquities without Rose's knowledge. Which was why kingpins and billionaires alike sought her out when they wanted to make a discreet purchase or sell an item the authorities didn't know about. Rose Leroux knew everyone, she knew their secrets, and that information gave her power. Incredible power.

"I understand you are in France."

"No one knows I'm here." He frowned. "Except you, somehow."

"Do not worry about whether I know. Worry if Olivier Lloris knows. He is not a man to be crossed. So, you are in France. Where?"

"I'm in Cannes."

"You were in Germany."

"I was. Did Joey tell you?" He waited. Silence. "I came here to find Saint Patrick's skull." An abbreviated version of his adventure came next. "I believe Agilulph's message points to Austria. To Lake Altaussee."

"You are traveling to Austria now."

"Yes," he said. Harry pulled the phone from his ear and consulted it. "A fourteen-hour drive, or a plane gets me there in under two hours."

"I suggest the plane."

"I agree." Harry's spirit perked up. "I have a question for you. I can't get ahold of Joey."

Another long pull from the cigarette, the crackle of tobacco burning, then the ice clinking in her glass. "Joseph Morello can use a friend right now."

"You know what the Piazza clan did."

"Carmelo Piazza is a fool." Her words sounded as harsh as the acrid scent of her tobacco that Harry remembered so well. "A fool with no idea what damage he caused. An impulsive man not fit to lead."

"He's Sicilian."

"He has a love for feuding. I suspect Carmelo thought this was his chance to make a name for himself." She sighed. "A chance Joseph may provide."

A dog yipped as it walked past. "What do you mean?" he asked.

"Joseph met with the other family heads a short while ago. The meeting only just ended."

"Care to tell me what they decided?" Someone at the meeting would have already told her what happened. Perhaps even Joey.

"Joseph asked for time."

"Let me guess. Nobody wants to give him time."

"The wiser family heads do. The more ambitious and hot-headed among them demanded a response."

"Albert Zurilli. He has his eye on Joey's seat." Harry considered. "Joey looks weak if he doesn't respond. But a response risks international conflict between Sicilian clans and the New York families."

"Which is why Joseph made a decision only he can make," Rose finally said. *"Il Codice."*

It took Harry a second. "The *code*?" A dusty memory surfaced, a story from the old country. "Is that still a thing?"

"It never left."

"'Don't talk to the police,'" Harry recited aloud. "'Never betray your family. Honor your father and mother.'"

Rose finished the most important part for him. "'And if there is a dispute between families, the head of each family is responsible for resolving it.'"

"Joey's going after Carmelo Piazza *alone*? He can't go to Carmelo's turf by himself. He'll ambush Joey and say it was a fair fight."

"We can only hope he will honor the code."

Rose knew the truth. "You know Carmelo will never honor it. He's a coward." Rose's silence was stronger than any agreement. "You have to stop him."

"My influence extends only so far," Rose said. "I believe it is too late."

Rose must have a source inside the Morello family. "He'll die over there," Harry said.

Tobacco burned. "As I said, what Joseph needs now is a true friend."

"He won't accept help. He's too proud. It's going to get him killed."

"I did not say he wants help. I said he needs it." A silence ensued. "Choose wisely," Rose eventually said. "Your journey is not yet over. Olivier Lloris deserves what is coming. Make sure he receives it."

She clicked off, having said all that was needed. Harry put his phone away. "Dammit, Joey."

Harry swallowed on a dry throat. Why now? Olivier Lloris was within reach. All he needed to do was follow Agilulph's trail to Austria, solve the mystery tied to Lake Altaussee, then deliver retribution. Nothing more. Except Joey was running into danger. Alone.

Harry shook his head. "Sara's gonna kill me."

He walked to his car, opened the door and got in. Less than an hour to drive from Cannes to the airport in Nice. From there he could fly nearly anywhere. He sighed and started the car. Charlemagne's relic and his date with Olivier would have to wait. Joey needed him. Even if he didn't know it.

Chapter 17

Sicily

A group of old men sat around a low table outside a café. They wore sweaters and scarves against the early winter chill. Tiles clattered, one man shouted in triumph, and a minor verbal skirmish broke out as the regular spectators offered their regular insults against fate and the victor. A dog yawned by the feet of one player. A second dog snored on the other side of the table. This wasn't the first argument of the afternoon.

No one paid attention to the solitary man sitting on a barstool inside the café door. A barstool offering a fine view of the community square ringed by local shops, a barber, and at least two other small cafés. The sort of square that had existed as the center of a neighborhood for centuries.

The barstool beneath Joey Morello creaked when he turned to sip his coffee, his second of the morning. Both had been consumed slowly, in the unhurried manner of one with plenty of time on his hands and not much to do with it. A book lay open in front of him. His easy movements and the slow pace of drinking let him blend in with the locals. The interior of the café was filled with shadows, a bartender, and little else. A bartender on Franco Licata's payroll.

Two days earlier Joey had flown from New York to Rome, where he rented a car and drove ten hours south to this island. Joey had connections here that he'd used as a starting point for his search. Connections sworn to secrecy. If that secrecy held, then maybe, just maybe, his plan would work.

He would follow *Il Codice*, the code that had bound men like Joey for generations to a system of honor. It was a gamble that would put his life in the balance. He cursed silently. Carmelo Piazza was right across the street. So close, but so far.

Joey had spent time asking subtle questions while seated on this stool. The bartender had answered every one, giving Joey a glimmer of an idea. Carmelo Piazza rarely left his base of operations without at least one bodyguard from among a rotating cast of foot soldiers, all fiercely loyal. Bribery would not work here.

The only true positive came when the bartender revealed a surefire escape route out of town, provided Joey could take care of Carmelo and get to a giant propane tank behind the café. The tank fueled the café's heating system and other operations, and had been artfully crafted to make it larger than necessary. The extra square footage concealed a trapdoor in the ground used by World War II resistance fighters. The resistance had built a tunnel system beneath the town. That tunnel system would give Joey safe passage out of Sicily.

Joey's only sighting of his adversary had been earlier this morning when Carmelo appeared outside his base of operations across the street. He may only have seen Carmelo once, but that didn't mean his reconnoitering had been fruitless. Carmelo had a small crew, small enough that Joey had a good idea of who in town was a Piazza foot soldier and who wasn't.

Noise squawked from behind the bar. A sports announcer was giving the play-by-play on television. Joey turned to find the bartender standing with a remote control in hand. Soccer highlights played as a commentator spoke in Italian so rapid Joey could barely follow along. The local team had a big match on tap, a rivalry game this evening. Joey checked his watch and turned back to study the front entrance to Carmelo Piazza's sprawling home. Almost noon. He finished his coffee and turned to the bartender. Time to order lunch. Then he'd stroll over to another café, perhaps stop at the bookstore down the street. A man with all the time in the world. He'd stay as long as it took to figure out how to deal with Carmelo.

"*Enzo!*"

Shouts filled the café's interior as a group of five men filed through the doorway, all crowding around the far end of the bar near the television. Joey kept his head down, eyes on his book. They were all Piazza clan foot soldiers. He looked intently at his book and leaned closer to catch every word they said.

"Those chumps are done." "We'll destroy them." "Send them back home to their mommies."

This and other juvenile insults showing the peak of Piazza creativity continued. Joey kept his eyes down, one thought running through his head. *If these guys are here, they're not with Carmelo. And Carmelo had only a small number of guards to watch him.*

The actual game wouldn't kick off for a few hours, but the pre-game coverage was intense. Joey's food came, which he picked at as the men down the bar kept drinking steadily. Their tongues loosened further with each round until the conversation turned to the man in charge.

"Carmelo is missing out," one man said. "I feel bad for the guys who stayed behind."

"Feel bad for them?" Another foot soldier made a rude gesture. "They eat and drink while we have to sit here with you."

The bartender spoke. "So, my food and drink are not good enough for you?"

"It is fantastic," the man said. He pointed at the man who felt bad for Carmelo's other guards. "He is the reason we are sad—we had to bring him with us!"

Laughter bounced off the walls, along with a few shouted epithets and more jokes at the man's expense. Joey lifted his empty coffee cup and the bartender came over. "How many are left with Carmelo?" he asked in a whisper.

"No more than five," the bartender replied, motioning to the television. "This is a rivalry game. They will be distracted."

"Will they be in Carmelo's headquarters?" Joey asked. The bartender said they would. "Do you know the layout?"

"I have been inside," the bartender said.

"Draw me a map."

The bartender hesitated. "I do not recommend going inside. You will be walking into the lion's den."

Joey lifted his empty coffee cup to cover his mouth. "Franco told me you had a cousin who lived nearby."

The bartender's face darkened. "Dante."

Franco Licata had assured Joey that this bartender would never inform Carmelo Piazza danger was on his doorstep in the form of Joey Morello. Carmelo Piazza was responsible for Dante's death. Carmelo had driven drunk one night and hit a bicyclist. The bicyclist died. Carmelo Piazza faced no consequences, because he was Carmelo Piazza. This bartender would do anything Joey asked as long as Joey provided revenge for his family.

"Give me five minutes." The bartender walked over to the Piazza crew, told them he needed to restock the bar and asked them to please not steal too much while he was gone. The men promised to ransack the place, though they remained in their seats when the bartender left, downing another round and getting a bit rowdier. Joey started when they broke out into a song about their local team, the notes lacking in harmony, but more than making up for it in volume and spirit. They were into their second rendition of the tune when the bartender returned. First, he topped off Joey's coffee. Then he refilled the Piazza beer glasses. That done, he returned to Joey and polished a few glasses that did not need to be polished.

"Here." Silverware wrapped in a napkin was placed in front of Joey. "On the napkin."

Joey unrolled the napkin, moved the silverware aside and slipped the napkin into his shirt pocket. "Thanks. Anything I should know?"

The bartender stopped polishing. Joey waited. "Carmelo had renovations completed last month."

"What changed?"

The bartender shrugged. "No idea."

Okay, that wasn't good. "How big a project was it?" Joey asked.

"Not sure. Five workers went inside every day for a month. That's all I know."

Joey ran a hand over his face. "The place could be very different. I don't know what's in there or how to find Carmelo. I don't have any backup, and I can't wait around forever."

"Do it while there are fewer men inside, and the ones still there are drinking and watching the game."

The guy had a point. Either Carmelo would catch on that Joey was in town, or the families in New York would run out of patience. Joey grumbled to himself.

The bartender spoke up. "Carmelo is not inside his headquarters now."

Joey looked up. "What?"

The bartender inclined his head toward the building across the street. "He is not in there."

"How do you know?"

"One of them just said so." This time his head tilted toward the rowdy Piazza goons. "Carmelo is watching the game at his winery. That is why they are all here together. He is not across the street."

"He has a winery?"

"Yes. There is a production facility there, and a warehouse for storing his wine. It is not far. Ten minutes on foot. The production facility is small, but the warehouse is large." He paused. "He will not be entirely alone." The bartender kept polishing as he said it. "Rocco will be there."

"Rocco?"

"A dangerous man. He is a giant."

Great. He'd have to tangle with the Sicilian version of Mack to get to Carmelo.

"I will give you a sketch of the warehouse," the bartender said. He kept his back to the Piazza men as he worked, his pen moving quickly over a napkin that he soon passed to Joey before going to check on Carmelo's men further down the bar. Joey stared at his coffee. The bartender's sketched map gave him a good idea of the warehouse layout. Carmelo and his men would be watching the game. They'd be distracted. A distracted man was easier to take down.

"How would I get back here if I needed to climb into your secret tunnel in a hurry?"

The bartender took the question in stride. "Run as fast as you can. They will be confused. Use their confusion against them."

"It could work." Joey let himself believe it for a second. "Or it could all go sideways."

This Rocco goon could get the drop on Joey. Or any other Piazza man might get lucky, spotting Joey by sheer chance as he entered the facility and sounding the alarm. Any number of twists or turns could flip his plan upside down and send Joey to an early grave. Going after Carmelo when he didn't expect it was smart. Doing so without a clear understanding of the building layout and what resistance he'd face was not. The rich scent of pipe smoke filtered in from outside. Joey bit the inside of his lip. This was far from perfect, but this sort of chance wouldn't come around again soon.

Joey shook his head. "Play the hand you've been dealt." He was alone. He would handle it.

Joey's phone sat atop the bar. He checked it again. No messages, no missed calls. Nothing could happen until he heard from Franco Licata. Licata was influential with the other Sicilian clan leaders, which was why Joey had to wait for Franco's call. Franco would ask each clan leader if they supported *Il Codice*. He wouldn't say who was involved; he only needed to know if they still honored the old ways. They would all almost certainly agree to honor the code. Unless the times had changed too much.

His phone buzzed and Joey read the message. His hand clenched into a fist. The clan leaders had agreed. They all still followed the code.

"I'm doing it." Joey repeated the phrase to himself. "Today." He looked up at the bartender. "The supplies I asked for are ready?"

The bartender's eyes flicked toward a small shopping bag behind the bar. "In there. Take it when you leave."

Two pistols, each with a suppressor, and plenty of ammunition. Joey looked up at the bartender again. "It happens today."

The bartender looked over Joey's shoulder and his eyes narrowed. The hair on Joey's neck went up.

A voice spoke in perfect Italian. "What happens today?"

Joey spun so fast he nearly fell off his stool. His mouth opened. Nothing came out.

Harry Fox stood behind him.

Chapter 18

Sicily

Harry Fox sat on the stool next to Joey. "Stop gawking," he said softly. "Those goons across the bar might notice."

Joey managed to turn back around without hitting the floor. It took him a moment to find his voice. "How?"

Harry ordered a coffee from the bartender. "How what?" he asked when the bartender turned away.

"How did you find me?" Harry didn't respond. Joey studied his friend's face. "Rose told you."

"She did."

A fair point. "You shouldn't be here."

"Too late."

"Go and follow Agilulph's trail. I have to do this myself."

"Who knows I'm here? Nobody. And you're not doing this alone."

Joey frowned. "Did Rose ask you to come?"

"She didn't ask me not to."

"This is between families," Joey said quietly. "Having someone help makes me look weak. It goes against the code."

Harry shrugged. "I see it as more of a guideline than a code."

Joey ran a hand over his cheek. "Most of the crew wants me to hit back hard, and they want in on it."

"They don't see how much damage a war between you and these guys will cause." Steam wafted up to briefly cover Harry's gaze as he drank. "It doesn't change the fact you cannot do this alone, no matter what you're trying to prove. So I'll ask again. What happens today?" Joey's hesitation gave his answer. "Then we have a plan to work out."

The bartender brought them food as Joey ran through what he knew so far. The soccer match, Piazza's goons here at the bar, and Carmelo himself at the winery facility. He finished with the escape route.

"Not exactly foolproof."

"I'm still working on it."

"You're right about today. The game will be a good distraction, and the fewer men he has nearby, the better. We need to know more about the layout inside the warehouse. It won't do us any good to take him out and then get caught trying to escape."

Joey's gaze flicked to the bartender. "My guy doesn't know the layout inside the warehouse."

"Then we need a second distraction," Harry said. "More than just a soccer game."

"I'm open to suggestions."

"Warehouses store lots of stuff," Harry said. "Stuff we can use to distract everyone." Harry got the bartender's attention. "You have a knife we can borrow?" The bartender nodded. "Thanks." Harry stood as the bartender put what looked like a large folding knife in the shopping bag and then set it in front of Joey.

Joey took the bag. "You'll be here tonight?" he asked the bartender.

"Until you get back."

"I won't forget this." Joey left an exorbitant tip on the bar before following Harry outside. "What are we going to use to distract these guys?" Joey asked.

Harry put his head down and started walking. "I'll tell you when I see it."

The sounds of the soccer match finally getting underway filtered out of an open window as they walked beneath gray skies. Harry sketched out the framework of what might generously be called a plan. "Sneak inside, find out where Carmelo and his guys are, and figure out how to get out of there."

They turned a corner and stopped. "That's the place," Joey said. "Carmelo's warehouse."

The two-story rectangular building resembled a smaller version of one of the big box stores littering the American landscape. It stretched for an entire block on the long side, while the shorter side appeared half as wide. Carmelo had apparently bought all the property on the edge of town, for this warehouse abutted a small factory where the wine was produced, which itself sat beside row upon row of grape-bearing vines stretching into the distance. The sun slipped out from behind a dark cloud for an instant. His gaze narrowed before the clouds returned, burying any sunlight, and brought a cold wind that ran down his collar. Joey licked dry lips.

"Big place."

Harry stuck an arm out and pulled Joey back into the shadows of a nearby doorway. "That's where we go in." He pointed to a dumpster along the warehouse's far wall. "Climb on that and go through that window."

"The window could be locked."

"It's older than we are. I can pick it, no sweat."

Harry dug into the bag Joey carried. He clipped the folding knife to his belt, checked the suppressed pistols, then secured one of them behind the small of his back. Joey stuck the other gun in his waistband. "Follow me," Harry said. "If anybody stops us, act like you belong."

"What if they recognize me?"

Harry didn't answer. All he did was tap the gun now hidden under his shirt.

Harry did a pullup on the window frame and pushed at the window. It slid up easily. He pulled himself through the window and dropped to the open warehouse floor. Nothing but big machinery, metal stairwells and the scent of grapes.

"All clear," he whispered to Joey. "Don't make any noise." He waited until Joey landed on the cement floor beside him. "Wait here," Harry said."

The metal warehouse walls amplified every step as he walked toward a rear exit door, unlocked it, and lodged a piece of wood between the frame and door to keep it open. He went back to where Joey was standing in the shadows of stacked wine barrels.

"That's our emergency exit," Harry said as he pointed to the now-open door. "If this all goes south."

"It won't."

He stood beside Joey and studied the interior. Walkways ran around the perimeter of the second floor, with open metal stairways allowing movement from one level to the next. Wine barrels dominated every available surface. They were stacked three and four high on the first level, some up against the walls, some in the middle of the floor. The effect of this was a warehouse maze. More stacks of barrels held in place by thick fabric straps were placed all along the upper-level walkways, leaving only the central part of the structure open.

"Those barrels." Harry pointed to the ones stacked across the upper-level walkway. "Those are the distraction we need." He peered deeper into the facility. "I bet the offices are close to the production line."

"That's where we'll find Carmelo."

"Stay behind me and don't talk unless you have to. They should have guards making rounds."

A bird flew through the rafters overhead, zipping between a ceiling-mounted track with chains hanging from it. Harry kept close to the wall, stopping at each row of stacked barrels to check for movement. A rolling bay door big enough to drive a bus through separated this storage area from the production section further ahead.

Harry lifted a hand when they were halfway across the warehouse. "You hear that?" he whispered to Joey. "Sounds like a soccer match broadcast ahead."

Joey nodded and they continued along the wall, trying to keep their pace slow until they reached the bay door and Harry leaned around the metal frame to peer into the production area.

Two rows of huge stainless-steel vats ran the length of the room, with various steel contraptions he didn't recognize near each vat. Curving wooden ribs supported the roof overhead. On one side a small area had been walled off to form a two-story office. It had windows on both levels and men were moving around inside. Harry frowned. *One of those guys is a monster.*

Harry knelt so his head was level with Joey's. "There's an office ahead. The men are in there."

"Even Carmelo?"

"Not sure. Pop your head around and tell me if you see him."

Joey did. "I don't see him," he said. "But I heard his voice. He's in the upper level. Sounds like everyone else is in the lower level watching the game."

Carmelo was separated from his men. All they needed to do was get into his office, handle this, and get out. The bodyguards might never even know it was happening.

"One guy looks massive," Joey said. "Must be Rocco."

The guy Joey had told him about. "Let's stay out of his way," Harry said.

"We may not need to distract anyone." Harry rose slightly to study the production layout. As in the warehouse, metal walkways ran the perimeter of the upper level, accessed by stairways at either end of the room. "Our guns have suppressors. If those guys stay downstairs while you can get up there, and if you time it, they won't know he's been shot until we're out of here."

"That's a lot of *ifs*."

Harry frowned. It was a lot of *ifs*. His gaze went back to the gleaming steel vats. "See those big wheels on the front of each vat?" Harry asked. Joey said he did. "Those covers are like entrance hatches. Twist the wheel open, everything pours out."

"It'll make a heck of a mess," Joey said. "Someone would have to clean it up."

Harry rubbed the stubble on his chin. "It could work." His fingers brushed across the amulet around his neck. "With a bit of luck."

"I'll get up to Carmelo's office," Joey said. "Once I'm in place, you open a wine vat and then you get out of here. I'll take care of Carmelo and be right behind you."

"Bad plan. I'll open a couple wine vats, then I'll wait for you. We leave together. You take the far staircase." Harry pointed to a set of metal stairs against the production area's back wall. "The vats will block you from view until you get to the second level."

"Carmelo could see me climbing up there. All he has to do is look out of his office window."

"Go to the front end of the facility, cross over toward his office, then circle back. He won't see you unless he looks in exactly the wrong spot."

"As I said."

Harry lifted a shoulder. "If he does, I'll spring the wine distraction early. Then we get out of here fast. Now get moving. It'll be halftime soon and those guys won't be glued to the game. Wait for wine to start flowing, then make your move. I'll meet you outside by the dumpster."

Approaching footsteps sounded from around the corner. Harry leapt for cover behind the nearest barrel stack, pulling Joey with him. They kept their backs against the barrels' rough wood planks as the footsteps grew louder, then stopped. Harry turned to Joey and mouthed a silent message. *He's right by the bay door.* Harry saw Joey's hand move toward the pistol in his waist. Harry shook his head and lifted a finger. *Wait.*

The seconds stretched on. A sound like fabric rustling came from the other side of the barrels. Harry reached into his pocket and slipped his fingers into his trusty ceramic knuckledusters.

Metal scraped on metal. A flame ignited, and moments later the acrid scent of cigarette smoke floated over.

Shouted Italian words boomed from the production room. "Don't smoke in there! Go outside."

A grumbled reply came back, deep and heavy, the same as the footsteps that moved away from the door. What sounded like an exterior door banged open and the footsteps crunched over gravel until the exterior door clicked shut and Harry tapped the top side of his wrist. *Time to go.*

Harry went first. He moved cautiously around the barrels with his back to the sheet-metal dividing wall until he reached the corner, where he poked his head around the edge of the rolling bay door. A collective groan from the assembled bodyguards confirmed the game was ongoing. Harry moved through the bay door to the nearest vat in the middle row. A look into the office found three men inside the room. Harry leaned back to watch Joey run along the wall toward a set of metal stairs, which he mounted two at a time until he reached the upper walkway and carefully approached Carmelo's office from the side.

Harry looked at the men's backs as they gathered around the television. He frowned. *They're all normal-sized. Where's Rocco?*

Harry looked up. Joey now knelt outside Carmelo's office door. Harry lifted his eyebrows. *Is he in there?* Joey nodded, then mimicked turning a wheel with his hands. *Open the wine.* One last glance toward the soccer fans. No sign of Rocco. It was go time.

His shoulder stayed against the vat as he circled around to the wheel. The middle row of vats provided cover, though Carmelo would see him from above if he stepped outside. The gleaming steel chilled his hands when he gripped it. He clasped hold tight enough that his fingers ached, set his feet, and twisted left to loosen it, leaning into it with his back and legs.

The wheel didn't budge. He shifted his weight until one foot slipped from under him and his chin nearly smacked off the wheel. He turned to look at Carmelo's office. Joey made a circling motion with one finger. *Hurry.*

Harry set himself to try again when a memory came back. His father speaking, one of the countless sayings he had. Sayings that appeared more intelligent with every passing day. Fred had often said to "work smart, not hard." What if this wasn't a question of brute strength? He stepped back to look at the wheel.

And spotted the clasp on the wheel's center. A simple, fail-safe device that required him to pull on one side of the clasp to loosen it so the wheel could turn. *Nice going, Harry.* It took all of one finger to lift the clasp and the wheel turned. Harry sent a silent thanks to his father as he kept turning it.

One second the cover was in place. The next, it flew open, Harry holding on for dear life as a torrent of wine erupted from the vat. A river formed in front of him, the wine surging and spreading out on all sides. He leapt up, ran behind the rear row of vats, ducked through the bay door, and sprinted back to a spot by the barrels.

Wine flowed into where the soccer match was playing, and a chorus of startled shouts erupted. Their distraction was on. He looked up to see Joey step through the door of Carmelo's office with his gun out. Harry headed for the steps leading to the upper walkway, his gaze on a set of barrels up there, secured by thick fabric straps. One hand went to the folding knife clipped to his belt. Time to make a bigger mess.

Gunshots exploded from inside Carmelo's office. Harry froze. Unsilenced gunshots. *That's not Joey's gun.*

Chapter 19

Sinai Peninsula

Sara's chest went tight as she studied a statue of Zeus inside the newly uncovered temple in which she'd nearly died. Hieroglyphs ran across Zeus's lightning bolt, a bolt carved from ten feet of lustrous white marble and held upraised by the god's muscled arm as though he were going to hurl it through the temple's front entrance.

"'*Here lies he who embodies Zeus as a man.*'" The dry air stole the words from her lips as she spoke them. She read the inscription again to be sure. "This is a tomb. It's not merely a statue. It's a monument *and a tomb.*"

Who was this person who embodied Zeus? Only someone of significant wealth and influence would be buried inside such a temple. The head priest? An Egyptian or Greek nobleman? Sara would find out.

"I need a GPR in here," she shouted over her shoulder. A ground-penetrating radar would confirm if anything was in the ground beneath this statue.

She continued examining the statue for another minute. "Hello?" Sara raised her voice. "I need GPR in here." Again, no response. Sara turned to find the two dig assistants who had been with her were gone. "Where did you guys go?"

First the electrical guys couldn't get the lights up and running. Now her assistants had disappeared. What was it with these new guys Ramy had brought in? The original dig support team had been top-notch. These replacements were anything but. She leapt up and marched toward the temple entrance. Somebody was about to be sorry.

"Hello?" Fading red sunlight washed over the dig site as Sara walked outside. "I need GPR." Two dig assistants were walking nearby between the tents. Neither of them looked up. "Excuse me. Over here."

Only after she marched over to one of the men did he turn to look at her. "Yes, Dr. Hamed?" he asked.

"I said I need a GPR device in the temple," she said. "As soon as possible."

"I see." The man looked toward the tent he'd been about to enter. "I will find someone to help you."

"Don't you know how to get it?"

"I do not."

"Which of you is in charge of the equipment?" she asked. Again, the man said he didn't know. She fought to keep the heat from her words. "Would you please find Ramy—actually, never mind. I'll find him."

The man watched as she turned and stomped toward Ramy's section of the dig. The wind died and the sun fell as a thought popped into her mind. Harry would be asking questions. Why were these replacement assistants unable to do even basic tasks?

She found Ramy exiting his tent. "Ramy," she called. "We have an issue."

He looked at her with wide eyes. Was Ramy Gad nervous? He'd spent years looking down his nose at his peers. The last effect she thought she'd have on the man would be to set him on edge.

"I need GPR," she said. "None of the assistants seem to know what one is, let alone where to find it."

He cleared this throat. "They are still acclimating to the site," he said. "They will learn quickly."

Her hands found her hips. "Why do we have so many new faces on site?"

"Ben brought them here," Ramy said. "I cannot argue with the man who has the money." He pointed to a tent not far away. "The GPR is in there. Why do you want it?"

"To check the ground. It's possible there's a tomb under the statue of

Zeus." She repeated the message inscribed on Zeus's lightning bolt.

Ramy's face came alive. "We must see what is down there."

He pushed past her and entered the nearby tent, barking orders at the closest assistant with each step. The man looked at Ramy as though he were a curiosity instead of the lead Egyptologist. Ramy repeated his request with less bite, and the assistant responded. In short order two assistants had a GPR device inside the temple. Sara explained where she wanted them to look. They looked at her. They looked at the device. One of them turned to Ramy and raised an eyebrow.

Tiny particles of dust glittered in the bright temporary lighting. It took Sara several seconds to understand. "You don't know how to use this, do you?"

The assistant stayed silent. "This is a standard GPR," Sara said. "Who does know how to use it?"

Both men shrugged. Sara turned to Ramy. "I need someone experienced in the use of this machine."

"I can assist," Ramy said.

Ramy's words made her take a step back. "You?" she asked. Ramy Gad was offering to act as a dig assistant? "Fine," Sara said. "I will be back shortly."

She marched out through the temple entrance and headed straight for the main tent, the one where she'd last seen Ben. *What was happening here?* Either Ben had hired an incompetent workforce, or there was a bigger issue at play.

Halfway across the dig site she changed course and went back to her own tent. The tent flap closed behind her and she went into her sleeping quarters, which consisted of a smaller tent-within-a-tent. She sat on her cot and pulled out her phone. Harry had told her more times than she could remember to trust her instincts. She angled her phone so it caught her features and unlocked.

"I'll never hear the end of this." She called Harry, already planning the mental gymnastics required to let him know his caution had been called for.

The phone rang. A second ring ended abruptly. She looked at the screen. Her phone had died. "What in the world?" She turned the power off and on. It reconnected, though when she tried to call Harry again it wouldn't make the call. She tried several more times, but none of the calls went through. Her grip on the phone grew tighter until she considered smashing it on the ground. *Easy.* She put the phone down and took several long breaths. "I need another phone."

Her instincts told her to use a phone not connected to the site. She walked back outside under the darkening sky and went directly to the supply tent. The tent flap fell shut behind her. Rows of shelving stretched out on one side, while tables covered with equipment and supplies filled the other. Odds were, if a phone was to be had, it would be over there.

The first table she passed had a chair tucked underneath it. A cup of coffee on top of a notebook sat on the table in front of the chair, steam still rising from the liquid, with a pen nestled against the cup. Alongside the notebook? A satellite phone. She grabbed the device and tapped the screen. *Perfect.*

No passcode locked it, so she dialed Harry's number and held the device to her ear. It rang through. Harry's voicemail picked up. "Harry, call me as soon as you get this. Something odd is going on here. Call me and I'll explain."

She clicked off and set the phone down. She picked the phone back up. *Always have a backup plan.* Harry's father had said that, and the advice had made its way to her. Advice she heeded by sending Harry a text saying basically the same as her message.

"Dr. Hamed?"

Sara looked up to find Ben standing inside the tent entrance. "Yes?" she asked.

"Is that your phone?" Ben stared at the device she held.

"No." She glanced down to confirm the text had gone through. "Mine wasn't working for some reason."

"Who did you need to call?" Ben asked.

"A friend." Her tone changed. "Why?"

Ben hesitated a moment. "There may be a problem with the site." Ben stepped into the tent, never taking his eyes off Sara. Another man appeared at the tent entrance. He stood there, blocking the exit.

Sara recognized him. "John?" It was the security team member who had placed the anti-tracking device on her phone earlier. "Is everything alright?"

"We're not entirely sure, Dr. Hamed." John stepped toward her. He was a lot bigger than she remembered. "There may be a problem. I'll need to check that phone." He put his hand out.

"Of course." Sara handed the device to him.

"It's nothing we can't handle," John said. He tucked the satellite phone in his pocket. "It is possible our communication links have been compromised."

"You think someone is trying to steal information?"

"Nothing is confirmed. However, we cannot risk word of what has been found here getting out." Ben stepped closer to her. "It's vital that we all maintain secrecy regarding the dig until we know if security has been compromised. Did the message you just sent jeopardize that secrecy?"

"It was a personal message. As I said, my phone is not working."

"I'm afraid that may be my fault," John said. "I assure you the situation will be resolved shortly. Please forgive the inconvenience."

"Certainly." What Ben said seemed plausible. "What sort of danger might exist?"

"My fear is there are individuals who could cause issues with our digging permit," Ben said. "Men with contacts in the Egyptian government."

"They could shut us down," she said.

"It's possible," Ben said. "But we are not without influence as well. Please gather any relevant notes you made. If we are directed to leave, even temporarily, we cannot leave anything behind that may aid those who are against us."

Sara agreed. Her notes, her laptop, all of the information she'd collected so far would go with her if they left the site. Sara stepped around John and left the supply tent, walking toward her own. Ben walked with her.

The rustle of a vibrating phone reached her ears. Ben pulled a device from his pocket. He read for a moment and his eyes went wide. "Hurry, Dr. Hamed. I fear our time here is short."

Chapter 20

Sicily

Joey's in trouble.

That realization sent Harry racing back toward Carmelo Piazza's office on the upper level. The vats hid him from the Piazza goons navigating the river of wine. En route to the same stairs Joey had taken he passed an open case of wine. Instinct made him grab two bottles without breaking stride. He made it halfway up the stairs when a man flew out of the office, banged off the safety rails and then vaulted toward the steps as though someone was shooting at him. It was Joey.

"Go!" Joey shouted as he ran directly at Harry. The silenced pistol in his hand never turned to aim at the office door as Carmelo burst through the it.

Sparks erupted off the metal walkway at Joey's feet as Carmelo opened fire. Joey was nearly to the staircase when Carmelo stopped to take aim.

Harry ran up the stairs and shouted. "Get down!" Joey dropped low. Harry pulled an arm back and sent a full wine bottle hurtling end-over-end at Carmelo's head. Glass exploded and wine flew in all directions to send Carmelo to the ground. "Get moving," Harry shouted. He spun and jumped to the concrete floor in one leap, then raced for the nearest row of wine barrels.

He turned as gunfire chased Joey through the door. Carmelo's men fired at them, although none had a clear shot. Harry looked at the distant window through which they'd come. "Keep going," Harry shouted over the thunder of flying lead. "I'll meet you outside."

"What are you doing?" Joey shouted as he ran past Harry. "This isn't finished."

"Just go. I'll be there."

Harry darted behind the rows of barrels toward a staircase farther down the wall. Up the stairs he went, two and three at a time, as Joey raced toward far exit. Joey stopped by the unlocked window, turned back and took aim with his pistol.

The first bodyguard to run out never made it. His foot slipped in the ever-growing river of wine, he went airborne, and when he landed Harry could hear the *crack* of his head hitting concrete. The guy wasn't dead, but he was out cold. The other two guards came around the corner and immediately hit the deck as Joey fired again. Joey ripped off a final shot before running to the open window.

Both guards looked around the corner of the giant doorway and spotted Joey running away. From his perch on the second-level walkway, Harry watched them come out from cover and start following Joey. The first guard remained flat on the floor after banging his head. One of the others winged a shot at Joey. Harry pulled the knife from his belt and used the blade to cut into the strap holding the line of barrels in place.

Come on. A little closer.

He sliced through the strap, put his shoulder into the upper barrel and flipped it over the safety rail. He flipped another barrel over, then another and another until the two guards went down under an avalanche of falling timber and he ran downstairs toward the open window through which Joey had vanished.

Outside, Harry turned back to find no one behind him. No one conscious, that is. Where had Joey gone? Had he tried to loop back to help instead of heading for the window? He could have been smashed beneath a barrel if that happened. Harry ran back to the destruction and threw broken boards aside until he found first one body, then another. Both Piazza goons. No Joey anywhere.

A door opened. "Joey?" Harry called out. "I thought you—"

A mountain walked through the door. The big man looked left. He looked right. He looked back at Harry. "Who are you?" he asked in Italian.

Rocco.

"Nobody." The word came out in English before he could stop himself.

A huge fist latched onto Harry's shirt and lifted him clean off his feet. Rocco threw Harry into a pile of barrels as though he were a child.

The knife in his grasp went flying. Harry fought to gain his feet until he stood upright in a fighting stance. Rocco growled at Harry, putting both fists under his chin in the stance of a man who knew how to use them.

Harry reached around for the suppressed pistol tucked at the small of his back. He found nothing but air. Harry instead slipped his fingers into his trusty knuckledusters, looking back at Rocco as the big man moved at him, already pulling a meaty fist back on approach. No boxer charged in like that.

Rocco pulled up short and feinted a wild roundhouse in the hopes Harry would duck and put himself in Rocco's sights for a massive blow from his other fist. Harry moved quickly, throwing a shot with his unarmored left hand at Rocco's chin that landed flush.

Rocco barely moved, firing back a booming punch to Harry's chest that lifted him off his feet. The force of landing knocked any remaining air from Harry's lungs. He rolled to one side and scrambled up and back as one of Rocco's giant boots crashed down by his head.

Rocco only needed to land one punch and this was over. Rocco was breathing hard as he trailed Harry across the facility toward the far wall, both men with their fists up.

Harry glanced toward the open window to judge his chances of just running for it. *Not good.* He circled Rocco and spotted a dangling fabric strap hanging down from the walkway. The barrels Harry had cut loose had rolled into other stacks of barrels and broken one of the straps lashing them together, a strap now dangling within reach.

He looked back as Rocco swung. Harry twisted, the blow glancing off his cheekbone with enough force to rattle his teeth and send him to one knee. He bounced up, feinting a shot at Rocco's face before kicking him in the kneecap. Rocco grunted and Harry slammed his boot on Rocco's foot before firing a jab that cracked the big man's nose. Rocco cried out in rage, launching an uppercut that caught Harry square in the chest and sent him crashing into the wall behind him.

Rocco moved fast for a man his size and caught Harry, lifting him with both hands off the floor. Harry kicked at Rocco's chest to no effect. Rocco pressed him against the wall and pushed, squeezing the breath from Harry's lungs before he pulled one fist back to finish it. Harry looked up. *That might work.*

"Had enough?"

Rocco hesitated at Harry's audacity. Harry didn't.

He crashed his forehead into Rocco's nose. Fire raged in Rocco's eyes as he roared and threw a wild haymaker that Harry ducked before shooting back up and launching another blow at Rocco's nose with his armored fist.

Direct hit. Rocco stumbled back but did not go down. *This guy's a tank.* Harry turned and jumped at the wall behind him, using it as a springboard to launch himself up toward the dangling strap.

Got it. His weight proved too much and the strap broke. The barrels came free, and as he hung on to the frayed strap Harry kicked Rocco right in his busted nose and Rocco fell back. The barrels tumbled down as Harry looked away.

He hung onto the frayed cord, spinning slowly, waiting for the awful gurgling sounds to stop before he let go of the rope and dropped to the floor. Rocco was done for.

Boom. A gun fired and a bullet smacked into one of the barrels beside Harry. He ducked as more shots came in to pin him down with his back against a standing barrel.

"You are dead," Carmelo shouted in Italian. He fired a few more rounds, then yelled again. "Joey Morello, you coward, get out here."

Carmelo was getting closer, firing after each sentence. "Get out and fight me."

He thinks I'm Joey. Harry had no desire to stand and disabuse Carmelo of the notion. A bullet came through the barrel and burned the hair on one side of his head. Harry leapt toward another fallen barrel beside him.

Sparks erupted on the ground and Harry froze. "Get up," Carmelo shouted. He didn't fire again, though his pistol was trained on Harry. "Get—*Harry Fox?*"

Harry kept his hands where Carmelo could see them as he stood. "Nice facility you have here."

"He brought *you?*" Carmelo apparently found this highly amusing. "A chump like you? I'm insulted. First Joey comes after me, then he runs and leaves you to finish the job? I can't believe it."

"He's not leaving," Harry said without emotion.

"Wanna bet?" Carmelo lifted his arms to either side. "You see your friend here? He's gone."

"He'll be back."

"He's finished." Carmelo's eyes narrowed. "So are y—"

A gun fired. Carmelo stopped talking, his pistol still aimed at Harry but now forgotten. Carmelo was too busy looking at the hole in his chest to pull the trigger. Still looking down in wonder, he collapsed in a heap.

Harry didn't move. "He could have shot me."

Joey Morello lowered his gun. "He likes to talk too much."

Harry walked toward Joey, giving Carmelo's body a wide berth as he passed. "Thanks for coming back."

"Don't mention it." Joey turned to look behind him. "Time to finish what we started. I'll meet you outside."

Harry went for the open escape door. Joey went over to the man who'd slipped in the river of wine when this all started and knocked himself out. A man who was now making the first noises of coming back to life.

Harry ran to a winery door leading outside, slipped through, then hurried to stand by the open window. He acted as nonchalant as a man soaked in wine and blood with the scent of gunpowder hanging on him could act. It didn't take long until the adjacent door opened and Joey came out.

"We're good," Joey said. "Time to leave."

Harry matched Joey step for step as they walked with purpose away from the winery. "What did you do?"

"I told him this was a personal feud, governed by the code, and now it's over. If any Piazza man comes after me again, they'll face the wrath of their entire island."

"The families in New York are going to think you're crazy."

Joey smirked. "Is that such a bad thing?"

They walked in silence. It didn't take long for Harry's thoughts to turn to an Austrian lake.

"You were there for me." Joey's voice startled Harry back to the present. "My work here is done," Joey said. "You still have a job to finish."

"I do. I'm going to Austria to unlock the earthly kingdom of heaven."

Joey blinked. "What?"

"I think that's where I'll find Charlemagne's final relic."

"Which will get you close enough to Olivier to pay him back."

"That's the plan."

"Austria it is, then. Let's go."

"Joey, you need to get back to New York. The city needs you."

"New York and the five families will last a few more days without me. We're in this together."

Harry knew that look in Joey's eye. He was the *capo dei capi*. The boss of all bosses. You didn't mess with Joey when he had that look in his eye.

Harry clasped Joey's hand. "Let's do it."

Chapter 21

Sinai Peninsula

Sara cursed as her laptop tumbled to the ground, bouncing and spinning until it landed against a metal container with a thud. "Well done," she chastised herself.

Ben, the dig sponsor, had received a call minutes ago from a contact in the Egyptian government. The contact warned Ben that competitors were working to revoke their dig permit. Revocation would open the door for another team to potentially take over at the site. The temple and whatever lay inside it would all be up for grabs.

"I need to preserve our find." The thought hit her out of nowhere. "Right now."

She shook her head. For a second, she'd considered not merely bending the rules, but shattering them. Of course, stealing artifacts from here made her no better than a common grave robber.

The arguments against it filled her head, though for the first time in her life they rang hollow. What they might find here could open a window into the history of a people and their culture. Sara looked at her reflection in the polished metal laptop case. She didn't see a grave robber. She saw a woman protecting history and standing up for what was right.

Unlike Ramy and Ben, it wasn't fame or riches she sought. It was the *truth*. About what they'd found and what it meant. Truth that she would share with the world. Sara had grown up in this country.

"I have to save at least one relic. One that will prove to the world what we say we found here is true." Prove the worship of Zeus had spread far beyond Greece centuries earlier than it was now thought. "And I'll return it."

What to take? Damaging the walls to remove any glyphs or imagery was out of the question. Same with the statues and the altar. Her gaze raced across the room. The golden scepter and the crown dotted with precious gems beneath the altar, left there as though the priest expected to return the next day to lead a service. She could take those in her pack. Her throat tightened. "That's what I'll do."

Sara jumped when her phone buzzed. Harry was calling. "Listen to me," she said before he could speak. "I have an issue." Sara described the possible permit loss and her departure. "I need to prove this place exists in case they try to steal everything."

"Who's they?"

"I have no idea," she said. "It doesn't matter. All that matters is they exist."

"Then take whatever you can lift. Something you can prove came from the dig. Anything you can prove ties back to the site, and only that site."

"Prove?" She put a hand on her forehead. "Oh, no. I can't prove anything came from here."

Harry let the quiet drag on as she worried. "There's another option," he eventually said.

"Which is?"

"You could take a picture," he said.

It took her a moment to respond. "Yes. Yes, I could." She cleared her throat. "As I've said before—"

"—I'm not entirely useless," Harry said. "Thank you. Now stop wasting time and take pictures. Get one of the temple with both you and someone else visible. That Ramy guy may be a jerk, but he's a well-known jerk. It would be hard to dismiss a claim from both of you."

"You, Harry, have never been more useful."

"Nothing like being damned by faint praise."

"That's quite enough." She walked toward the exit. "I'll call you when—hold on." Sara stopped walking. "You never told me what you're doing."

"Well, you're not going to like it."

"Are you still in Austria?"

"Not exactly." Harry launched into a story that began with him abandoning his risky plan to confront Olivier Lloris, and ended with a deadly encounter in a Sicilian winery.

"Are you hurt? Is Joey alright?"

"We're both fine."

"What about the others?"

"You mean Carmelo Piazza? He's not fine. Joey saved a lot of lives by doing what he did."

"And put yours in jeopardy to do it."

"What did you want me to do, let him go after Carmelo alone?"

"No." Sara kneaded the skin between her eyebrows. "No, I didn't. I would expect you to help him. He's your friend."

"Glad we're on the same page. I'm headed to Austria now."

"Alone?"

"Joey, too. He wouldn't take no for an answer."

"Tell him that if either of you gets hurt, you'll be sorry when I see you."

"I will." He paused for a moment. "You should think about leaving."

"What?"

"Tell me the truth," Harry said. "What's your gut say? Is something shady going on at that dig?"

She eventually said no, but it took her longer than necessary. Harry didn't miss it.

He wasn't buying it. "Ever been on a dig like this before?"

"No."

"Maybe you should be concerned. Or maybe there's nothing to worry about. If that's the case, the site will be there and you can come back."

"I'll be fine. You focus on staying safe in Austria. I'll worry about this site."

"I'll call you once I find something."

"Before you deal with Olivier?"

"Before I pay him back for what he did to my father."

He clicked off before she could respond. Sara cursed him for a good while before she stuffed the phone in her pocket and walked back outside in search of Ramy Gad.

"Ramy." She spotted him standing outside his tent. "I need your assistance."

Ramy mustn't have heard her, as he didn't turn to look at her, instead looking at the vast expanse of sandy ground stretching into the distance as he held a phone close to his ear. She walked closer and only then realized he was speaking rapidly and in hushed tones.

"Now? Why now?" Silence for several beats. "I do not—"

Sara tapped his arm and Ramy jumped. "What are you doing here?" he nearly shouted. Ramy's eyes widened as a voice emanated from the device in his hand, but Ramy looked only at her. "What is it?"

The disembodied voice continued speaking. She could only make out two words. *Stop her.* The voice had a distinct French accent. "I can wait." Sara pointed at the phone as she spoke.

Ramy looked down and realized the caller was still on the line. He jabbed at the phone to hang up. "It is fine," he said. "What do you need?"

"I need your help. Come with me."

Ramy didn't argue as she led him back to the temple and inside to the giant Zeus statue. "Stand beside me," she said as she took up a post next to him and in front of the giant lightning bolt. "Don't move." She snapped several pictures of herself and a confused Ramy. "Those are for our records," she said.

"Why? Is something wrong?"

"I'm worried about our permit," she said.

"Nothing has happened yet."

"Don't you think it's odd? I've never had an issue once a permit was approved. Have you?"

It was several seconds before an answer came. "I have not. However, our government can be difficult at times."

"By difficult you mean corrupt." Ramy shrugged as if to say *It is Egypt.* "What can we do?" she asked.

"We should speak with Ben."

"Is he still here? I thought he left to meet with his government contacts."

"He is doing that from here." Ramy pointed toward the exit. "Come with me."

This was a new Ramy. First sharing the dig, and now treating her as an equal.

"Let's do that," she said as he hurried out of the temple. It was only when they were halfway across the dig site, headed toward the central tent, that she caught up to him. Ramy seemed to know exactly where to find Ben, for he didn't break stride, didn't stop to ask anyone, but went straight for a tent to one side of the main area. There was a running vehicle sitting outside it. Ramy walked directly to the vehicle. The tinted windows reflected his face as they approached.

The door opened an instant after they stopped beside it and Ben stepped out. "I'm afraid we've run into a problem," he said.

"The permit?" Sara asked.

Ben nodded. "The Egyptian government has placed a hold on all archaeological activity here."

"What?" She threw her hands out. Her chest tightened. "Why?"

Ben raised a hand. "It is temporary. I am already working to handle the problem. I am confident we will be digging again within a few days."

The man seemed certain. Calm. Almost too calm. Sara straightened her back and drew in a breath. "That is good news. I am sure all will be back to normal soon."

"It will." Ben's eyebrow rose. "However, we cannot have our dig leaders returning to work without enjoying some well-deserved rest. It may be best if you returned home until I resolve this delay."

Sara looked around with unease. "What if someone disturbs the scene while we're gone? They could damage the relics, or even steal them."

"Do not worry about security here at the site." Ben tapped his chest with a finger. "That is my concern. I assure you all will be well."

A week back in New York wasn't ideal, but what choice did she have? "I suppose a few days won't hurt. I will return in one week even if the site isn't yet reopened."

"It's settled," Ben said. "A week to give me time to smooth this out, then the dig is back on." He hesitated. "There is one other issue I must discuss with you. I spoke with Dr. Gad about this a few minutes ago."

"What's that?" she asked.

"I am not the sole source of funding for this dig. I have a partner, and he is enthusiastic about preserving the past. He is a man with great resources. This is not the only site he is currently supporting." Ben lifted a hand to encompass the dig site. "He is impressed with your handling of the new finds. So much so that he would like to speak with you personally regarding other research opportunities. Opportunities you may be an excellent candidate to lead."

Oh. That's interesting. "What sort of opportunities?"

"He would like to discuss those with you in person. At his chateau in the Austrian Alps, near the German border."

Nightmares of multiple connecting flights sprang into her head. "How many airplanes will I need to ride to see him?"

"Only one. His."

That was better. "And who is this man?"

"He prefers to be called Antoine."

"Would I know this man?"

"Unlikely. Antoine is a private man. However, I will be happy to provide references if you wish."

"I do."

"Would you prefer to remain in Egypt until they are available?" Ben looked at his watch. "We cannot stay here. I suggest we travel to Austria now, and you can meet after you know more about him."

"I see no reason to wait here," she said quickly. "I look forward to reviewing those references."

"Excellent." Ben gestured to the running vehicle. "We depart for the airport at once. Gather the belongings you will need for a few days and meet me here."

Sara finally hesitated as she considered. "Now?"

"I'm afraid we have little time," Ben said. "The plane's schedule has been set."

Caution dictated this was too much, too fast. But perhaps she'd been away from Egypt for too long. This wasn't America. Situations changed quickly, and the Egyptian government was far less predictable than the German or American versions she'd grown used to. And opportunities to possibly run digs funded by wealthy benefactors didn't come up every day. *Take a chance.*

"I'll get my things."

Chapter 22

Lake Altaussee, Austria

"That's a big waterfall."

Harry squinted at the water as it exploded off the lake surface after falling several hundred feet. The morning sun reflected off the churning foam and flying spray bright enough to hurt his eyes. A brisk wind kicked up and made him pull the pack on his back tighter. "It's proof we're in the right place."

Joey looked over as Harry held out his phone so Joey could see the snapshot on it. The image that had broken Agilulph's last clue—the drawing of Bertrada here at Lake Altaussee. "It's the same skyline," Joey said. "Except that's only part of the message."

Agilulph's message had read *Time is counted behind the flowing life where Bertrada learned to be a fish. Here you will secure Charlemagne's empire. Use what unlocks the earthly kingdom of heaven. Follow the righteous path toward God.*

Harry had considered the cryptic words again and again on their flight from Italy to Austria, then countless times more before they snatched a few hours of sleep after driving through the night to this picturesque lakeside, and all to no avail. Odds were that *flowing life* came first. Focus on that, then worry about the rest of the message.

Harry locked their car and walked toward the lake. His breath fogged the morning air as he looked around. Not a single other person could be seen.

"What are you looking for?" Joey asked.

"Something that's been here for a thousand years." Harry hesitated. "I have a theory."

"Let me hear it."

"Sara and I believe Agilulph left a symbol of Charlemagne's power, hidden so that only a true follower of Charlemagne could find it in case things fell apart."

"After his death, you mean."

"Basically. To keep the peace Charlemagne brokered and protected."

"You had your nose in a book the whole way here," Joey said. "Find anything tying Charlemagne to this lake?"

"Only Bertrada and one other reference in the papers of one of Charlemagne's military officers. Apparently, part of Charlemagne's army not only came to Eastern Francia to test a new weapon, they came to this very lake."

"What sort of weapon?"

He held up his phone to show Joey the drawing of Bertrada and her children again. "First, look at this coastline by Bertrada. See the section to her left that juts out into the lake? We're standing on the same ground where Bertrada's family was sitting."

"I assume that matters."

"It does." Harry picked up on the none-too-subtle look from Joey to get moving. "The general describes testing a new type of weapon where we are standing. A trebuchet. Bigger and more powerful than any Charlemagne's army used before."

"They had those in Charlemagne's time?"

"Trebuchets first appeared in China around the fourth century B.C., and a thousand years later they'd become part of European warfare."

"I'm listening."

A solitary bird raced past overhead. "The general describes assembling a massive trebuchet. They built it here to do some target practice." Harry pointed across the lake to the waterfall. "That's what they tried to hit."

"The waterfall?" Lines creased Joey's head. "It's huge, but pretty far off."

"About eight hundred yards, I'd say. That's a longer range than any other weapon at the time. As to why they came here to test it, my guess is if the testing failed it would be easier to conceal that failure and save face with Charlemagne. The general references two teams of engineers. One under his command, and one reporting directly to Charlemagne. For his part of the testing, he talks about shooting from a narrow strip of land." Here Harry pointed at the commercial building. "One phrase stuck out to me in the general's writings. It's odd. He describes having a *perfect target* near the waterfall."

Joey looked at the distant mountain. He looked back at Harry. "What would be a perfect target?"

"I'm not sure," Harry said. "And I wonder why they had two groups of engineers working on it. Why not just one? What was the second group testing? Makes me curious."

Joey nodded slowly. "Are all your relic hunts this opaque?"

"Pretty much."

"I'll take running the five families any day." That got a chuckle out of Harry. "Seems we're stuck," Joey said. "What do we do now?"

"Use logic. We know Agilulph pointed us here. This is where Bertrada learned to swim."

"Agilulph left this path of clues so someone could unravel it and ensure a peaceful transition," Joey said. "To *secure Charlemagne's empire*."

Harry took a breath of the bracing air. "Agilulph uses objects or features that are in plain sight. Landmarks or buildings, or sometimes references to the stories of his time. My gut tells me he chose a geographical feature here."

"Then go with that," Joey said.

"One thing I don't understand is why the general's notes aren't precise," Harry said. "They seem vague. Intentionally so."

"Like he's hiding something?"

"Yes, but hiding what?"

"That's your department," Joey said. "I'm not in charge of this circus. You are."

"What would he need to hide out here in the open? It's a mountain lake. Not many places to conceal anything."

"Could be at the bottom of the lake."

Harry shook his head. "Clues are meant to be found. What we seek should be accessible on land. Visible, even. Agilulph's pattern has been to put the message in plain sight once you know where to look."

A full minute spent scanning the mountain and the trees standing by the fields on either side found nothing. He frowned. *It has to be here.*

"You see that?"

Harry turned to find Joey pointing. "The waterfall?"

"No, the plateau above it."

The mountain fronting Lake Altaussee didn't have a pointed peak. It had a plateau atop it, and it was from the center of this flat area that water tumbled into the lake below. "What about the plateau? It's solid rock."

"Maybe." Joey grabbed Harry's shoulder and pulled him close. "Look beside the top of the waterfall. You can see there's a different color of rock there."

Harry peered along Joey's arm to a spot on the mountain face beside the water flowing over the edge. "It might be darker. Or it could be the water."

"Then why isn't the rock on the other side of the waterfall darker too?"

"Good question." He stepped back from Joey as an idea took root. An idea that might explain it. "We need to get up there."

"Get beside the waterfall on top of that mountain? No way. One wrong step and it's all over."

"The government has banned hiking in the area. There are no barriers to access the falls."

"Good. Then we can't go."

Harry lifted an eyebrow. "I didn't say we *can't* go up there. I said we're not *supposed to* go up there. You want to stay here? I understand." Harry snapped a photo of the oddly colored rock and sent it off with a text message to Sara, then stepped around Joey toward a trail head. "I'm going."

Joey hurried to catch up. "Hang on. Why are you so gung-ho to get up there?"

"I think you're on to something."

"Slow down, Harry." Joey's words chased Harry as he kept walking. "Think about this."

"Suit yourself," Harry called over a shoulder. "I'm taking this path." He pointed at a route covered by snow. "There's a path along the lake that leads to the mountain. Follow that, take a different path at the base, and we'll get to the top."

"I don't see any path."

"Doesn't mean it's not there."

Joey appeared beside Harry, now matching him stride for stride. "And when we get to the top, then what?"

Harry grinned. "I'm still working on it."

Harry had studied the trail maps and knew the best path up the mountain was a winding route that looped around the base before it went up the rear side, through thick vegetation and towering trees, before finally depositing hikers near the plateau on the peak. A challenging climb, and one that ended well short of their true destination.

Harry glanced down at his phone as they ascended the mountain. He knew Sara would have thoughts on the picture and text he'd just sent her. Thoughts he could use right now.

"It's getting cold up here," Harry said. Snow crunched beneath their feet as the ground sloped upward and the trail led them in a direction away from the water's edge. The roar of falling water was much louder over here than it had been across the lake, a reminder to them of the immense power this giant hunk of rock possessed. Harry craned his neck to look up at the off-colored rock one last time. He had an idea. The outline of an idea, at least.

He grabbed his phone when it buzzed. Sara had responded. "'Keep in touch'?" he read, puzzled.

"What's that?" Joey asked.

"Sara." Harry read the message again. "She said 'keep in touch.'"

"What's wrong with that?"

"I thought she'd have more of an opinion. This is just, I don't know, weird."

"She's still at the dig, right?"

"Unless it was shut down since we spoke."

"What do you need from her that I can't provide?" Joey asked with a smirk.

"I need her take on that rock you spotted, and Sara isn't usually hesitant to offer her thoughts." He looked at the screen again. "Maybe she's distracted."

"By an incredible new site that now may have an expiration date on it," Joey said.

Joey was right. "Good call." Harry put his phone away and they set off again. The slope was growing steeper as they climbed. A few minutes later, he pointed to a narrow opening in the now-thick tree line. "That's where we go in. It should eventually take us close to the top plateau."

"But not to the waterfall."

"At the very top there is one level that we can access. The second, higher level overlooks the waterfall. It's blocked off so no one tries to get too close to the edge."

Joey pointed at the tumbling water. "That mountain plateau is the highest point around here. Where's the water source for the falls?"

"This plateau is the highest point on this mountain range, like you said, and there are multiple streams around here feeding it from flatter sections of the mountain range. The streams move fast enough that all the water runs across the plateau and spills down to the lake."

"I should have paid more attention in geography class."

Joey blew into his hands for warmth as they climbed onto the lower-level plateau and turned his face toward the sun. "This relic-chasing gig is hard work."

Harry ignored him. "Keep moving."

The lower plateau stretched out twenty yards to either side before vanishing in a vertical drop of several hundred feet. Heavy wind brought tears to Harry's eyes as they continued up the rise alongside the fast-moving river until they reached the second plateau. Joey raced ahead of Harry to near where the river fell over the cliff edge.

"This is amazing," he said, bending over to catch his breath.

The Totes Gebirge mountain range lay before them, its valleys cutting through undulating slopes and peaks, all of it covered with snow turned brilliant by the sun. Evergreens stood tall on the distant hills, and wisps of cloud hung suspended just above the rolling horizon. Harry had traveled the world and he could not recall a more incredible vista.

He set his jaw. "Let's see if I'm right." He walked directly to the waterfall, moving with purpose until the edge of the world seemed right in front of him. He pulled a rope from his pack and tossed one end of it to Joey. "Hold this," he said as he tied the other end around his waist before looping it under each leg to form a rudimentary harness.

Joey's eyes shot open. "What are you doing?"

"How else will I see if there's an opening behind the water? I think this is the target that Charlemagne's general wrote about in his journal."

Joey let the rope fall from his hands. "This is crazy. What if I drop you?"

"You won't." He pointed at the rushing water falling over the edge. "It was the off-colored stone you noticed. A section of the mountain face to one side is a different color than the rest. It's lighter in color. I think that rock isn't natural. I think someone altered this mountain. Altered it to *secure Charlemagne's empire*."

"Altered it how?"

"Something on this mountain drew the general's attention," Harry said. "And there was a team of military engineers up here. I think they hid the target by moving rock and dirt around. I think they diverted the path of this water."

The lightbulb in Joey's head came on. "To *hide* the target. On

Agilulph's orders."

"They diverted this water so the waterfall fully covered that target. I'm going to find out what it is. Now, are you going to help me or do I have to free-climb down?"

"Sara would kill me if I let you do that." Joey picked up the rope.

"Get ready," Harry said. "I'm heavier than I look."

"I have no idea what I'm doing."

"Put the rope behind your back," Harry said. "Thread it through your arms and around your back. I'll go over the edge, then walk my way down the cliff face. You let the rope out as I go. And don't fall in the river or we're both cooked. Once I see what's down there, you can walk back and help me climb my way back up here."

"This is a terrible plan."

"Just hold tight. I'll be back up in no time."

Harry watched as Joey secured his end of the rope around himself, then Harry tightly gripped the rope around him, looking at Joey as the river surged past. Joey leaned back hard, using his weight. The rope held firm. "I'll lie on the ground," Harry said. "With my feet over the edge, then scoot back until I start down. Two sharp tugs means start pulling me up."

Harry lay on his belly and moved backward until his lower legs and knees cleared the edge, then his thighs, until with one last move back his waist was over the edge and the toes of his boots got purchase on the sheer mountainside. He jammed one foot against the stone to get traction, then lowered himself another step. Joey held the rope taut, releasing just enough in increments that Harry could move down the mountain face. Progress was smooth and steady, step after step, until he moved through the waterfall's spray and could see clearly. He looked down.

Whoops. Several hundred feet of air waited below, punctuated by bursts of exploding water. *Keep walking.* He forced himself to look at the waterfall, continuing his slow descent. One step, then another, and he found it.

An empty rectangle on the face of the mountainside. Twenty feet from top to bottom, perhaps ten feet across, a natural opening that showed only darkness inside. The opening was entirely hidden by the thundering water.

A distinct, uneven vertical line ran up the mountain face in front of him. He reached out and touched the crevice separating the lighter stone from the darker parts. Yes, this rock had definitely been altered by human hands.

Harry tugged the rope twice. The pressure on his legs increased as Joey started pulling him up, his work letting Harry walk up the wall at normal speed. In seconds, he had both hands over the cliff edge and pulled himself up onto the ground.

Joey laughed between deep breaths. "You're heavy. Find anything?"

"it's there." Harry twisted until he stood, breathing hard and shaking his legs to get the feeling back. "It's down there."

Joey wiped sweat from his brow. "A target?"

"*The* target." Harry hauled Joey to his feet. "It's a cave hidden from sight behind the waterfall."

"They moved the water flow enough to cover a cave entrance." Joey shook his head. "I'm impressed. What's inside?"

"I couldn't see. There's an opening big enough to walk into."

"You think there's something in there."

"Don't you? They dammed part of the river to divert the flow and hide the cave. Nobody goes to all that trouble for nothing."

"You think anyone else knows that entrance exists?"

"I doubt it. The only way you can see the entrance is if you're suspended under the waterfall. Even a drone wouldn't easily spot the opening. There's too much spray. I barely saw it and I was right on top of it."

"Who would look under a waterfall to begin with? Unless you already knew something was there."

"I don't think anyone's been inside that cave for a thousand years."

Harry looked at Joey. Joey looked at Harry. Joey shook his head.

"You're crazy."

Harry shrugged. "Won't find anything standing around here. I'll need your help." Harry clapped a hand on his shoulder. "We split anything we find. Deal?"

"Do I have a choice?"

"I knew I could count on you," Harry said. "Dry your hands off. Time's wast—do you hear that?" Harry looked in every direction. "I hear something." Movement caught Harry's eye and he pointed into the distance. "I hear that."

A black dot moved on the horizon. It grew larger as it approached them, its *whump-whump-whump* drumbeat pounding the air until it vibrated in Harry's bones from his nose to his feet.

"I have a bad feeling about this," Harry said.

The helicopter came right at them, roaring until the chopper pulled up directly over them, the downdraft from the blades forcing Joey and Harry to lean into the wind. A helmeted pilot looked at them, and then the big bird descended, settling onto the ground not fifty feet away.

Harry's internal alarm blared at full volume as his fingers slipped into his pocket and found his trusty knuckledusters.

The twirling blades slowed and the engine finally stopped. One door slid open and a bearded man stepped out. Harry didn't recognize him. He had a pistol holstered at his waist. Harry took his eyes off the gun when a second man stepped out of the chopper, ducking beneath the slowing rotors with one hand holding a stylish hat atop his head. This man wore a suit, and his eyes were covered by sunglasses. Once he moved beyond the rotors he stood and looked at Harry.

The erect bearing. The expensive clothes. Recognition dawned. "Benoit?"

Benoit Lafont touched his hat. "Mr. Fox."

Joey spoke over the fading noise. "You know this guy?"

Harry didn't respond. Benoit, here on this mountain? The last time their paths had crossed was in Zurich when Harry had met Benoit to report on his progress hunting the Charlemagne relic for Olivier. "How did you find me?"

"We have tracked your movements with great interest. It appears you are near the end of the trail."

Harry glowered at the man. "This wasn't part of the deal."

"The previous terms no longer apply. You were not honest with my client. Your goal is not to deliver a relic to him. It is to exact revenge."

"I have no idea what you're talking about."

"You have been lying to us, Mr. Fox. You intend to harm my client."

Benoit never saw it coming. Harry stepped forward and slugged Benoit in the gut. Benoit dropped on the spot.

"Enough."

Harry looked up to find the bearded man aiming a pistol at his chest. A third man appeared from inside the helicopter, ducking below the doorframe before jumping out to land on his feet. A man Harry also recognized.

"You should have stuck to our deal." Olivier Lloris walked directly toward Harry. "What matters now is that you are close to finding the relic. I am here to be certain you finish your assignment." Olivier lifted a hand before Harry could respond. "With one change. I brought insurance."

Olivier pulled a handgun from inside his jacket. He didn't aim it at Harry or Joey, merely holding it pointed at the ground before he motioned to the bearded man, who put his own gun away and disappeared back inside the helicopter.

He reappeared a moment later, stepping down from the helicopter cabin before turning back to help another person out. A woman with dark hair.

An invisible fist slammed into Harry's gut. "Sara?"

Chapter 23

Lake Altaussee, Austria

Olivier re-holstered the pistol. He kept his jacket open so Harry could still see it. "She is here to ensure your cooperation. Nothing more."

"You made it more than that when you messed with my family," Harry said evenly. He drew in a breath. "You're funding the dig," he said to Olivier. "You orchestrated all of this to get close to me."

"Dr. Hamed." Olivier moved to stand in front of her. "I have not been entirely honest. My name is Olivier Lloris. You are in Austria. If all goes well, you will soon return to the dig site."

Sara blinked, and her face went from confused to something approaching incandescent heat. "None of it was real." She glared at Olivier. "The dig. The government shutting us down. The spotty communications. You orchestrated all of it."

"All of it necessary, and the dig is very real. You and your adventuring friend lured me into an agreement under false pretenses. The relic is being used to get close to me." Olivier gestured at the mountaintop they stood on and spoke to Harry. "You have come to the final step on Agilulph's path. Prove this is correct. Find the relic, sell it to me as planned, and we will all go our separate ways. You have little choice."

Harry bit back a sharp retort. "Let Joey and Sara leave. I'll stay and find your relic. Then we're through."

Olivier shook his head. "No. We may need her." He pointed at Sara, then at Joey. "And he stays as well."

"He can't help me." Harry ignored the look Joey shot him. "He'll get in the way."

"Joseph Morello runs New York's families," Olivier said. "He is far more dangerous to me than you are. He stays."

"And if I refuse?"

Olivier's response came softly. "Then I rid myself of you and find a new relic hunter. Do you understand?"

There was a long, tense silence as Harry weighed his options.

Finally, Harry turned and spoke to the helicopter pilot. "That'll be my anchor." He pointed at the falls. "I need to climb down and swing past the waterfall. There's a cave entrance hidden behind the falls."

"Ingenious," Olivier said. "And we have the proper gear on board." Olivier shouted over a shoulder. "Pierre." The bearded man snapped to attention before Olivier released a burst of French that Harry didn't catch, sending Pierre back into the helicopter. He came out moments later with a rifle strapped across his back and a metal case in his hands, which he opened to reveal climbing ropes, anchoring gear and safety harnesses. "Do you know how to use these?" Olivier asked.

Harry ignored him as he went to the case and quickly went about setting up a rappelling arrangement. Minutes later the lines were ready and Harry fastened a harness around his posterior. He didn't speak as he worked, finally cinching the safety harness under and around his torso. "I'll rappel down, then move over to the cave entrance."

"The two of us will follow," Olivier said. "Then Joey. Then Dr. Hamed."

"She stays here," Harry said.

"She goes." He pointed at Sara's forehead. "Her knowledge may be of use, so she goes."

Hard to argue when you'd brought knuckledusters to a gun fight. "Then she goes down right behind me." At least he could get a few minutes alone with her.

Olivier shook his head. "No. You first, then me, then him," he looked at Pierre. "Then Joey and finally Dr. Hamed. That is the order. The pilot and Ben stay here."

Harry looped an extra rope over his shoulder, walked to the cliff edge and turned to address everyone. "You will walk down the rock, using the rope to support you. Lean back as you go. Everybody got it?" Heads nodded, so he stepped backward until his heels hung over the void. A final tug on the rope. It held firm.

One step back and down, keeping the rope taut, and he began to move down the mountain. Heavy water spray pelted his face and gusts of wind tried to smash him against the mountainside. Soon, he was level with the cave entrance and moved toward it. The full force of the waterfall was now mere feet behind him, rushing hard enough to rip him loose if he got caught. He did not, and when he made it close enough to grab the side of the cave entrance Harry pulled himself over and with one final kick tumbled face-first into the opening.

He lay still, breathing hard. "Nothing to it." One hand spasmed as he pushed himself upright.

After securing a piton to the cave wall and threading a rope around it, he tugged hard twice on the rope to signal he'd made it. He slipped out of his harness and secured it inside the cave before Olivier came into view and approached the ledge. Harry threw Olivier a rope and helped guide him into the cave. "Get out of that harness and stay out of my way," Harry said.

More tugs, then Pierre came down, followed by Joey and finally Sara. Sara slipped free of her harness and laid it next to the others. Her flashlight came out of her pocket and she aimed it toward the back of the cave, revealing a tunnel. "The ground slopes downward," she said.

Harry pointed at Olivier and Pierre. "You two stay back. Don't walk past me, don't touch anything. Do that and maybe we all get out of here alive." He turned to Sara and motioned Joey over. "Here's what I think."

"Stand back here," Olivier barked as Joey began to move toward Harry.

Joey muttered something sharply in Italian but stood with their two captors.

"Agilulph's message said to find where Bertrada learned to be a fish,"

Harry told Sara. "We know that's here—Lake Altaussee. I think this will help us unlock the earthly kingdom of heaven." He reached into his pocket and removed the key from Saint Patrick's cross. "Look for any type of lock."

"What about the righteous path?" she asked.

"We'll know when we see it. Watch your step. Agilulph liked to leave nasty surprises."

His own flashlight beam raced across the damp stone walkway as they followed it. Sara walked at his side, the other three trailing behind. Pierre and Olivier kept Joey several steps ahead of them but they did not have their guns out. Harry studied the ground and the walls as they moved. The tunnel sloped downward, with no carvings or marks on the walls. Nothing but a cold tunnel with wind and the muted roar of the waterfall outside.

"This could extend a long way into the mountain range," Harry said.

"It's a natural cavern," Sara said. She pointed out the rough walls, the uneven floor, leaning close so only he could hear her. "What do we do?" she asked. "Olivier is lying."

"I know," Harry whispered. "Stay alert and follow my lead."

"What's your plan?"

"I'm working on it."

No sooner had the words left his mouth than the flashlight's beam revealed that the passageway ended ahead. The others caught up to them and they stood together before a vast, empty darkness.

"Stop." Harry lifted a hand and turned around. "Don't go past us."

"It's a giant cave," Olivier said. "I can't see the far side."

Harry stepped ahead, looking up at the rounded passage ceiling, which ended as abruptly as the walkway did. His flashlight beam faded quickly as blackness swallowed it. He leaned in further and looked to his left, then his right. "It's open on either side," he said. "Too dark to see how far back it goes."

Harry studied the surface of the wall to the left, then lightly ran his fingers over an anomaly in the stone. Sara noticed it as well. A square had been carved into the passageway wall, two feet on all sides, with text near the top. Latin. "You reading what I'm reading?" Harry asked.

"Charlemagne's signature. And there's a small hole."

"A keyhole."

"Let's hope so," she said. "There's a symbol below the keyhole. A snake."

"A moving snake," Harry said. "You know anyone who could make snakes move?"

Her eyebrows rose. "Saint Patrick. Well done, Harry."

Olivier stepped between them. "What is it?"

Harry put an arm out. "Don't walk any farther. It's not safe."

"It's an empty room." Olivier aimed his beam around haphazardly. "It is enormous."

"Just stay back. I'll handle this."

To Harry's surprise, Olivier did step back. Harry bent down to check the floor and found only dry stone. He stood and studied the image on the wall. A square with two symbols and one keyhole.

"You might want to stand back," he told Sara. "I have no idea what will happen."

"Do you have a key for this?" Olivier asked.

Harry pulled the bloodstone key from his pocket, deliberately holding it in Olivier's flashlight beam to make the red flecks erupt from the brilliant green stone. "Here."

"Where did you find that?"

"Saint Patrick's grave. Now get out of my way."

Olivier grumbled as he moved. Sara stayed beside Harry when he held up the key to inspect the notches. "I told you it was like an old skeleton key," Harry said.

"It has to be strong enough to open a mechanism made from stone."

The key fit neatly, sliding into the hole all the way until it hit something solid and held fast. Only then did Harry twist, slowly, then with more steam until a *crack* rewarded his efforts. He kept twisting with steady pressure to get another *crack*, then a third, until, without warning the key turned completely.

The cavern erupted around them. The floor shook and rumbled as though there were an earthquake, hard enough to blur his vision and make him crouch to touch the ground for support. Everyone else shouted or fell flat while he grabbed Sara's hand and pulled her down. "Look," he shouted over the noise. "The wall's changing."

Both of them aimed their flashlight beams at the distant wall. What had been a vertical piece of stone with grooves in it now revealed its true nature. The rear wall wasn't a large piece of stone. It was *two* pieces pushed together, and the groove was an empty space where the two stone blocks met. Stone blocks that now retracted into the walls to either side like a massive set of sliding doors. He kept hold of Sara and kept watching until the original rear wall had vanished, half of it retracting into the walls to their right and left.

The rumbling stopped. Harry was the first to stand. He aimed his light into the dust-filled air. He looked at Sara. "Stay close," Harry said softly. "You check your side. I'll check mine. We'll go straight for the back."

He ordered the other three to stay put until he confirmed it was safe. Harry waited until they were halfway across the room before he turned to Sara. "I don't like the looks of this," he said quietly.

Sara didn't speak until they stopped some twenty feet from the rear wall. Or what used to be the rear wall. "It's a puzzle," she said as she leaned back to look up. "It has to be fifty feet tall."

The rock façade, now gone, had covered Agilulph's masterpiece. He and his team of engineers had transformed the cavern's rear wall into a final test. A staircase of five steps stood on the left. It led up to a ramp that ran the entire length of the cavern wall. The ramp rose in elevation from left to right so that the far-right end was a good fifteen feet higher than where it began on the far left. The higher ramp included a standing platform and a wooden ladder leading up to another ramp, this one running from right to left and rising to a standing platform that was now thirty feet above ground level. Finally, a third ramp led back from left to right until it ended halfway across the cavern with another platform, this one nearly fifty feet above floor level.

"There's a ladder on the highest platform that goes up to the very top of the cave. Looks like there's a ledge to stand on up there." Harry pointed far above their heads. Whatever waited on that ledge was a mystery. "There are lines and markings in the wall along each ramp," Harry said. "I'll bet they aren't for decoration."

Sara touched his chin to redirect his gaze toward the beginning of the first ramp. "There is writing on the wall," she said.

"*Imperium Christianum. A solo deo.*" Harry turned to Sara and repeated it in English. "The Christian Empire. By God alone."

Sara didn't look at him. "Charlemagne was the first Frankish emperor to use that label for his empire. It wasn't a new idea—Emperor Constantine coined it five centuries earlier to describe his promise of eternal salvation for his Christian subjects."

Harry's thoughts went back to an earlier conversation in Brooklyn. "You told me about this."

"You listened to me?"

"Always do." He nearly kept a straight face. "Charlemagne planned a revival of learning and education among his people. At the time, monks and clerics were the only people who could read and write. Charlemagne needed literate messengers to be able to spread his God's word to the masses, and he also needed bookkeepers to keep the empire running."

Sara looked up at the rising walkway running across the face of the rear wall. "I see writing on the wall. The words are in the middle of some sort of design carved into the rear wall."

"That's not a design. That's a door."

"A door?"

"I see vertical lines connected by a horizontal line at the top. It's an outline of a door. One I'm not sure we want to open." He walked over to the beginning of the lowest walkway and knelt to examine it. "Look at this floor. More markings," he said. "And it's uneven in places. We don't want to step on those spots."

"Pressure triggers?"

"Looks like it. You can't get up the ramp without passing them."

Sara got it. "Agilulph left those as another test. Choose the wrong path—"

"—and that door opens. Whatever's behind it will knock you right off the path." He rubbed the stubble on his chin. "There's another set of markings farther up the ramp."

"What do we do?"

"We prove our worth." His gaze flicked toward the men standing by the entrance. "Follow my lead. Let's see if we can even the odds a little." He turned toward the entrance and then stopped, touching Sara's arm. "Look behind you."

Two ancient siege weapons stood in the shadows behind them, one on either side of the cavern entrance.

"Two trebuchets," Harry said. He pointed and raised his voice. "Look around the entrance," he told the other men. "Don't touch anything."

The trio did as ordered. "Are those things loaded?" Joey asked.

"Wouldn't bet against it," Harry said. "We can't walk straight up these ramps. Agilulph left a few presents."

"What does that mean?" Olivier asked.

"Traps. I've seen this before. Agilulph sets traps to catch the unworthy." Harry fell silent as he did a slow circuit of the room to check the floor. No obvious triggers, but having only one exit from this cavern made him nervous. "I don't think the floor is booby trapped." Harry spread his arms out to indicate the main cavern. "Come in. I want you to see what we're up against."

Olivier, Pierre and Joey came to the ramp entrance. "Agilulph protects the relics by securing the path," Harry said. "Only those loyal to Charlemagne may pass."

Olivier had been listening intently. "You go," Olivier said. "Dr. Hamed stays back with me."

Harry shook his head. "That's not how this works. You want whatever Agilulph left behind? Sara comes with me."

Olivier spoke with a coolness Harry had to admit he envied. "I have seen enough to know when I am at a disadvantage. Having her with me changes that. You climb the ramp with Pierre. She stays with me. And you"—here Olivier turned to Joey—"you wait by the entrance."

"Or what?"

"Or I shoot you."

One long look seemed to be enough for Joey to know Olivier meant every word. Joey turned toward the entrance.

"Wait." Olivier turned to Pierre and spoke in French. The bearded thug walked back to Joey, produced a zip tie and secured Joey's wrists to an outcropping in the cave wall. Olivier looked at Harry. "Cross me in any way and I shoot him."

A response came to Harry's lips, which he let pass unsaid. "I'll be back," he told Sara. "Trust me."

Olivier spoke as Harry turned to walk up the ramp. "Pierre goes with you."

Harry stopped, but didn't look back. "He'll only get in the way."

"This is not up for discussion."

What choice did he have? "Fine." He waited until Pierre joined him at the foot of the ramp. "Keep out of my way," Harry said. "Step where I step, touch only what I touch. Do anything else and chances are you get killed. Got it?"

Pierre nodded. Harry turned and took the first few steps up the ramp, his legs working hard to ascend the steep incline. He approached the midway point where a doorframe was carved into the wall along with markings on the floor. He raised an arm to signal Pierre to stop. Harry knelt and used his flashlight to study the floor. "Latin," he called out. "It looks like a step. I'm supposed to stand on it."

"How do you know?" Sara called from the ramp's base.

"It tells me to."

The same single word was carved into the ground in two places. Once on the left, and once on the right. *Pedites.* "Foot," Harry said to Pierre. "It wants me to stand there."

He stepped on top of the words, one foot on each, and waited.

Nothing happened. "Maybe it's stu—"

He sank. One moment, he stood; the next, the floor fell from beneath him. Fell a total of six inches. Arms out, knees bent, Harry caught his balance and stayed in place.

The floor ahead of him moved. A ten-foot section swung upward like a drawbridge to block the ramp and make any forward progress impossible. Metal shrieked from below, and Harry leaned forward and looked over the edge to find that the floor below the ramp wasn't as solid as it had seemed: now, a series of sharp metal spikes emerged from the floor and jutted upward toward the drawbridge. Dust erupted from the real walls by Harry's face as a section of the wall lifted like a window opening to reveal a message.

"'*Voluntas dei*.'" Harry translated to English and spoke louder. "'The will of God.' There are two words beneath it. I think they're supposed to be buttons you can press. One word is *grammatica*, and the other is *mathematica*. And below the buttons it says *A solo deo*. By God alone." A reminder to follow the one true god.

Sara shouted the first translation. "Grammar and mathematics. Two of the disciplines studied as part of the Carolingian Renaissance."

He'd gathered as much. "There were others. Logic, rhetoric, geometry. Subjects like that. Why list these two?"

Silence filled the cavern as he studied the words. No, not quite silence, for a distant rumbling behind the walls suggested that whatever ancient mechanics had been set in motion to reveal Agilulph's challenge were settling into place. Grammar and math. One based in language, the other numerical, both highly valued by Charlemagne. A connection existed, one Agilulph expected a true follower of Charlemagne to recognize. Harry realized this was a question of which mattered the most. Agilulph wanted him to choose which would be more important to Charlemagne. He needed to put one discipline above the other.

Sara's voice came from below. "Charlemagne modeled his Renaissance after Constantine's Christian empire, one based on Christian values. Charlemagne's purpose was to spread Christianity to the pagans."

Her voice lowered, as though she were speaking to herself. "What would be of more use? Grammar or math?"

Olivier had listened in silence until now. "Which is it?" he asked.

Harry's answer was to smash his hand against one word on the wall. His hand disappeared into it with immediate effect.

The drawbridge lowered so quickly he took a long step back to avoid being crushed. The ramp and its open path were restored, the stone bridge lowered back to where it had been, and his path was restored. "Grammar," Harry said. "Grammar allows people to share information."

He walked across the drawbridge. He was halfway over when Joey spoke from across the cave. "The spikes are still there," Joey said. "They didn't drop with the drawbridge."

"Shouldn't matter as long as the drawbridge holds," Harry said. He heard Pierre's footsteps coming from behind him. Harry took one final step and made it back onto the ramp, beyond the edge of the drawbridge.

His foot sank down several inches. He frowned and looked at the ground. "What is—wait!"

The drawbridge lowered. One instant it was a horizontal passage across the ramp, and the next it fell free. Harry leapt forward as his back foot slipped and he nearly went down onto the spikes. The breath shot from his lungs as he landed on the stone ramp. A scream split the air and was cut short.

He leapt to his feet and looked over the edge of the new precipice. He did not look for very long.

"What happened?" Olivier shouted.

"I stepped on a trigger after I crossed. The drawbridge collapsed when Pierre was trying to cross." Three words came to his mind. "*A solo deo.* By God alone." Harry leaned back and closed his eyes. "That's what it means. It's not about following one true god. It's about the path. You have to travel it alone."

Sara spoke. "With only God at your side. It's a warning. Only one person can go up the ramp."

"Keep moving," Olivier told Harry.

He ascended the remaining section of ramp without incident. The level platform at the end had a wooden ladder leading up to the next ramp, more than ten feet above. A thousand-year-old ladder he found to be in remarkably good shape. Pushes and pulls on the wooden frame did little more than make his hands hurt. Charlemagne's engineers knew how to build a ladder. He checked each rung before touching it on the way up, again finding nothing unusual, and it was the work of a minute to bring himself up to the second ramp. "There's more writing on this wall. It's halfway up again."

Harry walked to the end of this ramp and climbed a wooden ladder on the platform to get to the next ramp up, one leading back in the opposite direction. He moved slowly, alert for anything that seemed off. A smooth ramp and a barren rocky wall to his right side were all he found until he reached the halfway point, where he found more Latin writing on the wall. "The floor's uneven here. That's not good."

He walked slowly up the ramp until he could read the inscription. "There are two messages. One on top of the other. The first phrase says *hic sta*."

Sara translated it. "Stand here?"

"There's an *X* carved into the floor."

Olivier had a thought. "Follow the instructions."

"Good thing you're here." Harry looked down to make sure Olivier had heard him, then gritted his teeth and stepped onto the *X*.

The floor sank down several inches and a section of wall directly above the message slid down. At the same time, holes appeared in the wall, both above his head and by his feet, as well as holes on both the left and right. He kept very, very still. "My situation has changed," he called out, then described what he saw.

"There are likely spikes or arrows or some other weapon in them," Sara said at once. "Forget about it. What is the message?"

"Easy for you to say," he muttered to himself before speaking up. "I see two messages, and there are two crosses on metal chains hanging under the messages. They look almost like necklaces."

He peered more closely at the messages. "Hang on. These aren't identical. Each one is a slightly different version of the beginning of the Lord's Prayer," Harry said. "There's only one word difference. The left one opens with *Our Father, who art in heaven, hallowed be thy name.* The right version says *Our Father, who art in heaven, honored be thy name.* Both versions have the same first line, then one of them has *hallowed* and the other has *honored.*"

Why the difference? A test? To what end? Harry looked at the ground.

"Grammar." Harry turned to shout over the ramp edge. "I think it's a test of grammar, of literacy. Anyone ready to carry on Charlemagne's legacy should be able to recognize the difference between the two. I think I'm meant to choose the cross hanging under the correct version." The version with *hallowed.* He reached for that cross, though his hand stopped short. "It's a metal necklace," Harry said. "The links are sturdy. There's a cross at the bottom. Each cross looks to be solid iron on a metal chain. They've gotta be heavy." His eyes narrowed. "Here goes nothing."

The metal necklace rattled under his touch. It took a strong hand to get it off the hook. Only it didn't come off the hook. The hook rose with it, chasing Harry's hand as he lifted the metal jewelry, rising until it nearly touched the words above before stopping with a *click*.

Spikes burst from holes in the wall. Spikes above his head, spikes by his feet. An instant after the necklace came free, he was surrounded by rusted points as long as his arm, enough of them to turn Harry into a see-through lump of pierced flesh and shattered bone. Spikes protruded everywhere. Except for where he stood.

Sara shrieked.

"I'm fine," he yelled. "They all missed me." The *X* had marked a spot of safety.

As he stood still the spikes retracted without a sound. He waited until the last one disappeared then moved farther up the ramp until he was well clear of the holes. He looked back to find the deadly trap had reset itself, ready for the next intruder. *One more ramp to go.* He looped the iron necklace over his head and ascended the ramp, reaching the next ladder and climbing to the third and final level. "There's nothing up here," he shouted. "It's just a ramp."

"Keep moving."

Olivier sure was quick to risk Harry's neck. "No writing," Harry yelled down to Sara. "No markings. Nothing but the stone walkway."

One cautious step at a time, he checked the stone ramp and the cavern wall beside him, moving carefully until he stood at the end of the ramp, where a final ladder led up to a platform perhaps ten feet wide and half as long. It was a good fifty feet above the cavern floor.

He started climbing at a deliberate clip, again checking each rung before moving on to the next. In short order he reached the top and could see what the final platform held.

"What is it?" Olivier shouted.

Harry ignored him, using his flashlight to scan the small area. A metal chest sat against the wall, its surface studded with rubies and diamonds of every size and color that glittered under his light. The chest itself was made of gold and silver, and the entire piece spoke of exquisite craftsmanship. This chest was a work of art. An *Arabian* work of art.

Elegant writing ran across the side facing Harry. "*Allahu Akbar.*" An expression of holy reverence in Islam. *God is the greatest.* A powerful declaration of faith and peace. A phrase a caliph would use. The hair on his neck rose.

Olivier called out from below with more urgency.

"There's a chest up here," Harry yelled down. The description of it quieted any commentary. "There's also a message on the wall," Harry continued. "Not in Latin this time. It's Arabic."

Two words were inscribed on the wall. *Aqlib alsalib.* Harry said it to himself. "Turn the cross."

He shouted down what he'd found. No response from below. "Why use Arabic to talk about a cross?" He looked over at the chest. "There isn't a cross up here at all. Not on the chest, not on the wall, not any—"

The weight around his neck grew heavier. "This cross." He grabbed the iron cross around his neck. Was that what Agilulph meant? The cross he'd been given one level below? It had to be. He turned it back and forth in his hands. There was nothing at all on it to suggest what came next. Not on the outside. But what about the inside?

He latched tightly onto the lower vertical portion of the cross, gripped the horizontal part, and turned. Turned hard, gritted his teeth, and twisted again. It moved, and slowly, the upper half twisted away from the lower half to reveal that the cross was hollow. And inside? A rolled piece of linen. He set the cross down and unrolled the paper.

"*'Touch Harun's white circle for safety and replace the cross.'*" He read it again. Harun al-Rashid was the caliph with whom Charlemagne had made peace to secure a stronger future for both their empires. The white circle reference, however, made no sense. The moon came to mind, but what did an Islamic caliph have to do with the moon or with replacing a cross? Not a single connection came to mind. "Think, Harry. Agilulph wouldn't leave this unless you could solve it."

He put the paper back into the metal cross and looped the chain around his neck. Harun al-Rashid had been the supreme ruler of the Abbasid Caliphate, the equal of Charlemagne both in power and in devotion to his God. al-Rashid had courted other powerful rulers, striking accords with some, waging war against others. His influence had spanned the globe. What did a white circle—

"—the book." Harry shouted without realizing.

"What?" Sara asked.

"Hold on." His gaze flashed to the chest, to the decorations of rubies and diamonds and more. He looked right past them, past the glittering gold and exquisite craftsmanship. He spotted it.

"Got you."

Sara had been the key. Or, more precisely, a question she'd asked when he'd told her about finding the ancient book of folktales. A question about al-Rashid and pearls. "He loved pearls."

Sara had asked Harry if there were any pearls on the book. al-Rashid had loved pearls, had decorated his books with them, so pearls on the book might indicate it had belonged to the caliph. She knew he'd find pearls on the book. That knowledge mattered, because there was a massive pearl on this chest.

"It's the final test of knowledge," Harry said to himself. "I'd better be right." He leaned over, put his thumb on the pearl, and pushed.

Click. The pearl disappeared into the chest. Something had been activated, and the lid clicked open. The keys to one of the greatest empires in history lay at Harry's feet.

Chapter 24

"Sara."

His voice filled the cavern. "Sara, can you hear me?" Harry asked.

"What is it?"

"You were right."

More silence. "I have no idea what you mean."

Harry leaned over the chest. An object lay inside. Almost two feet long, half as wide and deep. He didn't touch it. There were too many delicate parts to simply grab it.

Metal rattled as a piece of the chest fell by his feet. He bent down and retrieved it. He'd picked up an iron cross. "Must have fallen off the chest," he said. "How'd that happen?"

A thought hit him and he studied the wall for a moment. That was all it took to spot the carving of a cross in the wall in front of him. A carving the exact shape and size of the metal cross he held. Even Harry couldn't miss this one. "In you go." He placed the iron cross in the hole. It *snicked* into place.

Nothing happened. He played his flashlight over the chest and discovered it sat atop a small raised pedestal. It looked like the pedestal had been placed into a hole carved into the ground. Could be the pedestal was a sort of counterweight, and if the weight of the chest atop it changed, the balance would be thrown off. Harry did not want to be around when that happened.

He pushed on the cross to make sure it was in place. Still nothing. His abundance of caution lasted several more seconds. "The heck with this." He reached inside the chest and lifted out what Agilulph had gone to such great lengths to hide.

A clock. Exactly as the stories had described it. A water-clock encrusted with precious metals and stones, its ivory face inlaid with gold. He stared at the highly polished wooden frame, the intricate dials and hands. A water-clock to dazzle and entertain, offering a new display of tiny figures to mark each passing hour. Clocks of such design wouldn't be seen in the Western world for five hundred years after this was given to Charlemagne. Arabian craftsmen had created a clock fit not only for a king, but also for an emperor.

"What is it?" Olivier shouted, breaking his focus.

"I found it," Harry said.

"Bring it down. Stand on the ramp by the spikes," Olivier said. "Use your climbing rope to lower it."

"You don't even know what it is," Harry said.

"I will see when it is down here."

He should drop the thing on Olivier's head. Sara would know to make her move and take Olivier out. Harry would run down, and they'd be out of this mess. Until Sara turned on *him* for destroying the clock. He put the idea in his back pocket in case everything went wrong. "Fine," he shouted back. "I'm bringing it down."

Climbing down with the water-clock proved a challenge, but he moved with care until he stood where the spikes had come out of the wall. Harry set the clock down on the ledge and put his hands on his hips. "I believe this clock was a present from Caliph Harun al-Rashid to Charlemagne to symbolize their peace accord," he called. "I can't just tie a rope around it. I'll walk it down." Harry pointed at the lowered drawbridge that had claimed Pierre. "I bet that will come back up when I step on the pressure trigger again. Agilulph wanted this treasure to be found. Not to kill every person who walks up here."

"No," Olivier said. "Lower the clock to me."

"All we want to do is go home." Harry waved a hand in disgust. "Keep the clock."

"I said lower it."

"Or what?"

"Or I shoot all three of you, beginning with Dr. Hamed. Are you willing to risk her life?"

He was not. Harry put the clock in his pack and tied a rope to one strap. Olivier's voice sounded as he worked. "Quickly, now. I don't want to be on this mountain when the moon is up."

Harry checked his knots one last time before he began lowering the clock. Olivier watched as the pack came down, moving at a steady pace before it settled on the ground. He removed his pistol from the holster and flicked it toward the clock. "Untie it," he told Sara. "Then back away."

Sara took her time. She didn't speak, moving with care to undo the knots, then loosening the pack to inspect the relic. The clock face appeared to be made of ivory, while the numerals were a dark gold. Gears could be seen in the open lower half, with revolving figurines of small men set among them. Smaller circular clock faces were on the front, while tower-like structures extended from the upper portions of the device. Each tower had human figures carved into the vertical sections.

"Enough." Olivier turned to Sara. "Climb the ramp until you reach the drawbridge portion."

Sara didn't look at Olivier as she walked up the ramp to the drawbridge level. She leaned over to look at the spikes below. "Now what?" she asked.

Olivier didn't respond. He was busy gaping at the water-clock. "Incredible. A piece without equal."

"You can appreciate it when we're out of here," Harry said. "Go ahead and leave. We won't follow you."

Olivier turned his gaze toward Harry. "You put the cross in the wall before you retrieved this. Why?" Harry explained how he suspected the chest on the pedestal acted as a counterweight, which had been deactivated when the cross was placed in the wall. "If that is correct," Olivier said. "The cross must stay in the wall."

Olivier turned without waiting for a response. He put the pack on his back and walked toward the exit, stopping on the threshold to put the clock down. "Both of you," he called out. "Lie on the ramp. Face down."

Harry didn't move, even when Olivier pulled the rifle from his back. "Do not worry," Olivier said. "I would already have shot you if that was my plan."

"Then what's the gun for?" Harry asked.

"To see if you are correct."

The gun boomed. A cannon-like explosion filled the air when he pulled the trigger. Harry ducked as lead hit metal with a *clang* and an odd sound followed, the sound an iron cross might make if it fell out of a wall and hit a stone pedestal below.

Crack. The first noise made Harry look up. A noise like the sound of a tectonic plate moving.

"Thank you for the clock," Olivier shouted above the cacophony as he slung the rifle over a shoulder, grabbed the clock and ran. Harry made it to one knee before movement caught his eye.

Shadows shifted in the two dark, recessed sections on either side of the cavern entrance. He jumped to his feet and shouted. "The trebuchets are firing!"

Ropes snapped, dust billowed and the counterweights at the front of each siege weapon dropped to trigger the main event. He made it halfway down the ramp before the elongated arms flew around and two car-sized boulders hurtled toward the far wall.

They hit with a sound like thunder, and an earthquake rattled the walls, the floor bucking and twisting to send him spinning across the ramp. He skidded to a halt before a section of the ramp broke free from beneath him and he grabbed hold of the wall to keep from falling with it. His legs hung over the sudden cliff.

Tremors rattled his brain as he got his fingers into a fissure and pulled himself back onto the ramp. The ground shook harder as Joey shouted from below. "The wall is collapsing," Joey yelled. "Sara's down there!"

The rumbling turned to a roar as the ramp lunged forward and he nearly went tumbling over the side. The two trebuchet blasts had destabilized the reworked back wall. A chunk of rock bigger than him clipped one ear as he looked straight over the edge and shouted Sara's name.

"A rock hit her," Joey yelled. "She's out cold."

His friend struggled against his cuffs, pulling and hitting the rock to no avail. Harry ran. A hunk of rock crashed into the ground one step in front of him and he hurdled it, stumbling when he landed to go down on his backside and slide down the ramp. He grabbed hold of a ladder rung as it slid beneath him, swung out and ended up with his feet on a lower rung and one hand still on the ladder. He slid down the ladder in one go without stopping until he hit the lower ramp and jumped off the edge, feet kicking and arms spinning as he fell to ground level.

He stood and found everything still worked. Dirty air burned his throat as he dodged through the debris field of fallen rock toward where Sara should be. Another boulder crashed down with a bang as he yelled her name, kicking rock chunks aside and pushing through. He found her lying unconscious amid the debris and put a hand on her chest. *She's breathing.* A quick check of her body found no obvious signs of injury other than a gash near her hairline that had clotted with dirt.

CRACK.

Harry looked up in horror as the ceiling disintegrated, a giant boulder detaching and dropping down toward them. Harry scooped Sara up in both arms and leapt back an instant before the massive stone thundered into the floor with the sound of a bomb dropping.

Joey's voice cut through the ringing in Harry's ears. "You okay?" he shouted.

"I'm fine." Harry coughed, pulling himself up to his feet, and then crouched to look at Sara. "She's coming around," he called to Joey. "Sara, can you hear me?"

"What happened?" she mumbled.

"Move your arms and legs." She did, cursing at him a few times when it hurt, but everything worked. Harry turned to find Joey standing beside them. "How did you get loose?"

"A sharp piece of rock."

"I think Sara's okay," Harry said. "Me too."

"I'll stay here," Joey said. "You need to move."

Harry shook his head. "I can't leave her."

"Go," Joey said. "I'll keep an eye on her. You can still get Olivier. Finish it."

Harry looked into the face of his closest friend in the world. "Thanks," he said.

Harry's footsteps echoed as he ran into the tunnel, his fingers brushing over his pocket and feeling the reassuring outline of the ceramic knuckledusters. Something told him they would come in handy soon. Olivier might have a gun, but he thought Harry was dead. The tunnel sloped up, and Harry accelerated until sunlight appeared ahead. He slowed, hugging the wall as he took the last few steps and stuck his head outside. The spray of falling water hit his face.

Olivier stood at the cliff's edge. A harness encircled his torso, and he had the pack on his back as he tied the knots that would hold him secure for a swing across the gap. After that, he could move up the cliffside to the waiting helicopter and be gone. Harry kept his back to the wall as he moved to where he could fully see Olivier, the roaring water covering his presence. Olivier never looked back. Ten feet away and Harry reached into his pocket. Five feet. His hand came out, fingers in the knuckledusters, his steps faster. Three feet.

Olivier looked back. His mouth opened, and as Harry lunged for him the Frenchman threw a hand up to knock Harry's punch aside. Harry kept moving, slamming into Olivier and knocking him off the cliff edge. Olivier went swinging into the void. Harry caught his balance and grabbed hold of the cliff face.

Olivier flew through the spray, a loose rope dangling from his waist. A rope with an unfinished knot. Olivier spun as his momentum carried him away from Harry, and then began swinging back. As he drew closer, Harry tensed. *That's my chance.*

Harry launched himself off the edge, flying across with nothing but air below him before crashing into Olivier. Harry grabbed the Frenchman around his shoulders and held tight, his feet dangling over the abyss.

Olivier punched him in the face. Harry growled, pulled his head back and smashed his forehead into Olivier's nose, letting go of his adversary with one hand as he reached for the loose rope. *Got it.* Harry's fingers went to work.

Spittle landed on Harry's chin when Olivier shouted and kicked the cliff side. Harry's grip slipped as they flew away from the rock face before swinging back, Olivier's weight crushing Harry against the mountain. Harry grabbed a strap on the pack across Olivier's back, working it loose as Olivier threw a punch that missed. Olivier pulled back for another shot. Harry grabbed the dangling rope with one hand, held the backpack strap with the other, and pulled. Olivier's harness came undone.

Harry twisted as the Frenchman fell, moving so Olivier's arm slipped out of the strap as Harry clung to the rope. Olivier went down. Harry did not.

Harry twisted gently as he watched Olivier Lloris fade to nothing before a spot on the lake erupted like a geyser. The Frenchman's last screams echoed in the air.

"Harry!" Joey Morello stood behind the waterfall, Sara at his side. "You good?" he called.

"Yeah, I'm good. Hold this." Harry tightened the straps on his pack and checked the clock was secure. "Hang tight. I'm going up. I'll toss a harness down in a minute."

"Hold on." Joey bent down and picked something from the ground. "You might need this." He held out the pistol Olivier had dropped in the struggle.

Harry tucked the pistol into his waistband and ascended the rope until he reached the cliff edge, sticking his head over to make sure no one was watching before sliding over the edge and back onto the plateau. The helicopter had not left. The pilot and Ben were sitting inside.

Harry crept up to the passenger door, leaned in, and stuck the pistol in Benoit's face. "Bad news." Harry grinned. "Your boss lost."

Benoit looked at the gun. He looked at Harry. "Perhaps we can make a new agreement."

"Unlikely."

Benoit hesitated for only a moment. "I *was* his attorney. That has ended. It would be my pleasure to facilitate the sale of Olivier's extensive collection of antiquities—exclusively through your business."

Harry frowned. "What's your cut?"

Benoit blinked. "I leave that decision to you."

"Toss all your weapons out onto the ground." A pair of pistols landed on the grass beside him. "I could use an attorney."

"I am at your service, sir."

Harry knelt in front of the ornate clock. "Watch this. See this pearl?" Harry pointed to a single pearl set into the clock face, directly in the center of the moving hour and minute arms. "Harun al-Rashid loved pearls. There was a large one in the chest holding this clock. It was the key to safely opening the chest."

"You believe this pearl has a similar purpose."

"I do." Harry put his finger on the pearl. "I think it's the key to everything."

He pressed the pearl. It slid into the clock face. A soft *snick* sounded from the clock's rear as a small compartment popped open.

What Harry lifted from the compartment jingled as it moved. He held it up for Ben to see. "Care to guess what these are for?"

Epilogue

Brooklyn
One Week Later

An electronic chime dinged as Harry pushed open the door to Fox and Son with one hand, the other holding a takeaway cup of coffee. The wind sent snowflakes chasing him inside as he closed it. "Morning, Scott."

Scott Marlow did not look up from his computer monitor as he sat down behind the counter. "The new catalogue is on your desk."

Harry sipped from his coffee cup. "You look at it?"

"Before you had a chance to see it?" Scott smirked. "Of course I did."

"What do you think?"

"About your acquisitions? Not bad at all."

It was about the highest praise Scott would ever offer. "Glad you like them. Collectors will go nuts when they see the new artifacts. Even at these premium prices."

Harry walked through the showroom to his office, where he grabbed the catalogue Benoit Lafont had compiled showing the artifacts Harry was offering from the late Olivier Lloris's estate. A conservative estimate of Harry's profit for facilitating the sale was in the millions. Should bidding wars occur for some of the pieces, the profits would be significantly higher.

Harry finished scanning the catalogue and set it down. He spun in his chair and moved to the large office safe nearby. The locks clicked open when he put his palm on the access panel and he opened the door. Among the objects inside was a small box, roughly the size of a harmonica case. He took the case out and set it on his desk.

The lid flipped open. Harry lifted the set of keys from inside. Two small keys, each resembling an ornate skeleton key from the past. He turned them over in his hand. These two keys had the power to send the world into an uproar.

The keys had been inside Caliph Harun al-Rashid's clock. A clock that symbolized the peace accord between the Frankish empire and the Abbasid Caliphate. The keys had been a gift from the caliph to Charlemagne, a symbol of that peace agreement, a symbol in which Charlemagne saw an opportunity for much more. He knew these keys could ensure a peace that would outlive him. He had directed his personal abbot to lay a trail to hide the keys, a trail meant to be followed by someone dedicated to maintaining peace through generations. A person who shared Charlemagne's belief system and was able to protect the peace. A person who, it turned out, never came, and without them the Frankish empire spiraled into civil war.

A war that would be but a prelude to the conflict that these keys might yet cause, for these were the keys to the most contested real estate on the planet. The city of Jerusalem.

Harry smiled. The legend had been true. Harun al-Rashid had given control of the city to Charlemagne as the ultimate proof of trust. The keys unlocked the gates that had once separated Jerusalem from the outside world. Today, those keys held just as much power as they had when the caliph gave them to Charlemagne.

Harry shook his head. Whoever held these keys could claim ownership of Jerusalem. They could literally stand before the ancient gates guarding the city and open the locks, because those locks still existed.

Harry put the keys away. He needed time to think.

His phone buzzed. Joey Morello was calling.

"Morning," Harry said.

"Don't talk." Joey's voice brooked no dissent. "Just listen. Gary Doyle will call you shortly. Do what he tells you, and remember that I'm here for you. We're in this together."

A beeping sounded in his ear and Harry checked his screen. "Gary Doyle's calling me right now."

"Remember what I said."

Harry clicked over and kept his tone neutral. "Morning, Gary."

"I have a visitor coming to my office shortly," Gary said without prelude. "An official with the Italian government. He is based in Sicily."

Uh-oh. "And you're telling me this why?"

"It has the potential to be very challenging for you. Please come to my office. Now, if possible. I want to help you. We can't do this over the phone."

"Should I bring my passport?"

"Not necessary," Gary said. "But this Italian official wants to speak with you immediately. I'm honestly not sure how this will go. The best way I can help is if you come to my office now."

Sara had returned to her dig only a few days ago to take over the site from Ramy Gad, who had left unexpectedly on an extended vacation. She was under strict instructions to avoid any caverns with strange lights in them, because those odd colors she'd seen before the explosion turned out to be lights on small explosive charges laid by Olivier's team to cause the collapse. "I'm on my way."

He clicked off, retrieved his passport from the office safe, hesitated, then removed a large envelope as well. Harry did not lock his office door as he walked onto the sales floor. "Hold on to this for me." He set the envelope in front of Scott. "Don't tell anyone you have it. There's a chance I'll need it quickly. And discreetly. Can you do that?"

Scott lifted the flap on the unsealed envelope. He barely blinked at the amount of cash inside. "You need a receipt for this?"

Harry laughed. "It's twenty grand. I trust you."

"You tell me when and where," Scott said. "I'll get this to you. Count on it."

Harry thanked him and headed outside, making his way to the subway entrance before hopping a train that deposited him a block from the district attorney's office in Manhattan. Harry went inside to the front desk, said he needed to see Gary Doyle, and immediately found himself on a private elevator to the D.A.'s floor. The elevator doors opened to reveal the fiery red beard of newly minted district attorney Gary Doyle standing in the hallway.

"Thanks for coming so quickly." Gary offered his hand and pulled Harry close when they shook. "I'm still learning about the reason for this man's visit," Gary said. "Don't talk unless I tell you to."

Harry followed Gary into his personal office. Two people already sat at a table in one corner. One looked an awful lot like some of the gangsters Harry had battled with last week in Sicily. Odd. Harry stood beside the table as the pair rose to face him.

The first was a short, compact man, and the second was a very tall woman. She spoke in English. "Hello. My name is Chiara Girelli." She towered over Harry as she stepped forward and offered her hand. "This is Walter Scalzi." The diminutive man gave Harry a handshake he would not soon forget.

"What's this about?" Harry asked.

Gary jumped in. "Agents Girelli and Scalzi are with an Italian governmental agency called the Carabinieri Headquarters for the Protection of Cultural Heritage, or T.P.C. for short. They wish to speak with you about a current criminal investigation in Sicily. They understand that you are here as a courtesy only."

"This is not an official meeting," Chiara said. "In fact, should anyone ask, this meeting is not happening." Her English was flawless, which made Harry nervous. "We know you have a close relationship with District Attorney Doyle. We appreciate you coming here today."

That put Harry on high alert. Flattery was never good.

They all sat around the table. Chiara shot Walter a look, and moments later a manila folder lay on the table between them. "This folder contains evidence from an investigation into multiple murders that occurred last week in Sicily. The deceased individuals have ties to a Sicilian clan led by Carmelo Piazza." Chiara smiled with icy cool. "I am not asking if you know Mr. Piazza."

"The murders occurred in a small wine production facility." She flipped the folder open to reveal a photograph. "This handgun was found at the scene of the murders," Chiara said casually. "You will note the attached suppressor. They are illegal." She watched Harry as she spoke. He did his best not to notice. "This is the fingerprint report." Chiara moved the photograph aside to reveal a page packed with dense Italian. "Your fingerprints were found on the suppressed pistol. Our ballistics reports are still in process, but we expect to confirm this weapon was involved in the murders." She frowned when Harry didn't blink. "Even if it was not. Mistakes can happen." She shrugged. "They can take a long time to correct."

Gary Doyle put his elbows on the table. "What is it you want from us?"

"We can place Mr. Fox at the scene of these homicides. We have surveillance footage of a man resembling you in Sicily on the day of the murders. This is more than enough to request extradition for you to face charges." She put the pictures away and closed the folder. "None of which matters to me. Our agency combats art and antiquities crimes against the Italian people, and we are determined to win that fight." Her face darkened. "However, there are parts of the antiquities world we cannot easily access. Private groups, collectors, relic thieves. People who we want to bring to justice," Chiara said, then paused. "You are a man whose reputation for acquiring antiquities is well known. Legal acquisitions, from what I can see. Still, there are rumors that you have experience in less lawful activities as well."

"You hear all sorts of rumors in my line of work." Harry lifted a shoulder. "Why are you telling me all of this?"

Chiara frowned. "I will speak plainly. We need your help. The T.P.C. is aware of efforts being undertaken by certain private organizations that have nearly limitless funding from certain governments."

"These organizations or governments have names?"

"Not that we can share. One organization is rumored to have found information concerning a relic of extreme historical importance. One not yet recovered."

"An Italian relic?"

"A relic belonging to a nation with Italian ties. Of the very highest order."

Harry closed his eyes and leaned his head forward. "You're talking about the Vatican."

Chiara looked at Walter. Walter looked at Chiara. "This unnamed nation has requested our assistance. We have hit a wall. That is where you come in."

"This sounds an awful lot like blackmail."

Chiara shrugged. "Let us say you would become a partner in preserving our cultural heritage." Her voice lowered. "Though this concerns far more than the acquisition of one relic. This antiquity could spark a global catastrophe. Millions may die if it falls into the wrong hands."

Harry couldn't help himself. "What's the relic?"

Chiara shook her head. "The relic is our focus, but it is not the true mission."

"Then what's the mission?"

"Preventing a maniac from initiating a modern-day religious war the likes of which the world has not seen for over seven hundred years."

Harry started. "A Holy War that started eight hundred years ago? You're talking about—"

"—a crusade." Chiara's expression made his chest go cold. "Eight major crusades were undertaken in our history. Millions died. We now face a ninth crusade. We need you to find a missing relic to prevent this catastrophe."

Harry looked at Gary. "Sara's going to kill me." He turned to Chiara. "What are we looking for?"

Author's Note

The Harry Fox adventures are rooted in fact, though I have taken many liberties with the truth, stretching it in certain places, or outright wrecking it with a battering ram in others, though always in the service of telling a better story. The tales I enjoy reading blend fact with fiction artfully enough that it makes me question if what I'm reading could be true—and often sends me searching to find where the facts end and the fiction begins.

This adventure brings Harry's struggle against Olivier Lloris to a close, though to finally overcome a man who has haunted his family for decades forces Harry to dive deep into the past, not only to the time of Charlemagne, but much further back, as Sara must contend with challenges tied to Greek mythology—a familiar topic in a very unfamiliar location. But we'll get to that in due time.

Harry's troubles start right off the bat when he finds himself in a war zone near the city of Kharkiv in Ukraine *(Chapter 1)*. The message inscribed inside Charlemagne's crown instructed him to travel to where a man named Anthony of the Caves led his disciples. Anthony of the Caves did exist, and today is venerated as a saint in the Russian Orthodox and Ukrainian Orthodox churches. Anthony co-founded the Kiev Monastery of the Caves in 1051, an apt name as the monastery truly did start out as a cave. Given that humans first lived in caves many thousands of years ago, it is natural that the structures would be used for religious gatherings, and over time the cave monastery where Harry wreaks all manner of havoc on the Russian army grew from a small collection of outbuildings to the sprawling structure that exists today. Fortunately, the city is not and has never been under Russian control, though in February 2022 the invading Russian forces attempted to take Kiev. They were repelled by Ukrainian forces, and as of this writing the city remains in

Ukrainian hands despite being subjected to frequent air strikes.

Agilulph's path from Kiev requires Harry to demonstrate his knowledge of a man who opposed Charlemagne. Information about the life of the Saxon king named Widukind is in short supply, though it is certain that he led his Saxon armies against the Frankish forces of Charlemagne in the Saxon Wars. Widukind didn't roll over when Charlemagne came to spread his religious beliefs, something the Saxons would have little interest in hearing about as they worshipped Germanic pagan gods, of which there were many. Odin was one of the largest gods in their religion, and it is almost certain Widukind and his warriors would have prayed to Odin, Loki or Thor for protection before going into battle against the Franks. However, the eventual defeat of Widukind by Charlemagne is accurately told in this book, including how Widukind was baptized by Charlemagne as part of their peace accord. Not that Widukind had much of a choice, given that the alternative would have been death. Where this baptism occurred is a mystery, though it certainly wasn't at Cochem Imperial Castle *(Chapter 2)*, as the castle wasn't likely completed until three hundred years after Charlemagne defeated Widukind. The castle is real, and does appear mostly as described, though there are no repurposed pagan churches inside with any hidden tunnels. At least as far as I know, that is. The castle was not given to anyone related to Charlemagne, and about those tunnels, I'd recommend speaking with the true owners, the town of Cochem, as they may know the truth.

I should also mention that German nobility no longer exists in any official capacity. Barons, counts and every other title ceased to exist in 1919 when the Weimar Republic abolished royalty and nobility in the new German Constitution. Hereditary titles are permitted as part of a surname, so someone with "von" or "zu" in their name may at one time have possessed a title, but today those do not officially exist. The party-loving and mostly absent Baron Schweinsteiger *(Chapter 2)* certainly does not own a castle, and if he did, he'd be treated as a normal citizen like every other German.

The Charlemagne Accord

Sara is thrust into this adventure (or at least her personal side quest) when she is asked to join the excavation of an ancient temple in the Sinai Peninsula, a Greek temple dedicated to Zeus *(Chapter 2)*. As strange as the idea of a Greek temple in Egypt may sound, incredibly, it is true. In 2022 the ruins of a Greek temple dedicated to Zeus were uncovered in the Sinai Peninsula. Excavation at the site is ongoing today, with archaeologists having uncovered evidence the massive structure may have been toppled by an earthquake in ancient times, though in its heyday the temple allowed hundreds of worshippers to gather far from Greek shores to worship Zeus.

Harry's explorations beneath Cochem Castle *(Chapter 7)* on Agilulph's trail have him locating hidden passages inside a formerly pagan temple. These passages lead to another of Agilulph's tests, which Harry passes to uncover a book that appears quite out of place. A very valuable book, in that it's *the* first edition of the collection of Middle Eastern folktales commonly called *One Thousand and One Nights*. Today this collection contains many well-known tales, including *Aladdin and the Wonderful Lamp* as well as *Ali Baba and the Forty Thieves*, both of which were not part of the original Arabic versions, but were later added to the collection by a French translator who enjoyed each story. As a factual matter, the earliest evidence of these folktales being gathered in a single volume is found in writings from the tenth century, which is roughly a century after Charlemagne died, so based on the historical evidence it's unlikely this book would have been gifted from the Abbasid Caliphate to any Europeans. However, a hundred years isn't much when it comes to looking back this far, and it is possible earlier versions of this collection existed and moved between the two empires. A simple lack of evidence does not confirm such an exchange never occurred, and for this book, I'm saying it did.

Another liberty I've taken with history involves the language of clues Harry finds while under Cochem Castle. I refer to Charlemagne's spoken language as *Old High German*, which is in fact a great oversimplification. In truth, the classification is much murkier, as his language would have descended from Old Dutch, and without hearing him speak, it's hard to say what language he used. For story purposes I called it Old High German, though I want to be clear that's not the exact answer.

A familiar name Harry comes across in this story is the man who drove the snakes out of Ireland, and a man who sells more Guinness beer than we can imagine. Saint Patrick is a historical figure we know was born under Roman rule in Britain in the fifth century, and according to the history books he was in fact captured by pirates before eventually escaping. There is no record indicating he completed his education at Lerins Abbey, nor did he likely receive a tonsure upon graduating, though he did truly study at the abbey and tonsures were quite common at the time for men in his profession, so it's entirely possible something akin to what I describe occurred. Alas, Saint Patrick's grave is not and never has been at Lerins Abbey, and there are no wolves on an adjacent island with any sort of ruins. The tie between Saint Patrick and the quartz-based mineral called bloodstone *(Chapter 14)* is fictional, though I'd like to think the symbolism of such a vibrantly green gem would have appealed to Saint Patrick if he were ever in the market for jewelry. As to whether there are tunnels running under any abbey structure, the monks have been silent, though if you visit the abbey and visit the working vineyard, maybe you can share a bottle or two of their wine with a monk and learn a secret or two. Let me know if you do.

Joey Morello is faced with a challenge to his rule in this story. A Sicilian challenge, and to address this he uses an ancient tradition known as *Il Codice (Chapter 12)*. This ancient and honored tradition is also entirely fictional. I was inspired to create this for a few reasons, the main one being it allowed Joey to further cement his position atop the hierarchy, but also because it reminded me of the Mafia code of silence called *omerta*, which is well-documented and real. Omerta is not only a code of silence, but the code also covers how to act in an honorable fashion, conducting oneself in accordance with the Mafia values and practices. Forgetting the fact omerta was often a way of covering up a murder, the societal pressure for those involved in organized crime to accept this code isn't far removed from other codes of conduct we must navigate every day, both spoken and unspoken. That Joey and his crew would have such a code in their history, a code that Joey revives to be alive and well, is one of the lesser stretches of the truth in this story.

Harry opens a cross made of bloodstone (that Saint Patrick certainly would have created if he knew of the mineral) to uncover a message discussing Charlemagne's mother, Bertrada. This Frankish queen truly existed and was Charlemagne's mother. She is commonly called Bertrada of Laon due to being born in the Frankish city of that name, but she is also sometimes referred to as "Bertrada Broadfoot", for reasons that are unclear. I mention this simply because I found that nickname to be most unfortunate. Harry researches Bertrada's background and discovers the answer to Agilulph's riddle can be found as part of an illustration showing Bertrada swimming near Lake Altaussee in Austria, supposedly near where she was born. That is not true, as Bertrada was born in what we now call France, not Austria. I changed her birth nation because I really wanted to use the lake in this story, for reasons I'll reveal momentarily. As for Bertrada, some historians claim that her influence on Charlemagne upon his ascension to the throne played a key role in his many successes, mainly due to her diplomatic skills. Perhaps Bertrada was central in facilitating the peace accord between Charlemagne and the Abbasid Caliphate. If so, this entire story exists in no small part because of her.

From very early on in drafting this adventure I knew I wanted the climax to take place at Lake Altaussee in Austria. An image came to mind as I wrote the first draft of this story, of a man piloting a boat on a serenely calm lake. Mist shrouded the land to either side, though shadows suggested tall peaks hid behind the fog, and as the boat approached a far shore the land came slowly into view with the promise of an adventure only just beginning. The man driving the boat is actor Daniel Craig as he portrays the British spy James Bond in *Spectre*. That scene captured my imagination, so I decided to pay homage to it by setting the climax of this story at the same lake. That being said, I did fudge some serious geographic details—starting with the waterfall, which is my creation.

There is no waterfall at the lake, and there is no plateau in the vicinity (other than on top of my imaginary waterfall). Should you find yourself in Austria, you are able to hike trails around the lake and appreciate an incredible view from every angle.

The image of Bertrada swimming which leads Harry to the lake is my creation, and as far as I know, no army engineers serving under Charlemagne ever visited the lake. The mountains which lend themselves so well to the scene in *Spectre* are much farther away than I depict them, so any trebuchet shots an army may have fired would have fallen woefully short of their targets. While the geography around the lake has been altered, the idea of trebuchets in Charlemagne's time is very real. Trebuchets first appeared in China around the 4th century BCE. and were used in European warfare beginning around 700 A.D. The maximum distance they could throw a 200-pound rock—that's around 90 kilograms for my metric friends—was around 300 yards, or less than half of what I say. These deadly weapons could bring down the walls of imposing fortresses or towering castles, but it had to happen at a much closer distance than what Agilulph orchestrated by firing boulders at a waterfall. Finally, should you find yourself in need of outdoor gear in an Austrian airport, you will almost certainly be out of luck, as I have not found any sporting goods stores in Austrian airports—though perhaps there should be.

While working the Sinai Peninsula dig under false pretenses, Sara is led to believe the Egyptian government may try to shut the dig down in an effort to steal the find *(Chapter 19)*. While this is fictional, the threat of unethical or outright criminal activity by governmental bodies to seize cultural relics is widespread throughout history and well-documented. An old joke asks "Why aren't Egyptian pyramids in the British Museum? Because they are too heavy to carry."

First, museums have incredible value and are one of humanity's crowning achievements when it comes to educating the public about different cultures. Without institutions such as the Smithsonian Museums, the Louvre, the British Museum, or the newly-opened

Egyptian Museum in Cairo—which Harry and Sara know quite well!—our collective familiarity with and understanding of human history would be greatly diminished. Museums are for everyone, and they show us we live in a great, big, wonderful world with so many incredible people who are not like us—and these differences are fantastic. They truly do make us stronger, more educated and, in my opinion, better people. I truly believe this. And I also believe that sound you just heard is the other shoe dropping.

Museums are a monument to the invaluable contributions and achievements of every civilization that ever existed. They are also, at the core of their beings, institutions of conflict. Between nations, between cultures, between ideas. Several of the wonderful museums I referenced would not exist if it weren't for the fact that they curated such diverse collections through acquisitions from other cultures. I stood in awe of the Parthenon Sculptures in the British Museum. I couldn't help but linger by the Horses of Saint Mark inside Saint Mark's Basilica in Venice—not exactly a museum, but pretty close. That they are available for anyone who can walk in the front doors is incredible. How they came to be there for so many to enjoy? A different story. The Parthenon Sculptures were removed from Athens in the early 19th century by the British ambassador to the Ottoman Empire, which was the governing authority over Athens at the time. The horses were looted first by Venetian forces during the sacking of Constantinople in the Fourth Crusade in 1204, only to be later stolen from Venice by Napoleon in 1797, though after his forces were soundly defeated in 1815 the horses were returned to Venice. Does outright theft justify keeping such treasures in new locations? That question is very difficult to answer.

Joey Morello's final confrontation with his Sicilian nemesis takes place on Carmelo's Piazza's turf *(Chapter 20)*. A bold move by Joey that thrust him into the heart of danger, for he had to attack Carmelo in the middle of his clan's stronghold. However, Joey's mission was made easier in this story as I reduced the size of a typical Sicilian clan to make the sequence of events in this mini-climax more realistic. Typical Sicilian clans have a few hundred members, with some potentially numbering close to a thousand. The Piazza clan I created is much smaller than that, so if you find yourself in a dispute with a Sicilian clan, think twice about heading over to the island to work it out.

High above the factual Lake Altaussee, Harry must face down Olivier Lloris and settle the score once and for all. To do so, he navigates the last step of Agilulph's path, facing a series of tests which includes understanding the idea of *Imperium Christianum*. This label is one Charlemagne truly did place on his empire, one depicting the idea of an empire devoted to God in which all subjects receive the promise of eternal salvation for their submission to a leader's oversight. Not a bad way to keep people in line and get them to follow orders, and Charlemagne wasn't the first to take this approach. The idea originated with Constantine the Great, who, as Roman emperor, oversaw the beginning of the empire's spiritual transition which ended with Christianity being the official religion of the Roman Empire. I found it interesting that though Constantine did in fact cease persecuting Christians, there is scholarly debate as to whether he was merely paying lip service to the new religion and remained a pagan at heart. I wouldn't be surprised if someone who made it to that level of power proved capable of such a crafty deception.

A second test Harry faces relates to the Carolingian Renaissance. Most everyone is aware of the cultural movement simply called *The Renaissance*, the period of great social change that saw an explosion of human achievement in art, science, literature and a host of other disciplines, but it is less widely discussed that an earlier period of history mirrored the latter. The first Renaissance, mentioned above, began in roughly the 14th century and continued through the 16th century. The Carolingian Renaissance *(Chapter 23)* occurred in the 8th and 9th centuries, including when Charlemagne ruled. Harry's knowledge of the *quadrivium* and *trivium* not only saves his life in this book, but they are actually real. As Sara notes in her impromptu lecture, the trivium is a term indicating the study of seven liberal arts, including grammar, logic and rhetoric. The quadrivium focused on arithmetic, geometry, music and astronomy, which truly was considered at the time to be more useful in unlocking god's mysteries.

Harry manages to overcome Olivier Lloris and recover what Agilulph left behind so many years ago. However, that is not the end. Harry loves adventure, and adventure loves Harry, though in what form it will arrive it is impossible to say. Upon his return to America Harry has little time to relax before Gary Doyle calls with an ominous message: Get to my office and get here now. Harry arrives to find two unfriendly faces waiting, a pair who traveled across the Atlantic to meet him. These two work for the Carabinieri Headquarters for the Protection of Cultural Heritage, or T.P.C. for short. And do they ever have a story to tell. While what happens because of this meeting will be revealed soon (just below!), the agency these two agents represent is real. The T.P.C. was created in 1969 and is a part of the Italian national police force—the *Carabinieri*—and is responsible for combatting the arts and antiquities crimes which prevail in Italy. I couldn't resist using this real-life task force to expand Harry's world and get him into a whole lot of trouble, which I hope you will enjoy.

I hope you enjoyed reading this adventure as much as I enjoyed writing it, and I hope this made you seek out the truth about a piece of Harry's adventure at least once—history is truly amazing. Harry may have closed the book on Olivier Lloris, but his troubles are not over. What has until now been a series of relic hunts tied to Harry looking into the past will change as Harry finds himself fighting for a place in a new world, one much larger than what he has been used to dealing with. New alliances will be formed, new foes will arrive, and Harry will tackle challenges he couldn't have imagined a short while ago.

I can't wait to share the next adventure with you soon.

Andrew Clawson
April 2025

Excerpt from
THE CENTURION'S SPEAR

To continue the story, you can purchase a copy of THE CENTURION'S SPEAR at Amazon

Chapter 1

Venice, Italy

Maybe four smoke grenades were too many.

Broken glass crunched as a man raced away from the building, moonlight glinting off windows as he raced toward the nearest canal. A gondola thumped softly against the wooden pilings of a small dock. The man turned a corner and pressed his back against the wall. He steadied his breathing and listened. He heard nothing. *I told him four were too many.*

A siren blared. Harry Fox grinned. "Three were perfect."

Black smoke poured from the broken windows at ground level on a building behind him. Raised voices filtered outside, men shouting and coughing as their world descended into chaos. Men Harry was counting on to follow orders. He pressed a phone to his ear and waited for the call to connect.

"I told you to use more grenades."

Harry nearly laughed. "Four are plenty. Did you cut the water?"

"Does it sound like I did?"

Harry lifted his ear toward the not-quite-burning building. "They're plenty mad in there." The shouting grew. "Yeah, I'd say you cut it."

"Of course I cut it," the voice said. "Their fire suppression system is suddenly out of water. Lucky for them there's no actual fire."

"They don't know that," Harry said. "Good work. See you tomorrow."

"Follow your plan, Harry. Don't improvise."

"Wouldn't dream of it."

He clicked off and pocketed the phone. A look at his watch told him to stay patient. Follow the plan. Handle his business here, get what he needed, then slip away down the winding canals to a waiting private water taxi. Nothing to it. He narrowed his gaze.

A side door alongside the house had his eye. A door that opened to a narrow canal and a private dock. A dock with two powerful boats moored at the ready. If what Harry knew about the man who owned the building with smoke pouring from its windows proved true, those boats wouldn't be idle much longer. A thought ran through his head for the hundredth time that day. *This better be worth it.*

Fabio Maldini was not a man to be trifled with. The heir to one of Italy's most legendary fashion houses, he had far more money and taste than sense. Unfortunately for Harry, a good deal of that money went into security for the building Harry had just bombarded with smoke grenades. The men shouting inside who were now discovering their fire sprinklers didn't work would not take kindly to his actions. Harry could only grin. *You should have sold it to me.*

Fabio Maldini collected cultural antiquities. Provenance mattered little to the fashion heir. If he wanted a relic, he bought it, throwing enough money at any problem until it went away. Harry knew this because he'd sold a relic to Fabio years ago, a relic the Italian government would love to get its hands on, and if it could toss Fabio in jail in the bargain, all the better. Fabio's lust for historical treasures made him accumulate one of Italy's more notable private collections, though the public had no idea as to the true extent or contents. Harry Fox, however, did. And Fabio had something Harry Fox wanted very badly.

The steel door banged open and the first man came out. The pistol holstered at his waist was impossible to miss. He turned and shouted as two more men came out carrying a large trunk, immediately followed by two more who also carried metal containers. Harry knelt and stayed in the shadows as more trunks and cases were loaded, the men moving in and out with a practiced efficiency until the first boat was full. Harry watched as they worked. *Where are you?*

The first siren sounded in the distance as the first boat engine roared to life, the second following suit. A final trunk came out of the building and went onto the second boat. Harry's jaw tightened. *It's not there.*

The last guard turned and slammed the metal door shut behind him before leaping into the second boat. A long, narrow container hung from his shoulder as he jumped. Harry's eyes narrowed. *Got you.*

Harry turned and ran on a course parallel to the canal. The escape plan for evacuating Fabio Maldini's prized relics called for the boats to be loaded with specific relics from his collection, his most prized pieces and anything susceptible to fire damage, before being whisked to safety at another building Fabio owned nearby. An evacuation plan should the fire suppression system ever fail. Which, thanks to Harry's interference, it had. The ball had started rolling. Time to see if he could stay ahead of it.

Both boats pulled away from the dock and headed on a path that would take them beneath a single stone bridge before they turned and made their way to the second building several blocks away. Harry ran at full tilt so that he was standing on the stone bridge by the time the first boat approached. He held a large stone perched on the bridge ramp with both hands. A stone so big he'd wheeled it here that evening on a dolly. A stone big and heavy enough to crash any boat it hit. Harry reached into his pocket as the lead boat came closer. If the rock didn't do it, another smoke grenade definitely would.

The lead boat's bow moved under the bridge. The second boat trailed close behind. Harry leaned over the rock, balancing it on the edge of the bridge ramp, holding it steady. Wait for it. Wait. *Now.*

He shoved the rock forward. It vanished over the edge as the bow came fully into view, crashing onto the windshield with a *bang* to shatter it and send the three occupants scrambling out of the way. The smoke grenade Harry dropped on board next caused one man to stumble and fall overboard. Harry turned, ran to the other side of the bridge, and looked down to find the trail boat had stopped directly below him, the three guards aboard it looking and pointing as they shouted at the lead boat. Harry stepped onto the ledge and jumped.

He landed on the closest guard, who went down in a heap. One punch knocked a second guard overboard before he ever knew what happened. The third guard was quicker on the uptake, throwing a haymaker at Harry that he easily avoided before ducking low to let the man's momentum carry him forward onto Harry's back. It took no effort at all to flip the guard up and over the edge. Two in the water. Harry grabbed the prone guard by the shoulders, heaved him up to the edge, and slid the narrow container over his arm before dumping him on top of his two friends. The boat had been taken.

Harry strapped the container over his shoulder and grabbed the wheel, hitting the throttle as he spun the craft around and aimed it back the way they'd come. Shouting came from the three soaked guards as they scrambled to get away from the twisting boat. Smoke still engulfed the first boat when Harry looked back, and he pushed the throttle forward so water churned behind him and he shot forward in the canal, off to freedom without so much as a shot fired. He let out a breath and grinned. *Nothing to it.*

Gunshots filled the air. Lead zipped by his ear and Harry ducked low, turning back to see the lead boat shoot through a wall of smoke and give chase. One guard leaned on the shattered windshield and fired shot after shot, all of them slamming into the hull of Harry's boat. He held the long container tight with one hand as he shoved the throttle ahead, gaining precious space before the gunman could get him in his sights.

Another canal branched off ahead. Harry took it at speed and sent the metal containers zipping around the interior behind him to crash against the other side. The fiberglass hull took the worst of it with a *crunch*. A map of the Venetian canals came to mind. Follow this one past two canals on either side, then take a left at the next canal, a wide one. Then he could open it up and make his getaway.

More gunshots. The first boat was behind him again. Harry veered left and right, bouncing off a crafted tied to a dock. The late hour meant these side canals were empty, though plenty of craft were in place to serve as bumpers when he flew past. A man shouted and waved his fist as Harry zipped by. The man stopped shouting when another shot rang out. This one shattered Harry's windshield. Too close.

One canal zipped past, then another. The third canal waited ahead. He kept his bow pointed forward until the last second, ripping the throttle back and twisting the wheel with no time to spare so the boat seemed to leap over the water and bounce across it before settling down, his throttle goosed as the engine whined to fire him into the larger canal at pace. He veered around an idling *vaporetto*, the giant water taxi rocking under his wake. The second boat came out close on his heels and threw up twin plumes of water as it shot after Harry.

Golden light illuminated the night sky ahead. The wider canal wasn't the largest in Venice. That would be the Grand Canal, which lay ahead. Spray stung Harry's eyes as he peered into the distance, toward the golden light. He looked back to find the other boat getting even closer. They weren't shooting now, not with so many witnesses around. And if they caught him those three guards wouldn't need bullets to overpower one man. The window to make his getaway was closing. He hadn't planned on anyone giving chase. Time to do what he'd promised he wouldn't. Improvise.

He veered onto the Grand Canal and pointed his boat toward the golden light. Around a bend, his wake set every boat in sight bouncing and moving as he went straight for the most famous landmark in all of Venice.

St. Mark's Basilica loomed above him. The vast *Piazza San Marco* stretched from the water's edge to the towering cathedral church several hundred yards distant. St. Mark's clocktower stretched to the heavens on one side, while two long arcades of shops framed the wide central piazza on the other side. The piazza was decidedly empty at this time of night, with only a cluster of tourists visible in front of the church's façade, people out for a nighttime tour. A tour Harry was about to make much more interesting.

He used precious seconds getting his boat close enough to a dock without crashing to leap off and hit the dock running. All the relics save one were left in the boat. The long, narrow container remained strapped across his back as he ran into the piazza from the south, veering around the southern arcade and running diagonally through the piazza. A thundering crash told him the chasing guards hadn't been so adept at stopping their boat, though their wreck had put them on dry land faster than Harry, their pounding footsteps chasing him across the open square as he raced toward the gleaming basilica façade ahead.

The piazza would be a shooting gallery, Harry the easy target. He wove left and right, never moving in a straight line, doing anything to throw off their aim. The echo of his racing feet on the shopfront walls was the only sound in his head. He wove back. Why weren't they shooting? A look behind him found two guards on his tail, one with a phone pressed to his ear. The guards were gaining on him. Harry looked ahead toward the pack of tourists, a few of whom now looked his way. The guards weren't shooting. Because of the tourists? Or nearby police? Hard to say and it didn't matter. Harry straightened his course and accelerated.

Two guards on his tail left one in the boat. A wrecked boat, hopefully, but he wouldn't count on that. Four bronze horses stared down at him from atop the basilica as he raced toward the darkness at the church's side. Horses plundered during the sack of Constantinople during the Fourth Crusade. Harry glared as he ran. The Crusades. *That's why I'm in this mess.*

The puzzled tourists and unflappable tour guide went by in a blur as he darted into the street alongside the church and turned back to the Grand Canal. Movement on the water caught his eye. A water taxi, pulling to a stop in front of a tall building alongside the water. A taxi with a long, flat roof. A building with an exterior fire escape. Inspiration struck.

Harry hit the gas and raced toward the water. The men behind him fell off the pace, buying him enough space to reach the three-story building seconds before they did. Harry didn't go for a side door, didn't try to find a way into the dark structure. He aimed for a dumpster underneath a streetlight, accelerating as he approached. Harry never stopped running until he leapt on top of the dumpster, pounded ungracefully across the top and then jumped to grab the lowest rung of the retracted metal fire escape ladder hanging above him. A pull-up got him to the second-floor platform. He kept going, the metal stairs rattling as he raced back and forth, reaching the upper level when the two men chasing him had only just climbed to the lowest platform.

Harry ran across the roof until he could look over the roof's edge to the water below. The taxi was pulling away from the dock. A taxi at least twenty feet below him. He looked back. The two guards were at the top platform level, about to get on the roof. He waited. Water churned as the taxi pulled away from the dock. One guard landed on the roof and ran at Harry, his hand going to his hip and coming back up with a pistol. Harry lifted two fingers to his forehead and saluted the guard. Then he turned and jumped.

Gravity took hold and ripped him down, pulling harder than Harry thought it should, his arms wheeling and feet kicking as he flew toward the rapidly-departing taxi roof. Wind whistled past his ears. Dim light made the boat roof impossible to gauge. He hung suspended for an instant, the entire world stopping, and then he hit.

Harry crashed onto the roof at full speed, trying, without success, to roll as he hit, his crash-landing sending him tumbling across the roof with a disastrously loud noise they could hear in Rome. He flew toward the edge, unable to stop himself, careening out of control until he zipped past the side of the roof and flew toward dark water.

He grabbed hold of the roof and hung on. Dangling by one hand, his feet hung above nothing, his face pressed against a window with no one on the other side. *That was close.*

A shout and a splash sounded behind them. Harry looked back in time to see water plume as though someone had leapt from the roof toward the boat and come up short. An instant later another scream sounded, then a splash erupted as the second guard followed his friend into the drink. The water taxi surged onward. Harry readied himself. When the taxi came in line with the boat Harry had stolen, still docked by the *Piazza San Marco*, Harry steadied himself. The pungent scent of salt water filled Harry's nose as he leapt from atop the taxi and dove into the water, the salty water quickly stinging his eyes and biting his tongue as he swam directly for his abandoned boat, the narrow container across his back.

Fabio's first boat remained at the shore's edge. The third guard who had remained behind after slamming it into the stone wall along the river bank was still in the boat. He didn't notice Harry's jump from atop the water taxi, didn't see him swimming to his stolen boat. He didn't see this because he had wandered to the edge of the piazza and was looking in the direction his compatriots had vanished.

Harry hauled himself aboard the craft without drawing the guard's attention. He was about to fire the engine when shouting and splashing reached his ears and the guard on dry land turned around. His wet colleagues had grabbed his attention. Harry started the boat and maneuvered away from the dock an instant before the guard on land raced back to his boat, leaping aboard as Harry gassed it to send his bow skyward and his craft shooting ahead. The white spray glistened behind him as he veered toward the Grand Canal, whipped around a corner and headed for a narrow waterway. Gunfire erupted from the boat now chasing him. Too much gunfire. Harry spun to find three muzzles flashing nearly simultaneously from the boat on his tail. The dry guard had picked up his wet friends, and they were angry.

He took the first narrow waterway and zipped down it at a reckless pace, whipping the wheel over at an intersecting canal and flying further into the city. He did it again, turning back in the direction of the Grand Canal and getting far enough ahead that the shooting abated. That gunfire would soon draw attention from the police. He couldn't get arrested, not with a stolen relic on his back. Escape was the only option. More gunshots rang out and bullets slammed into his hull. Time to end this.

He shot across the Grand Canal, caught sight of a church he'd visited earlier while reconnoitering the city and pinpointed his location on the map of Venice in his mind. Inspiration struck. He had a plan. A bad one.

The wake his boat left behind might as well have been a map. Harry spotted another intersecting canal ahead. He zipped beneath a bridge before veering around the early morning's first refuse collection boat and coming to the intersection, forced by the narrow confines to slow to a crawl while going in a circle so that he was soon facing the way he'd come. The garbage collection boat puttered past him. Harry took the sole reason he'd come to Venice to risk his neck off his back, angled closer to the garbage boat, and tossed his prize away. It landed atop a metal refuse container on the side of the boat closest to the sidewalk. The garbage boat trudged onward, passing Harry as it moved deeper into Venice. The narrow metal container did not fall off. Harry turned his running lights off.

His adversaries appeared ahead. They barreled into the canal, racing forward without seeming to notice the boat sitting in the middle of the canal. Harry waited, holding steady as they plowed on. One hand rested on the throttle, and he picked up a short length of rope with other. A beat passed, then another. *Now.*

He slammed the throttle forward. His boat jumped, erupting from a dead stop as the engine whined and water filled the air behind him. The roar of his engine in the small confines drowned out everything, doors whizzing past above him at ground level on either side, lights nothing but a blur as he flew on a collision course with the other boat ahead. Harry looped the rope around the steering wheel and the broken windshield in front of him to hold the wheel steady. The two crafts came at each other without slowing. Not ten seconds from impact, Harry flicked his lights on.

The white eyes of three terrified guards lit up in front of him. Harry climbed over the destroyed windshield, onto the forward deck, and crouched. Five seconds to impact. He leapt.

Leapt off the racing boat an instant before it passed beneath a bridge. He flew over the bridge's edge and crashed into the far side, bouncing back and landing unceremoniously in a heap. He blinked, and thunder erupted beneath him.

Harry scrambled to his feet, then immediately fell back as fiberglass shrapnel filled the air on either side of the bridge. Shards clattered all around as Harry covered his head, waiting for the barrage to cease before leaning over the edge. Three men splashed and sputtered in the brackish water. They would survive. The relics they were charged with rescuing would as well. Once they were pulled from the canal bottom.

Harry strolled off the bridge and down the sidewalk. He soon caught up to the garbage boat, leaning over to pluck his narrow container from atop the garbage box before heading toward a hotel along the Grand Canal where a private water taxi waited to take him to the airport. He had a flight to catch, and a relic to inspect. The relic strapped on his back. A relic from English royalty. His boots squelched on the sidewalk as he walked, his thoughts already turning to the question that brought him here.

What did a scepter belonging to an English king have to do with the Crusades?

To continue the story, you can purchase a copy of
THE CENTURION'S SPEAR at Amazon

GET YOUR COPY OF THE HARRY FOX STORY
THE NAPOLEON CIPHER,
AVAILABLE EXCLUSIVELY FOR MY VIP READER LIST

Sharing the writing journey with my readers is a special privilege. I love connecting with anyone who reads my stories, and one way I accomplish that is through my mailing list. I only send notices of new releases or the occasional special offer related to my novels.

If you sign up for my VIP reader mailing list, I'll send you a copy of *The Napoleon Cipher*, the Harry Fox adventure that's not sold in any store. You can get your copy of this exclusive novel by signing up on my website.

Did you enjoy this story? Let people know

Reviews are the most effective way to get my books noticed. I'm one guy, a small fish in a massive pond. Over time, I hope to change that, and I would love your help. The best thing you could do to help spread the word is leave a review on your platform of choice.

Honest reviews are like gold. If you've enjoyed this book I would be so grateful if you could take a few minutes leaving a review, short or long.

Thank you very much.

Also by Andrew Clawson

The Parker Chase Series
A Patriot's Betrayal
The Crowns Vengeance
Dark Tides Rising
A Republic of Shadows
A Hollow Throne
A Tsar's Gold

The TURN Series
TURN: The Conflict Lands
TURN: A New Dawn
TURN: Endangered

Harry Fox Adventures
The Arthurian Relic
The Emerald Tablet
The Celtic Quest
The Achilles Legend
The Pagan Hammer
The Pharaoh's Amulet
The Thracian Idol
The Antikythera Code
The Charlemagne Accord
The Centurion's Spear

About the Author

Andrew Clawson is the author of multiple series, including the Parker Chase and TURN thrillers, as well as the Harry Fox adventures.

You can find him at his website, AndrewClawson.com

or you can connect with him on Instagram at andrew.clawson

on Twitter at @clawsonbooks

on Facebook at facebook.com/AndrewClawsonnovels

and you can always send him an email at:
andrew@andrewclawson.com.

Made in United States
Orlando, FL
04 May 2025